Astral Amour

Astral Amour

by
Willy

Translated, annotated and introduced by
Brian Stableford

A Black Coat Press Book

Visit our website at www.blackcoatpress.com

ISBN 978-1-61227-563-5. First Printing. October 2016. Published by Black Coat Press, an imprint of Hollywood Comics.com, LLC, P.O. Box 17270, Encino, CA 91416. All rights reserved. Except for review purposes, no part of this book may be reproduced or transmitted in any form or by any means, electronic or mechanical, including photocopying, recording, or by any information storage and retrieval system, without permission in writing from the publisher. The stories and characters depicted in this novel are entirely fictional. Printed in the United States of America.

Introduction

"Amour astral" by "Willy" (Henry Gauthier-Villars, 1859-1931), here translated as "Astral Amour," was originally published as an eight-part serial in the *Nouvelle Revue* between December 1900 and April 1901. It does not seem to have been reprinted in book form, although it is not at all clear why that should have been the case, as the author had a captive market in the publishing company run by his younger brother. It seems probable, however, that it was not conceived, as almost all the other works bearing the same signature were, as a straightforward commercial exercise, but more as a *jeu d'esprit*.

A letter from Gauthier-Villars dated 21 August 1900 to the poet and editor Félix Jeantet (1855-1932), auctioned in 2010 and quoted on the auctioneer's website, was included when the author submitted the text—or a section of it—to the *Revue Hebdomadaire*, of which Jeantet was then the literary editor. The letter mentions that approximately a third of the text had been cut from the manuscript, but appearances suggest that the version eventually published in the *Nouvelle Revue* was the full text. The fact of the prior submission to Jeantet adds further plausibility to the suggestion that it was not written as a commercial exercise.

Gauthier-Villars says of the novel in his letter: "It is a kind of review of the *fin-de-siècle* (oh, that stupid term!) is which the 'personalities' of thinking and esthetizing society file past, under pseudonyms, in new and exact décor. I have not wanted it to be fantastic, with no more of Hoffmanesque mummery than tricks borrowed from the Châtelet; the extranatural always appears in the aspects foreseen by the pseudoscience of the occultists. And the hero is a good old young man, still somewhat ingenuous, although blasé, seeking to reconcile his unavowed love 'of realities' (as the pestilential

Célimène puts it[1]) with his desire to soar in elevated meta-physics. The heroine, forged with the elements (in accordance with the theories of certain hermeticists) is illusion, and also irony, personified in the eternal feminine. You might say that, by virtue of its hero, a recent avatar of the neurasthenic dilet-tante, the novel is arriving 'at its time.'"

Timely it might have been, but Félix Jeantet apparently did not care to publish the novel in the *Revue Hebdomadaire*, and it is possible that the author's brother did not like it either, and also rejected it. It might be the case, therefore, that its existence in print was entirely due to the experimental spirit of the editor of the *Nouvelle Revue*, Pierre-Barthélemy Gheusi, who had bought that periodical from Juliette Adam in 1899. During the years of Gheusi's ownership the fiction published in the magazine was strikingly innovative, particularly in re-spect of various kinds of non-naturalistic fiction. Gheusi co-authored with Charles Lomon the extravagant heroic fantasy *Les Atlantes* (1905; tr. as *The Last Days of Atlantis*)[2] and also published the interplanetary fantasy *Les Terriens dans Vénus* [Terrans on Venus] (1907) by Sylvain Déglantine. The manag-ing editor he hired, Henri Austruy—who took over the period-ical completely when Gheusi left to become the managing director of the Opéra-Comique in 1914—wrote several strik-ing fantastic stories for it pages, including "Le Statue" (1901; tr. as "The Statue"), "Le Pays d'Humanie" (1902; tr. as "The Land of Humania") and *L'Eupantophone* (1904; tr. as "The Eupantophone").[3] "Amour Astral" was not the only novel dealing with fashionable occultism to appear in the *Nouvelle Revue* during Gheusi's tenure as proprietor, having been pre-ceded by Jacques Le Lorrain's earnest and tentative *L'Au-delà* [The Beyond] (1899-1900), but it was the most adventurous,

---

[1] Célimène is a female character in Molière's *Le Misanthrope*, seductive and flirtatious but much given to criticizing people behind their backs.

[2] Black Coat Press, ISBN 978-1-61227-456-0.

[3] Black Coat Press, ISBN 978-1-61227-293-1.

and is certainly a more revealing testimony to the editor's desire to push the envelope of contemporary fiction to as many new extremes as he could find.

The same section of Gauthier-Villars' letter to Jeantet that offers his account of "Amour astral" adds that the writer's wife has been seriously ill, and is only just beginning to recover; although it makes no connection between that datum and the description of the novel, it is perhaps worth bearing in mind that the novel was presumably written, at least in part, during that illness. The wife in question was Colette (1873-1954), who subsequently became far more famous than her husband; the latter's reputation was permanently prejudiced by the fact that he sold the copyrights in her first four novels to his brother, who published them under the "Willy" pseudonym in 1900-03. Colette must have been writing either *Claudine à l'école* (1900; tr. as *Claudine at School*) or *Claudine à Paris* (1901; tr. as *Claudine in Paris*)—in the intervals when she was not ill in bed—in parallel with "Amour astral." She eventually succeeded in reclaiming full credit for the four novels in question, in opposition to her husband's conviction that they ought to be reckoned collaborative works, whose themes he had chosen and whose texts he had edited.

It is generally reckoned that many of the other works appearing under the signature "Willy" were partly or almost wholly the work of other hands, and that, with the exception of "Amour astral," it was effectively a "house pseudonym" employed by the family publishing company. The letter to Jeantet seems to establish that "Amour astral" is Gauthier-Villars' own work, but that appearance might be deceptive; the unevenness of its style and the drastic change of tack part-way through the story could easily engender the suspicion that another writer might have taken over the writing at that juncture. The mutation might, however, simply be a result of the evident fact that the author was making up the plot as he went along, with no clear idea of exactly where it was heading or how to get there.

7

Gauthier-Villars had met Colette in 1889, and they had married in May 1893. The marriage was not dissolved until 1910, although the couple had separated in 1906, and their relationship had been disturbed by several extramarital affairs. The exact state of the marriage in 1900 is difficult to determine, but it is unlikely to have been untroubled. How much bearing that might have on the peculiarly jaundiced view that "Amour astral" takes of the frustrations of sexual attraction it is impossible to determine, especially given that the author, in sharp contrast to his hero, was a notorious and supposedly cynical rake, but it must at least be reckoned a significant factor in the emotional environment in which the story was conceived and composed

As Gauthier-Villars' letter to Jeantet alleges, the novel provides, in its early chapters, a satirical depiction of the literary community of *fin-de-siècle* Paris, offering a bitterly sarcastic depiction of the esthetic ideas current at the time. That section comes to an abrupt conclusion, however, when the hapless protagonist and the enigmatic "heroine" leave Paris and embark on a strangely cursory world tour, during which they encounter a series of characters representative of the contemporary mythology of the occult revival, treated with a curious mixture of credulity and skepticism.

The author's assertion to Jeantet that he did not intend the story to be fantastic seems blatantly disingenuous, given that the supernatural is perennially present in the plot, but it is always presented in a very distinctive fashion, in which characters routinely give the appearance of being outright charlatans even while occasionally working manifest miracles, leaving the true character of many of them—most obviously that of the "heroine"—crucially ambiguous, and their motivation permanently mysterious.

Given that that the ostensible subject-matter of the greater part of the text is what occultists call "the mysteries," it is perhaps not inappropriate that it should remain stubbornly mysterious itself, especially given that novels of the period that set out to provide hypothetical clarifications and explanations of the classic occult mysteries invariably seem unconvincing, if not frankly bathetic, but Willy's treatment does make for a certain frustration. As an account of the social and psychological aspects of the occult revival, however, "Amour astral" does have the advantage of a unique originality, which is something always to be commended. It is more a commentary on occult fantasy than an occult fantasy in its own right, although it is blithely willing to use the fantastic as a casual literary device for the purpose of that examination. As the author's letter says of the heroine, she is illusion and also irony—and the same alchemical combination applies to the entire text, which is simultaneously all illusion and all irony.

As a study of the "eternal feminine," as the author's letter also claims it to be, the story might well appear to be blatantly misogynistic—as one would surely expect of the work of a notorious *fin-de-siècle* Parisian rake. It is worth noting, however, that the novel's plot has significant affiliations with a number of works by Théophile Gautier, notably "La Morte amoureuse" (1836) and "Arria Marcella" (1852). That might simply result from the subversive appropriation of one of the earlier writer's favorite story-arcs, but it surely also reflects, in a more conscientiously disenchanted fashion, a similar consciousness of a certain fundamental paradox of sexual attraction. In that sense, the novel is not a study of the "eternal feminine" at all, but actually a rather painfully self-critical study of the "eternal masculine," viewed as a hankering after an impossible ideal. It is, therefore, not so much misogynistic as wryly misandric. The real focal point of the narrative is its male protagonist, and his perpetual ludicrous failure to grasp, let alone to accept, that what he is chasing so assiduously is something unreal, and essentially unattainable: not a woman but an "elemental," an essentially mythical creature.

Seen from that viewpoint, the narrative frustrations of the story are not merely appropriate but essential, and its dealings with the occult and "extranatural" are purely symbolic. The novel is, at any rate, sufficiently unusual as an oblique commentary on the occult revival and the more general esthetic sensibilities of the *fin-de-siècle*, as well as in its analysis of the paradoxicality of amour, to retain its interest as an intriguing historical artifact. It was always undeserving of the oblivion into which it was effectively cast by its relegation to periodical publication without—until now—publication in book form.

This translation was made from the relevant volumes of the *Nouvelle Revue* reproduced on the Bibliothèque Nationale's *gallica* website. The translation was awkward because of the author's extreme fondness for esoteric terminology and a frequent tendency to neologism. I have anglicized most of his invented words straightforwardly, without adding explanatory footnotes, and I have transcribed many terms borrowed from contemporary occult literature directly, only adding annotations where the context does not supply the meaning adequately. Nor have I attempted to footnote the majority of the author's extraordinarily abundant references to his contemporaries, whether they are straightforward or disguised, restricting myself to annotating a few that seemed to me to be most in need of further explanation.

Brian Stableford

AMOUR ASTRAL

I. The Heartsickness of a Student of Occultism

In his library, even more sumptuous in its works of art than its books, Enogat de Sothermès, was dreaming, his eyes gazing into infinity.

The grayness of a dismal dusk inundated the vast room, gradually drowning the corners in which the gleams persisted of the bronze of a statuette, the enamel of a porcelain vase, the pewter of a tankard, the ivory of a netsuke or the lacquer of a casket, putting the finishing touches to the symphony of colors played by the exotic bindings in their ebony bookcases. There was a melancholy in the air that evening, and our dreamer was subject to its emprise when his *valet de chambre* came in and announced:

"Monsieur le docteur Callidulus!"

Almost immediately, a fat man appeared, with a cheerful expression and a twinkle in his eye, who exclaimed from the threshold, following the custom of the mages of old: "As above..."

"...So below," Enogat concluded, swiftly, hastening to meet his visitor. And without transition: "Oh, dear master, how timely your arrival is!"

"I'm delighted to hear it. Do you desire to elucidate some grave question?"

"Exactly! And I have more need than ever of your enlightenment..."

So saying, Enogat pushed a vast Louis XIII armchair toward the doctor; and, having sat down on a Medieval stool, he commenced: "Don't you think, dear master, that the *feminine* education of women is greatly neglected nowadays?"

"Ahem! I won't say no," murmured Callidulus, taken by surprise.

"Personally, I affirm it. No one understands the true social role of woman. Certain gracious and tender qualities are praised in her, and certain domestic virtues, but the development and refinement of her sense of the Beautiful is neglected..."

"That observation reveals your spirituality," the doctor put in, amiably.

"Even in the aristocracy," Enogat went on, "people are only preoccupied with forming bourgeois wives, irreproachable waltzers, or, sometimes, exhibitors at the Salon. By virtue of that culpable negligence, an intelligence of delicate culture cannot find in society milieux a complementary individual, a sister-soul."

"Have things really reached that point?"

"That very point, dear master. If only that refined intelligence, that *aristie*,[4] could find a suitable companion elsewhere...alas, since the Revolution, the world of gallantry, completely degenerated, no longer produces anything presentable."

Callidulus shook his head, ingenuously. "On that terrain, I'm short of documents, I must confess..."

Leaning back slightly, raising his left hand, Enogat made a reassuring gesture.

---

[4] *Aristie*—here misrendered in the original, but given correctly later in the chapter—which has no obvious English equivalent, is a term derived from Classical philology, where it refers to a series of exploits accomplished by a hero in an altered state of consciousness, which makes his name worthy of being sung. Enogat cheapens the concept in his perverted definition, although the real significance forms a backcloth of sorts to the central thread of the plot.

"Don't regret it. A courtesan is no more than a dress-maker's dummy, and moreover, she reeks of the concierge's daughter, no matter what adornment enlivens her. Don't ask her to create herself a costume or to make the most of her planetary type. Don't ask her, either, to radiate beauty; she has lost the secret of eurhythmic attitudes, and style is a closed book to her. Stupid enough to make a gander yawn, as pretentious as a reverend, she doesn't know how to dress, to talk or to shut up. The more one tries to ornament her, the more her poor grimaces and original flaws stand out."

"However, I've read in fashionable novels..."

"Oh, novels! Which? Those of Monsieur Bourget, Monsieur Zola or Monsieur Prévost? Novels! There are editors who dictate them all, and that's why they care so little about exactitude in matters of psychology. The time of great courtesans is past, long past! Even Cora Pearl is dead. There's no longer anything but *grisettes*, and worse! The throne on which the likes of Ninon de Lenclos, Montespan, Gabrielle d'Estrées and the Imperia reigned is still awaiting a queen of wit and beauty; I doubt that the white and subtle majesty in question can be, I don't say discovered, but even glimpsed, even among our most superb socialites."

"I would have thought that there were still a few characters to be found in that milieu," Callidulus objected, whose optimism was frightful.

"Eh? What scepter could a woman hold, pray, who allows herself to be enslaved by her dressmaker and her upholsterer?"

The fat man with the twinkle in his eye breathed out softly. "Well, if that's the way it is...but why, damn it, Sothermès, my friend, are you telling me all this?"

"One moment...I'm getting to that," Enogat replied, earnestly. "I need, first, to demonstrate to you that there probably no longer exists a single woman capable of giving the illusion of amour."

"Obviously, we're attributing to that word its meaning of transcendent spirituality."

But Enogat, without paying any heed to the doctor's words, folded his arms and, entirely given over to his discourse, continued, with a vibrant conviction:

"And why? Because none of them any longer has the intuition of the principles of Eroticism. Once, remarkably endowed individuals were able, without special study, to apply its complex laws, but those creatures belonged to the category of great intuitives; they were the artistes of amour. For the crowd, a method and an initiation are absolutely necessary. Oh, we require the advent of the august thinker with the ability to trace that method and establish an initiation!"

"The fact is that that new Orpheus would render humanity a signal service," underlined Callidulus, benevolently.

"By not making the modern woman an artiste of amour, with a doctorate in Eroticism, the antagonism of the sexes has been created. And that antagonism is the sole source of the mysterious malady of which modern societies, exhausted and neurasthenic, are dying. What women are worth, my dear master, fatherlands are worth!"

"It's necessary not to exaggerate that axiom, however, for..."

"Pardon me! A country in which women no longer know how to love or to make themselves loved is a country that is sliding toward ruin, because all the baseness of instinct can be unleashed there frenetically. Well, go search, in our society, bastardized by democracy, for a Phryné who is simultaneously a Hypatia and a Laïs, who, beneath her golden chignon, has the melodious genius of a Sappho of Mytilene, who could cry, without lying, 'I have something here!' while indicating, not her strong-box but her head or her heart!"

"That's agreed. Furthermore, it's certain that materialism, on the one hand, and clerical obscurantism, on the other, have spoiled everything..."

"Absolutely everything, dear master, and now we're in accord! You understand now what perplexity is mine, when I confess to you that my bachelor life, in spite of me, is beginning to drive me mad."

"What, my dear friend, that's it?"

"That's it. For three weeks I've been living in a strange languor..."

"Perhaps it's purely physiological," said the fat man with the cheerful expression, winking. "Well, you're about to turn thirty-five, a delicate age for intellectuals. Men also have their menopauses."

"No, the malady from which I'm suffering has deeper roots," sighed Sothermès.

"Don't allow yourself to be cajoled by melancholy; that would be to attract to your *self*, as you know, the baleful influence of Saturn."

"I'd like nothing better than to react," said Enogat, stifling a second sigh. "But how, alas? It's necessary, at all costs, that I find a companion worthy of me. Without a soul-sister, is life anything but a glacial penitence?"

He stifled a third sigh. The doctor looked at him fixedly, and murmured, half seriously and half in jest, while the increasing shadows blurred their pallor, as in a painting by Carrière: "In short, Sothermès, it's a Fay that you desire?"

"You've guessed it, my master.

"Damn! It's just that the Fays are beginning to need persuasion."

Feverishly, Enogat exclaimed: "Let's create one!"

Callidulus fixed his interlocutor with his piercing gaze again.

Becoming impassive again, however, Enogat continued: "Yes, let's create one. The alchemists of the Middle Ages fabricated homunculi; why shouldn't we, who've pored over the hermetic books of Nicolas Flamel and Cyliani,[5] attempt to create a woman? Come on, master, is it really so crazy?"

---

[5] "Cyliani" is the pseudonym attached to a narrative text entitled *Hermes devoilé* (1832; tr. as *Hermes Unveiled*), which exercised a considerable influence on a subsequent school of French neo-alchemists.

"Not at all. At least that one would be the woman of your desires. Truly, my friend, you've imagined such a project?"

Enogat emphasized his reply with a forceful affirmative gesture.

"So be it," said the other, his hands clasping the twisted arms of his chair.

And for a moment, the two men looked at once another in silence.

The issue of an insolently rich family, brought up among the refinements of an unusual luxury, Enogat de Sothermès had, from an early age, organized his life in accordance with the *Carpamus dulcia* of Persius,[6] elevating egotism to the level of a religion. Master of his fortune at twenty-five, he had hastened to banish all those whose aspect or conservation displeased him, and to create himself a tower, not of ivory but chryselephantine. Everything that modern industry has invented of the comfortable, everything that the art of stylistic epochs presents of decorative marvels or curiosities, was brought together in that residence, reminiscent in more than one way of the palace of the Temple under the Vendômes. And like the dilettante lords of the great century, Enogat had a court and gave fêtes. No one was admitted there without sponsors; furthermore, all postulants had to have given proof of artistry; exception was only made in favor of painters and sculptors of sovereign originality.

For Enogat, *aristie* consisted of not being ignorant of any the little-known works of the past or present, of possessing a multitude of details and anecdotes regarding their authors, of frequenting the exhibitions, concerts and theatrical performances of the most daring innovators and the most guileful tricksters—in sum, in keeping up to date with all novelties of the intellectual or artistic order. He had read, from the Homerides to Jean Moréas, from Panyasis to Raoul Ponchon,

---

[6] *Carpamus dulcia* means: "Let us pick sweet things". The quotation from the satirist Persius continues, in translation: "For when we are dead we shall be but ashes and a story."

From Hecataeus of Miletus to Élémir Bourges, poets and prose writers of whom more than one rare writer only knows the name. He ferreted through anthologies, and his eyes had scanned the majority of typical philosophies and so many histories and memoirs that it was almost frightening.

To tell the truth, he had not gone deeply into any text, and scarcely paused to meditate on the merest page; philosophers only interested him from the historical point of view, and historians from the literary point of view; he was naturally inclined to cephalgia. Studious in a rather peculiar fashion, studious with nonchalance, that "amateur" demanded of books motives for delectation, hours of cerebral intoxication, not themes of comparative study. Incurably eclectic, he supposed that a literate person ought not to be preoccupied with principles and causes, nor, in consequence, in creating an all-encompassing opinion. Rather than espousing some doctrine, it was far more important, in his view, to express intelligent opinions elegantly. He knew everything and he knew nothing. He was a perfect dilettante.

Enogat had exhausted all the mediocre enjoyments furnished by our society at the age of thirty. Libraries had been devoured, precious trinkets accumulated without counting them—and so many women! But of the emptied cups he only retained distaste, and from his reading, images and words. Blasé about everything, his lassitude no longer enjoyed anything of his desires. Like Arsène Houssaye, of cherished memory, he could sing:

I've made the tour of things a hundred times.
Going from Moses to Zeno...

However, although he was a feminist—or because he was a feminist—he could not add:

I only love the intelligence of roses
And the wisdom of Ninon...

We have seen what he thought of contemporary woman-hood.

Now, in passing such a general judgment, the gentle Enogat could only be mistaken. An observer devoid of synthetic vision and rational argument, a critic devoid of psychology, he knew a few women, but not Woman. So, in spite of what he thought, he remained vulnerable to the schemes of a coquette. His fortune having permitted him to surround himself with a particular atmosphere, and his taste drawing him to stylish reading, he thought himself virile, energetic, aristocratic and the master of his senses; in truth, no one was more at the mercy of a sensation than that man of elegant weakness.

So, having past thirty, he had resolved to change his life. In his state of mind, seeking new sensations was limited to modifying his reading.

A great deal of noise was then being made about Occultism, which several sects claimed to be reviving; the novelty of that movement was bound to attract Enogat.

Lightly tinted with metaphysics by the glosses of socialists and bourgeois exegeses, the nostalgia for the Beyond, Mystery and the Invisible, and its relationship with human beings had not solicited him. Finally, after a great deal of reading, the only thing that still interested him was magic. With a childlike fever he had thrown himself upon that new toy; he consulted those unknown volumes, at first as fairy tales, and then as treasures of wisdom, and gradually, fascinated by that tinsel, he allowed himself to be intoxicated by their deceptive effluvia. A year later, he was no longer content with texts; he wanted to be an initiate.

Immediately, he made the acquaintance of a kabbalist of great renown and solicited from that "doctor of occult sciences" the favor of studying under his direction. The illustrious master skillfully took the neophyte under his wing and deigned to prepare him for the initiatory grades.

That formation was to last nearly three years, during which Enogat took a dozen lessons a month at a louis each. On the advice of his master, he joined an occultist study group, and very gently, like schoolboy "cramming" himself dutifully he had prepared for one of the examinations that the new Rosicrucians—the authentic ones—had just organized. Now he held a baccalaureate in the kabbalah. He was proud of that. If only that contentment had been sufficient...

That success proved the new adept's excellent memory and nothing more. As denuded of mystical sentiment as of metaphysical intelligence, Enogat had only recalled from his occult reading the marvelous aspects, more interested by the fabrication of homunculi than the practices of spiritual embellishment. An initiate, as he understood it, was a hedonist in possession of all the means of enjoyment, and the culture of pride that constitutes initiate asceticism had only fortified him in that agreeable opinion.

Now, at that moment, sitting on a Medieval stool, his legs crossed and arms folded, gravely silent in the gloom, he looked at Callidulus.

Dr. Callidulus...my God, he was something else entirely. A mage! Well, yes, but who gave less the impression of a mage, even a modern one, than a country doctor scarcely rough-hewn, almost clumsy. Nevertheless, he had not had to scratch his head for long to discover one of those superficial intelligences which, unlike profound intelligences, are alert, sharp and redoubtably cunning. A doctor in medicine devoid of fortune and clients, he had succeeded in creating a prosperous situation for himself by setting himself up, by means of the pen and vocally, as a director of occult ideas.

Laborious and ardent, possessing the skill of a diplomat, with a sense of current affairs that a great reporter would have envied, that stout fatherly figure with the cheerful expression and the sly gaze, was a star in the small world of renovators of the kabbalah and other grimoires of that kind. But if he served the cause with zeal, he understood above all how to make it serve his intimate welfare; that is why he left no stone unturned in taking advantage of his notoriety in an entirely material fashion, and no matter how far his high wisdom went, it never forgot to call in at the bank on the way. He was, in the meantime, most amiable man in the world, and the most expert at hiding his true sentiments under a mellifluous false bonhomie that captivated the cleverest.

Certainly, when Enogat had clearly expressed to him the desire to create a homunculus, the excellent doctor remained silent for a moment, his hands clutching his armchair. Soon, however, he offered to direct the "operation."

"Although, Sothermès, my dear disciple, the endeavor presents great difficulties," he insinuated, shaking his head. "It's necessary not to hide that. And we mustn't hide, either, the fact that we're far from being the equals of the glorious alchemists of the Middle Ages. And yet...yes, with powerful conjurations and persistent efforts... In any case, my friend, your project appears to me to be of such superior interest that it's necessary, at any price, to attempt its realization. I don't know of any field of study more admirable, and then again, what a stimulus for our brethren!"

"You think so, master?"

"Oh, undoubtedly. The occultists of these sorry times imprison themselves too much in theory. Instead of applying themselves so much to recruiting adherents from the pen-pushers of the Town Hall and the idlers of the bourgeoisie, it would be better to devote themselves to experimentation, to restore honor to practical magic. A fine advance, when we have gathered together a few hundred affable cretins! Have we reconstituted Rosenkreutz's Rosy Cross only to imitate the freemasons and open one more chapel to universal boorishness, or to form true adepts? History, in accord with tradition, cries out to us: 'The doctrine is nothing without the works!'"

"You bear the seal of the true Magi," said Sothermès. "Oh, Callidulus, dear Callidulus, if only all our brethren were like you!"

Callidulus braced his shoulders and, almost convinced, pronounced: "Our brethren are quite remarkable, but they lack faith. Too many erudites among our candidate hierophants! And then, dear friend—just between us—too many universitarians, deprived of the spirit that vivifies. What's the point of our lectures? Are they just a Sorbonne for the usage of demoiselles? When one wants to conquer the great public, you see, one always expends oneself with students and no longer finds time to work with adepts. Now, without serious endeavors, we'll disgrace esotericism and become magicians within the reach of socialites—a sad destiny, Sothermès. So I can't congratulate you too much for wanting to undertake one of the projects extolled by our venerable masters. Are they reflections sister to mine that have inspired this project in you? Are they…but tell me, what are your special requirements of a homunculus?"

"I'm thinking less of an Egeria than a Theano. Without a companion, my home is becoming a tomb, and you'll understand that I need an ideal companion, a creature of ethereal essence. I manifested to you just now my desire to live with a being superior to the humankind of our cycle; it's a being superior to femininity that I should have said."

Callidulus made a sign of assent.

"The idea is still beautiful; I can only bow to it. I understand your heartsickness, dear friend, and I observe with pleasure how you have already taken advantage of esoteric information, since you have discovered by yourself the only appropriate remedy: a spiritual union with a supraterrestrial, and hence highly enlightened, feminine soul. When do you want to start work?"

"As soon as you please, dear master."

Callidulus frowned, placed his index finger on his temple, and spelled out in a low voice: "Let's see…the time to consult certain texts…"

Night had fallen completely; the conversation, somewhat special in that phantasmal atmosphere, did not lack character.

Two lamps brought in transformed the scene. There was a brief silence.

In a louder voice, the doctor asked: "Does six or seven days suit you?"

"Entirely at your orders. And believe that my gratitude…"

21

Callidulus having sketched a gesture of protest, Enogat, his eyes shining with a vague anxiety, went on: "The operation will take a long time, won't it?"

"At least nine weeks; that's what it normally requires; but those two months will seem short to you, in spite of your impatience, so busy will our days be, and submissive to the unexpected. Oh, don't hide it from yourself that a great many fatigues await us! Will you have the strength to go on to the end?"

"My determination will sustain me."

"One final word: this work will be very expensive, as you doubtless suspect?"

"Reasons of that kind won't deter me; let's march on boldly, without counting the cost. In any case, dear master, it will always be less ruinous and more agreeable, in every respect, than the conversation of a contemporary woman who squanders money without a care for the expense, a *demi-mondaine* merchant of smiles..."

Or an entire *mondaine!*" suggested Callidulus, getting to his feet.

II. The Anadyomene of the Matras

Enogat de Sothermès "dilettantized" in the Rue Vaneau, in a vast house with a garden, built in the seventeenth century, and which, thanks to the conservative spirit of its successive owners, had escaped "modern embellishments." While augmenting the comfort of the old dwelling, its proprietor had refrained from touching its architecture, which at least had the merit of presenting a courageous unity of style; and—an even rarer virtue—he had respected the trees.

The utilitarian accessories that brought a contemporary cachet to the new installation had been successfully dissimulated, or presented in a discreet fashion. The furnishing of the abode, however, had not been disposed with a similar tact; an amalgamation of elements of all ages and all materials, it did not present any concordance with the style of the building—with the consequence that Enogat seemed to be camped in the midst of a opulent bric-à-brac, although he scarcely suspected that, and would not have changed it for an empire, for his dilettantism delighted in contemplating so many disparate objects, so many divergent effects and curious contrasts. In dispersing his loving power thus he thought he would enjoy it more; in truth, he exhausted his sensitivity day after day by blunting it.

Yes, certainly, when he had launched himself into occultism, Sothermès had only changed his reading; thus, it had been sufficient for him, in order to satisfy his new hobbyhorse, to add an annexe to his library. How could he have foreseen then that he would one day devote himself to alchemy, and that a laboratory would become necessary to him? Now, caught on the hop, he did not know what to do. To eat into the kitchens was not practical; to encroach on the garden would not be esthetic. He therefore proposed to the doctor to rent space somewhere.

"An alchemist's laboratory can't be improvised," Callidulus replied, smiling. "Use mine, dear friend, and be sure that it's a joy for me to put it at your disposal."

And the excellent doctor, always amiable practical, completed the extraction of his disciple from embarrassment by charging him for all the purchases and all the material supplies, certain of drawing a good and honest profit therefrom.

Monsieur Callidulus, in whom love of the family was abundantly developed, lived in Bellevue, in a very stay-at-home, almost provincial fashion, with his wife and three children, in one of those banal villas of which the environs of Paris offer so many bourgeois examples nowadays. It was there that Enogat went every day, as soon as "the Work" had commenced.

The doctor's laboratory was vast and congruently furnished, for he hired it out to colleagues in hermeticism, but like all those of contemporary alchemists it did not present anything particular, save for a few pentacles or esoteric signs painted on the walls; it had the same instruments as chemistry laboratories. Nevertheless, Enogat, not being familiar with any of them, was greatly amused by the spectacle of retorts and flasks, and ecstatic in beholding the ease with which his master moved in the midst of so many mysterious objects.

In truth, Callidulus almost never did any practical alchemy; he was nevertheless a very skillful chemist, and his unrelenting ingenuity permitted him to overcome the worst obstacles. This project of Enogat's was too good an opportunity for him to devote himself, with expense, to costly experiments, in order that he might devote himself wholeheartedly to the task. Thus, it was marvelous to see him setting an example of activity and patience to the two domestics that Enogat had placed at his disposal.

He came and went, served and spun, taking one ingredient with a musical name and another with a barbaric name, mixing them, filtering them, and kneading them as prescribed. Another ingredient: "Bring me the large crucible!" And yet another: "Light all the furnaces!"

Undoubtedly, the preparations for the operation were rather laborious. They only required, however, a relatively short time. O joy! Soon, the mixture destined to produce a living being was in a very solid glass matras in the shape of an egg, and that matras, hermetically sealed, was enclosed in the athanor, a furnace specially designed to heat all kinds of vessels.

For five weeks, day and night, fire was maintained in various hearths at a high temperature. In addition, the success of the "work" still necessitated various manipulations, periods of fatigue, solicitudes and emotions of every order for the two alchemists.

The two? To tell the truth, Callidulus, the only competent one, considering his honor at stake, was obliged to have a hand in everything, to supervise everything, and to direct the smallest tasks. Enogat who did not want to get his hands dirty and was exhausted by long periods standing up, gave himself a great deal of trouble in order to be almost useless.

As soon as the fourth week, the unfortunate dilettante, superlatively impressionable, was wondering with such anxiety what was going to come out of the matras that it did not take long for fever to invade him. He no longer did anything useful, but, still resolved to do *something*, and believing himself to be important, he wandered around the laboratory, quivering, bewildered and lamentable. He became so exhausted that Callidulus retained him, sleeping downstairs, under his own roof.

The sun rose on the thirty-fifth day, expanded, and rose slowly in the sky. Then, as it began to oscillate toward the Occident and its decadent splendor striped the window-frames of the laboratory with gold, the doctor—O joy!—suddenly caressed his short beard and in a solemn tone, declared the operation concluded. Then having had a kind of aquarium brought, about one meter sixty long and twenty-four centimeters broad, he took a minuscule piece of silver, approached the matras, in which the corpuscle was finishing simmering, and, triumphantly, he brought it out.

"Behold our creation," he said.

It was something more reminiscent of a bazaar doll than a living being, for that homunculus measured no more than twenty-four centimeters, and its grossly sketched forms did not even exhibit the concern for reality of archaic statuettes. Without losing a moment, Callidulus deposited it in the aquarium, which he immediately had his aides fill with filtered water. Then, he applied an ox-bladder to the upper part of the receptacle, which he moistened on which he placed his right index finger. Having then pronounced magic words above the sacred envelope, he sealed it with one of the ample seals that have the virtue of binding spirits, in order that the "creation" could not escape if the desire should take it.

In spite of the information that he had been given regarding the "Work" Enogat not suppress an exclamation of disappointment at the sight of the corpuscle. What? Was that the result of five weeks of prodigious labor, ardent care and sovereign attentions? A derisory manikin covered with a crust? What kind of woman would that myrmidonesque abortion become, even if the operation had not failed completely?

Seeing his disciple's alarmed disappointment, however, Callidulus hastened to console him.

"That result astonishes you," he said. "It's not what you expected. Well, believe me, Sothermès, and rejoice with me, for the success surpasses my hopes. As a beginning, it's veritably marvelous. Ah, my dear friend, Messieurs the chemists can sneer at us, the jokers, with their *encheirisis naturae*,[7] to which Goethe did full justice. Sunk, the artificial production of urea! Surpassed, the concepts of Liebig! As if sages, knowing the Aour of the kabbalists, the Telesme of the hermeticists and the Universal Mercury of the alchemists could be embarrassed in obtaining a spiritual link with the organic forms that they constitute! Yes, truly, we're in a position to communicate life to matter. And this is what proves it in a peremptory fashion,

---

[7] "An intervention by the hand of nature." The phrase is cited by Mephistopheles in Part One of Goethe's *Faust*.

for you'll observe, Sothermès that our 'creation' is well and truly alive like you and me. All right, she doesn't look like much; she seems very fragile, but don't worry—she'll grow!"

The artiste was still dejected, and in a dreamy voice, his eyes blinking, he murmured: "She'll grow! Oh, my dear master, are you sure?"

"Perfectly sure; not a shadow of doubt, since the Work has succeeded."

"Truly, that inert corpuscle possesses a vital spirit?"

"It possesses one, no matter how much it displeases the Wöhlers and their successors."

"And it was our...your conjurations that attracted it?"

"It's also the internal spirit of the homunculus. In such cases the internal spirit attracts the external spirit, which descends from the heavens and, uniting with it, renders generation possible."

"How thankful I am to you, dear master; but while waiting for her to grow, what sufferings will I not undergo! The waiting is so difficult for me."

"Because you're not yet sufficiently elevated in the asceticism of magi," the doctor proffered, gravely. "Remember, friend Sothermès, one of the principles of initiation: it's necessary to be able to consider what one desires with the greatest indifference—the sole means of rendering oneself the master of it. Patience! Nature never proceeds in leaps, and the alchemist can't proceed by any other laws than those of nature. There is no supernatural; there is an extranatural, the Isis of old Egyptian temples, of whom the initiate must succeed in lifting all the veils. With that, think of the sweet compensation that awaits you, and let's complete our work...."

He had spoken; and the two aides, immediately commanded, transported the aquarium into the depths of the garden, where Callidulus was keeping in reserve a sufficiently large quantity of mule-dung. That was the fodder necessary to

27

the development of the homuncula.[8] And when the aquarium had been buried under that trivial tumulus, the doctor sprinkled it with a liquid prepared, not without difficulty, in accordance with the formula of certain alchemists. Immediately, vapors emanated from the dung-heap, as if it contained some extraordinary fire.

Then Enogat put his handkerchief to his nostrils with evident signs of disgust. But with a satisfied and seemingly fixed smile, Callidulus explained: "The odor is nauseating, I gladly agree. You should be joyful too, because that stink is an excellent augury. Along with those swirling vapors, it testifies that the liquor leaves nothing to be desired. You know, Sothermès, that it has been composed with almost innumerable ingredients. Isn't it admirable that such vile materials can, by the miracle of alchemy, become so nobly and radiantly useful?"

Then, addressing the servants, who were not hiding their repulsion either: "Come on, my friends, a little courage for the love of science! It will be necessary for you to repeat that fecundating sprinkling every day from now on."

And, expansive in the manner of a satisfied artist, Callidulus led his disciple away, who expression remained discomfited. And two or three days went by, which Enogat lived in a mute and febrile disenchantment.

During the four weeks that followed, the doctor concocted a kind of paste destined to nourish their "creation": one little pellet every three days or thereabouts would suffice for her sustenance, he affirmed. And when he had kneaded about an ounce of the substance, which, by virtue of its pink color, resembled redcurrant jelly, he put it in a silver box.

Those days were interminable for Enogat, who did not succeed in recovering his calmness. So he continued to live

---

[8] This is a bowdlerized version of the formula for making a homunculus specified in *De natura rerum* (1537), attributed (probably apocryphally) to Paracelsus, which recommends keeping the quasi-embryo in a putrefying mare's womb and nourishing it on human blood.

more at Bellevue than in his own house. He went into the garden at the slightest pretext, and often, as he heard sighs and bizarre cries coming from the aquarium, he was tempted to lift it out or to clear away the dung in order to see whether the doll was growing. But Callidulus, sagely pitiless, did not permit the disciple to fail in the prescriptions and thus compromise the definitive success of the Work.

The impatient Sothermès was obliged to confine himself strictly to his role, which consisted of practicing magical conjurations over the tumulus. Even that ceremony only took place twice a week, on Tuesday and Friday, and in the presence of the doctor.

How slowly the time passed! It seemed to Enogat that the hours were months. Anxious and tormented, he was so profoundly sunk in the anguish of waiting that he was struck by amazement when he learned that the day of the exhumation had come.

May had begun. Stimulated by the caresses of the matinal wind, the garden quivered, enraptured. The cherry-trees, the apricot-trees and the beautiful peach-trees, expanses of pale green sky in which pink nebulosities were palpitating, the hawthorns, the lilacs, the sovereign rose-bushes, the meek glory of the world, the syringas, the wisteria and the lilies-of-the-valley, all the trees and all the plants embalmed, rejoiced and intoxicated the air. And the sun powdered them with blond, orange and nacre and further away, higher up and everywhere extended its enchantment over things...

At eleven o'clock exactly, the servants dug up the tumulus and disinterred the aquarium with infinite precaution, while Callidulus, clad in a long ceremonial robe, gravely pronounced formulae in accordance with the magical rite, assisted by Enogat, very pale and emotional, anxious and yet proud of also appearing in broad daylight in the vestments of an adept. The aquarium was quickly transported to the laboratory, where the water it contained was poured out. Then the little woman, withdrawn unconscious from her glass prison, was placed in a bed of warm sand, where she was to dry out for three times twenty-four hours.

Miraculously developed, she now measured a meter in length, and her forms, clearly outlined this time and delicately modeled, were no longer those of a child; nevertheless, she gave the impression of a work of art rather than a living creature.

Enogat seemed to recover his courage. An imperceptible rosy tint appeared in his cheeks. Having looked again at the bed of sand where the little woman lay, he even uttered a profound sigh of hope, of delightful deliverance. Finally, in a surge of enthusiasm, he drew near to Callidulus, shook his hands for a long time and exclaimed:

"Oh, dear master, that a theurge you are! I salute in you a realizer of the septenary of septenaries that puts on the philosopher's brow, according to the expression of our Khunrath, 'a divine glory greater than the sacerdotal miter or the royal crown.' Allow me to call you Anthropopoios!"[9]

"Do so, then," replied Callidulus, condescendingly.

On the morning of the fourth day the homuncula was uncovered, and the doctor, having ascertained that she was in excellent condition, although still unconscious, plunged her into water again. With her delicately-contoured body and her sweet face, ringed like a silky diadem by abundant blonde hair, she seemed a true princess of Lilliput. The most misogynistic assessor could only have criticized her fingernails, which might have been thought to be in a period of formation such as to promote the jealous admiration of the aristocrats of China. This time, the "Work" was completely finished. It only remained to maintain the vitality of the Lilliputian. Callidulus declared that to be easy, for a man as well-versed as him in the magic of transmutations.

"What!" groaned Enogat. "She won't grow anymore?"

---

[9] The epithet Anthropopoios [Maker of Human Beings] was applied in antiquity to the sculptor Demetrios.

"Not an inch. Her growth has attained its limit, and in that too, the success surpasses my hopes. The glorious alchemists of the Middle Ages might never have achieved such a result. Homunculi rarely exceed fifty centimeters."

"That's very little," murmured the disciple, lowering his eyes.

"The present state of our scientific knowledge and the imperfection of our spirituality doesn't yet permit us to do better," the doctor regretted, vaguely. "But truly, what we can already do doesn't seem too bad. Look, then, at our creation—isn't she pretty? Look at that irreproachable anatomy, and the grace of that posture! Tell me, as a connoisseur of works of art, don't you find her charming?"

"Assuredly, her beauty recalls the most exquisite of the figurines modeled in Florence by the *quattrocentisti*, and I'll willingly call her the Anadyomene of the Matras, although she has fingernails that are a trifle long and pointed. But by the ten Sephiroths, how tiny she is!"

"Do you think that Monsieur Berthelot could do as much, eh? And am I unjustified when, in comparing myself to that professor, I qualify him as a laboratory assistant?"

"Oh, certainly, I recognize, and admire more than ever, your knowledge and your art, my dear master; Paracelsus himself couldn't have realized a more astonishing homuncula; I express my eternal gratitude and I shall remain eternally obliged to you. However, I can't help deploring the exiguity of those proportions; I confess that I had counted on a...figure of natural size."

But the stout Callidulus formed a subtle smile; then, emphasizing the first words, he replied: "Well, my dear friend, she'll render you the same services, for lucidity is not in proportion to stature. Soon, we'll interrogate her, and you can tell me what you think."

"Agreed. However, I would have preferred an individual less prophetic and more similar to ourselves, externally. I had so many plans for her! I saw her already doing the honors of my salon..."

"That's no problem. If you're desirous of showing her to your friends, her size can't be an obstacle."

"That's easy for you to say. It's quite impossible. Beside one another, we'd be ridiculous, and can you see us going out together? No, can you see us? I'd seem to be taking my daughter for a walk."

"Your tendency to forge torments for yourself is getting the upper hand again, it seems to me; it's the malign influence of the moon that's incessantly troubling your imagination. Are you forgetting, then, Sothermès, that from this day forward our homuncula can't live outside her element? Look, since she's immersed, she hasn't yet recovered her senses, and every time the water in that recipient—her dwelling henceforth—is renewed, she'll remain unconscious like that for two or three hours. That's why the renewal ought to take place as quickly as possible, and only every six or seven days."

"Aiee! It's absolutely necessary that she stays in the water? She can't live like a fish?"

"What! Haven't I told you? Paracelsus informs us that every elementary spirit lives in its 'chaos' and dies in any other. Now, a homuncula engendered like ours has many similarities with the spirits of which the genius author of the *Book of Nymphs* speaks."[10]

"What? She's not even an amphibian? I'll be reduced to keeping her in a bottle, then, like a gherkin! I'll only be able to have a relationship with her through that translucent wall?"

"That adds mystery and doesn't lack charm; think about the princesses captive in enchanted towers of whom the old legends speak."

---

[10] The *Liber de nymphis* (1566), the scholarly fantasy from which the modern mythology of elemental spirits is derived, is apocryphally attributed to Paracelsus, but he had been dead for some time when it was published. The idea of elementals was popularized in France by the enormously popular *Comte de Gabalis* (1670), a work of fiction that greatly elaborates the notion of an elemental marriage sketched in the earlier text.

"Very evocative, indeed, but not very cheerful for me, who...doesn't have the mind of a Maeterlinck. So permit me to leave this aquatic princess in your laboratory, where her place seems to me to be entirely indicated..."

"You no longer want her!" the doctor exclaimed.

Peering sadly at the little princess, Enogat said, with the gesture and tone of a man resigned: "Undoubtedly, since her principal qualities are prophetic. My dear master, you devote yourself to abstruse research, so you have much more need than I have of an oracle close to hand; and besides, she's cost you so much difficulty, that creation, that it would be a great injustice to steal her from you..."

"And this is another! But I made her for you, friend Sothermès!"

"My confusion is augmented by that. I wouldn't have asked that service of you if I'd suspected the labor it would demand."

"Haven't you paid for it liberally?"

"What's a little money for a work of this kind? No, no, dear master, in truth, I won't dispossess you."

At that moment, the little princess woke up, stretched herself, stood up, opened her large eyes, the irises of which were a somber sapphire in hue, and fixed the two men with an astonished and interrogative gaze.

"Look," said the doctor, "isn't she as pretty as a picture? Can it be that with your sentiment of the beautiful, you won't obtain any felicity from the contemplation of that jewel? Look at those eyes!"

"Yes, velvet, it seems, and of an almost sumptuous shade. Why do they have to illuminate the face of a dwarf?"

"Isn't your disappointment, dear friend, drawing you into a hyperbole that your lunar influences are rendering pessimistic? What importance can you attach to the stature of that being and her conditions of existence? Why not accept her as she is, since you recognize in her a perfect specimen of her species?"

"Eh! Because I wanted to make her my companion, in the most human sense of the word."

Callidulus shrugged. In a low voice, he pronounced: "Ah, that's different. Why didn't you say so sooner?"

Then, in an exceedingly low voice, Enogat de Sothermès said: "I thought you'd understood."

"Oh dear! Were you dreaming, then, of something other than platonic love? Oh, my friend, to what perils you'd expose yourself then! Beware from sacrificing to material passions like a simple man of the world; you'll lose all the fruits of your efforts, you'll compromise your ascension through the initiatory grades."

"I'll beware, master! In any case, don't worry; I have no desire to wallow in the mire of bourgeois sensualism, or to pluck the petals from paradoxical roses in the already-obsolete canthares of Baudelairean lust. I'm not asking for anything but a companion worthy of sharing my life. Can one not marry a creature constituted by the science of the Magi?"

"Ha ha! That would be another matter! Nothing prevents the trial, so far as I know. What a subject of study and meditation for our brethren! Yes, in the interests of science—the true science, ours—the experiment ought to be tried."

Enogat raised his head entirely. A vague joy invaded him, and then an anxiety. "Tried in what manner?" he asked.

"Attempting a materialization by means of a medium," Callidulus replied. "Our brethren in Italy have a surprising one at present, you know, Eloa Chevalier, the one who surpasses Madame Hannecart and Home himself. You could borrow that rare subject and render, by the same token, a signal service to our group in Paris."

"Indeed—a Katie King[11] would suit my purpose admirably. Why didn't I think of it sooner? Oh, what happiness you're causing me!"

---

[11] Katie King was a "materialized spirit" first associated with the teenage medium Florence Cook in the early 1870s, who succeeded in convincing the physicist William Crookes of her

"Anyway, it's easy for us to discover whether that's what you need. Our Anadyomene of the Matras will inform us perfectly..."

The excellent doctor pivoted on the tip of his right foot, and, going to a little dresser of composite style, he picked up a little silver hammer. His disciple, motionless, considered it attentively.

Three times, Callidulus waved his silver hammer in the air. Then, three times, he struck the magic seal. Then, after a brief conjuration, he interrogated the homuncula.

The latter, with a perfect amenity, responded that the projected materialization would succeed marvelously, thanks to the collaboration of an elemental. The creature thus obtained would give Monsieur de Sothermès much satisfaction, as much by her intelligence and taste as by her dazzling beauty, if the Monsieur maintained himself in her presence in the sidereal regions of sentiment or the higher spheres of thought.

When Enogat hastened to enquire whether he could marry such a creature, however, the homunculi did not understand the meaning of the word at all; all that she could see in the astral was that the elemental would live like a mortal woman beside Monsieur de Sothermès, and that she would inform him of the conduct that he ought to maintain in her regard.

As for events reserved for the couple, they would consist of travels, at first through strange milieux, the vision of which made the little sibyl burst out laughing, and then through sumptuous decors under admirable skies, which plunged her into a vague ecstasy.

But Enogat soon enquired of her: "Will it last long? How many years?"

---

reality. She became so famous that other mediums began to manifest her. She sometimes appeared naked at Cook's séances, adding to her notoriety and encouraging scurrilous rumors about the precise means she had employed to convince Crookes of her materiality—rumors that Enogat appears to have heard.

The humuncula having expressed her stupefaction by means of a very eloquent mime, the doctor shook his head gently, and, leaning over his disciple's shoulder, murmured: "Time is naught for spirits."

"Then let her tell us the denouement?" begged Sothermès.

Shortly thereafter, the seeress exclaimed, in an inspired fashion: "As the dog returns to its vomit, the man who returns to the abjections of the world of Rupa will see his happiness vanish in smoke."

It was impossible to get any more out of her.

"It's a sibylline pronouncement," the doctor concluded. "If I grasp its meaning correctly, you ought to conduct yourself as a veritable adept with the elemental that destiny accords to you."

"I can marry her, then?"

"In truth, the best thing is to ask her...herself!" replied Callidulus, not without a hint of irony. And, terminating the conversation: "Let's procure, then, as soon as possible, the indispensable medium."

III. In which we become acquainted with elementals
and the heroine of the story

It was in Milan that the Eloa Chevalier lived whose reputation as a medium extended all the way to America. Her case
did not only interest occultists and spiritualists; several doctors
in medicine and a few serious scholars were studying her passionately, so all the experimenters wanted to take possession
of her as much as possible. Callidulus had to enter into veritable negotiations and trumpet the interests of science very loudly for his Milanese colleagues to consent to lend her to him for
a month; then it was necessary to pay the subject royalty, who,
sensing that she was indispensable, had imposed conditions on
her displacement like those of an opera singer.

Eloa Chevalier arrived in Paris on 15 May. A tall and
stout young woman, in her gait and visage she was reminiscent of a camp-followers of the bersaglieri. In reality she was
a former schoolteacher for whom the glory of revealing the
dark mysteries of the ABC to bambini had been insufficient.
Rapidly, with her soldierly appearance and her schoolmistress's bun on top her head, she had conquered a veritable reputation in the world of the curious and the scholarly occupied
with psychic matters. Her portrait had appeared in two or three
of the occult periodicals that were prevalent in Italy, and the
Tribuna had just published a photograph of her recommending
the famous Menelik soap to transalpines.

Knowing the signora's self-esteem and anxious to please
her, Enogat had a room prepared for her in his own house,
and, in spite of the impatience that clawed him, he invited her
to fix the date for the first séance herself. Eloa did not abuse
her host's generosity; she only took three days to rest from the
fatigues of her journey. Nevertheless, when that period of time
had elapsed, Callidulus restricted himself to submitting her to
ordinary experiments, because he wanted to "try her out" first.

Delighted by those preliminaries and certain of being able to manipulate her as he wished, he put her in a somnambulistic trance on the afternoon of the following day, after the obligatory conjurations and evocations made in concert with Enogat.

When the signora was entranced, the two men established the chain and waited in silence, in complete darkness. The window of the room where they were had been carefully covered with thick curtains, for the yellow rays of the solar spectrum, and the red rays even more so, are injurious to the emission of vital fluid.

Eloa had only been asleep for a moment when she felt a sharp pain at the level of the heart; immediately, she went into the lethargic state. A pale light, an indefinable blue-gray in color, emanated from her body and gradually enveloped her in such a way that she appeared to be clad in misty muslin.

"That's the astral fluid exteriorizing," the doctor murmured to the dilettante, who was invaded by emotion.

Then that vaporous vestment tore, or rather split, into narrow bands, which condensed and formed a long drapery, from the summit of which surged a coldly luminous ball, similar to a rough sketch of a head modeled in clay.

"That's our elemental condensing around itself the matter that it's borrowing from the medium," Callidulus explained.

The ball stretched into an oval and, by virtue of a mysterious labor of construction that seemed to be the work of an invisible hand, it took on a characteristic form. The surface was modeled into a human face, the projections becoming a nose and a chin, between which lips were silhouetted; flat areas were transformed into cheeks and cavities suddenly illuminated two eyes.

As the head began to come to life, Enogat noticed that luminous matter had condensed in one of Eloa's hands, and imparted his astonishment to Callidulus, who replied in a whisper:

"Oh, yes, the phosphorescent stone! It's the medium's astral fluid condensing."

"One might think they were snowballs."

"Petrified—look carefully, because it's not without importance; some claim that the idea of the philosopher's stone owes its origin to that phenomenon."

Abruptly, that condensation paled, and was then extinguished, while the glow of the body in formation increased in intensity. The medium's face then became perfectly distinct; aged by several years, she exhibited the state of fatigue particular to people exhausted by some chronic malady. But they did not have the leisure to devote their attention to Eloa, who was still in lethargy. The face of the elemental was palpitating with life, and the fluidic drapery that linked it to the medium was transformed into the white robe of a priestess of Isis. The spirit became a woman and appeared in all her beauty,

Opening eyes in which gold circled an emerald,[12]

smiling and resplendent beneath the hieratic coiffure that heightened the Venetian red of her hair.

Dazzled, the two men admired her silently and held their breath. Suddenly, Enogat, whose gaze had just met the charming, suave gaze of the apparition, felt his entire being vibrate and, invaded by an almost religious tenderness, let himself fall to his knees.

Before he had recovered from his surprise, the "procreated" individual, her arms raised above her hair, slightly inflected in such a way that they formed a crescent, proclaimed in a crystalline voice, simultaneously caress and music:

"In Keter, Hokhmah and Binah, greetings to you, dear curious! You have called me, and here I am!"

As Enogat remained motionless and indecisive, his heart beating rapidly, and Doctor Callidulus, astonished, perhaps or

---

[12] The line is from Henri de Régnier's "Tel qu'en songe" from *Poèmes 1887-1892*.

the first time in his life, could not believe either his ears or his eyes, the radiant apparition lowered her eyelids slightly, and, her shoulders swaying slightly and her nostrils imperceptibly tightened, already coquettish, she went on:

"Am I such as you desired me, Enogat de Sothermès?"

Still on his knees, the interpellated individual shivered and replied: "Oh, a thousand times more beautiful than my imagination dared dream of you."

"Your form declares the beauty of the idea to which you give light, dear daughter of the concepts of a literate adept," said the doctor, whose aplomb was beginning to return. "Your head bears the planetary types that we desired of you, the triple signature of Mercury, Venus and Apollo. Your spirit certainly responds, therefore, to the aspirations of the one who procreated you on the terrestrial plane. Be welcome among us, amiable reflection of the astral world."

"Very well, let's talk, dear friends, let's become acquainted. Mutual desires have brought us together ; let a sympathetic communion now liken our souls."

And the apparition, advancing toward her "procreators," extended her delicate hands to them politely; in response to the plea of her gaze, Enogat rose to his feet.

"But first," she continued, "put an end to this darkness; light does not inconvenience me at all. I even think that it is becoming necessary to me."

Callidulus approved: "Yes, you need light, for, materialized, you won't take long to lose your photogenic radiation. In fact..."

He interrupted himself abruptly. He clapped his hands.

Enogat had just drawn the curtains; and quickly—very quickly—the apparition was deprived of her supernatural appearance without any deterioration of her marvelous beauty. She gave the impression of a young foreigner; her face bearing the inscription of the character of the ancient Egyptian race. And on seeing her so alive, the doctor gesticulated, clapped his hands again, and pirouetted, no longer able to restrain his joy.

"Behold," he cried, "something that far exceeds the experiments, conclusive as they were, of Crookes, Aksakov, Zöllner, poor MacNab and James Tissot![13] And how many hours will you remain thus, during each séance?"

"In this terrestrial state? I could remain for months, if you wish."

"Certainly, yes, we wish it," said Enogat, with an affectionate energy, his eyes bright with an enamored gleam.

"What! You could do that?" said Callidulus.

"I could, with your help."

"Ah! Science of the Magi! Decidedly, Katie King is surpassed. It will be necessary..."

"What will be necessary?"

"For us to give you a name, dear girl!"

"I've already received one. An elementary adept who, since his arrival in the Kamaloka, has always testified generosity toward me and given me advice, drew my horoscope when he was certain that I would descend to this planet, and after seeing the role that destiny traced for me, he named me Neurocyme."[14]

Callidulus bowed. "We accept and respect such a baptism; long live Neurocyme! In fact, how can we conserve it for you, this life?"

---

[13] Tissot was actually an artist, but he produced a famous painting, *L'Apparition médiumistique* (1885), after attending a séance held by the English medium William Eglinton, who allegedly summoned the ghost of Kathleen Newton. The preference to "poor MacNab" is enigmatic.

[14] *Cyme*, derived from a Latin word meaning "summit," is used in both French and English to refer to a flower-head, especially one not yet opened. That might have more to do with the author's improvisation than the fact that the term "neurocyme" was used in some 19th century biological textbooks to refer to a hypothetical "wave" passing along neural fibers.

"It's the simplest thing in the world: by maintaining the medium in lethargy and nourishing her with a catheter. It will be sufficient for her to assimilate thus the juice of certain plants, which I shall designate to you when the time comes. For the moment, it is merely a matter of letting her sleep."

"Very good; we shall only occupy ourselves henceforth with your person. Now, tell us, although you have come to ours, have you conserved a precise, lucid memory of the world from which you have descended?"

"My spirit has not forgotten anything."

"And can you reply to the questions we address to you regarding that invisible world and the beings that are encountered there?"

"I will probably be unable to satisfy your curiosity immediately, for no one receives with impunity a light too intense after a long sojourn in obscurity, but I promise to do my best to prepare you to receive elevated revelations."

"An adept of my grade is no longer languishing in the tenebrous regions; are you unaware that I am a hierophant?"

"What are your terrestrial enlightenments for the Selves moving on the divine plane?"

"Oh! But to what Neshama have we the honor of speaking? The oracle we consulted announced an elemental, one of those the Hindus qualify as kamamanasic. Is that what you are?"

"Yes, if you wish," said Neurocyme, allowing trills of irreverent laughter to escape.

Nonplussed, the doctor murmured: "Why *if I wish*?"

"Yes, yes," replied the mysterious individual, "the pretended theosophists of Europe and American attribute strange things to the Hindus of past centuries."

"But I have nothing in common with those people," Callidulus protested. "Our orientalists..."

"Oh, they're not very well-informed on the subject of elementals. We're not at all—not in the least—what you believe us to be down here."

"But the secret doctrine can't be mistaken on the nature of elementals!"

"To what doctrine are you alluding, Doctor—that of your contemporaries or that of the ancients?"

"You're not going to tell me that modern occultists have deviated from the essential principles taught by their ancestors?"

Neurocyme applied a charming index finger to her mouth. "We'll discuss that later. Today, your amazement would be too great."

As she pronounced the last words, Neurocyme had a slight smile in her eyes, but the rest of her beautiful face remained enigmatic; and, allowing the doctor to trace gestures of protest in the air, she turned to the dilettante, who had not ceased gazing at her with an affectionate and rather naïve delight.

"And you, Seigneur Enogat," she interrogated, "do you also deny that I'm a elemental, even kamamanasic? A scarcely graceful name, in truth."

"Oh, what does your origin matter to me?" sighed the ecstatic, his hands raised and joined. "For me, you're the Princess of the Fays."

"You speak more truly than you think," she said. "My peers were, in fact, long mistaken for Fays by your ancestors, and there are still Celts in Scotland who believe in us and offer us milk and flowers every evening."

There was a momentary silence.

"I see, dear unknown," Callidulus resumed, suddenly, "that it is necessary to submit to your pleasure. You must know how eager my disciple and I are to penetrate the arcana. When will it be fitting for you to commence your revelations?"

"As soon as I know you better," Neurocyme replied. "I intend to measure out carefully the doses of knowledge that it is appropriate to dispense to you."

Her eyes were still smiling...

The doctor, reiterating his solicitations, attempted to persuade her to describe the impressions she had felt when she materialized, but his persistence was in vain; the mysterious individual did not reveal anything precise. Then, not without some resentment, he snapped: "At least, are you content, at present?"

"I'll tell you that later, when I've observed your fellows at close range," she said, evasively.

Callidulus withdrew.

"A singular character," he ruminated, on the way. "Scarcely materialized on our plane, she's already a woman. And what a woman! She'll be the finest of our sly creatures, or I'm only a layman! Yes, a very curious character! And not to succeed in knowing her precise origin! Oh, Science of the Magi, divine Sun, how many mysterious veils still remain for you to pierce!"

While he was muttering in that fashion, while walking along with his hands behind his back, Neurocyme, after having remained pensive momentarily, as if indecisive, slowly drew nearer to Enogat de Sothermès.

"He has amusing ingenuities, the good doctor," she declared, in a tone that expressed with mockery and pity, "and a great many illusions yet!"

"Him! The most theurgical Magus of the era!" protested the dilettante, surprised.

"Child!" the extraordinary creature continued, with a caress in her voice. "Dear child! You'll see later, when I have lifted before your astonished eyes the veils that will reveal their mysteries."

"Oh I care very little, I confess, about knowing the unknowable, any more than I care about contemplating the stars, now that I can admire your eyes. Consent to stay down here, that's all I ask of you; deign to choose this as your dwelling, and you'll be treated as its sovereign. Are all the secrets of the absolute worth as much as a single one of your radiant glances?"

Her eyes widened, and with a fleeting transport of joy, quickly stifled by an exclamation of mischievous impertinence, she said: "For a dilettante in the latest style, you're very sentimental. However, I like your enthusiasm; at least you, dear literate seigneur, have not yet been dried up by pride."

He became more excited. "I don't want to have any other pride than that of serving you as a knight serves his suzeraine," he proclaimed, "because I love you; I love you, Neurocyme! Your ineffable fluid raises unknown energies in my triple nature. I love you as Pygmalion loved the statue in which he had molded his ideal, as the epic poet loves the creation of his thoughts. Are you not, Neurocyme, the creation of my amour?"

"Enogat..."

"Daughter of Viviane, you have enchanted me! Oh, may your apparition not be fugitive, in order that I might believe that I am not only being lulled by a beautiful dream!"

"That would, however, be more ideal," the feminized spirit sighed, ironically.

"In losing you, a masterpiece of the Demiurge, I would lose my reason, I sense it! To give your supreme beauty the radiant life it merits, to testify my love to you by an incandescent worship, is that not also an ideal?"

"Perhaps."

The eyes of the apparition gleamed.

"I beg you on both knees not to return to the astral. Grant, at least, that mercy to a devotee who wants nothing except to adore you. From this day on it is only up to you to take the astral ascendant over your servant..."

Lyrically and hectically, the dilettante intoned his peroration:

"My heart is a mystic rose that owes its blossoming to you; can you see, in my eyes, dazzled mirrors respectful of yours, and on my cheeks, once livid, the gold and crimson that are the grateful sap of that new rose? That mysterious flower, I believed desiccated, faded, incapable henceforth of blooming in a mud as sad as my being. That sap, I believed forever dried up in my heart; but now it has opened and is blossoming, that mystic rose; permit, then, O Neurocyme, that I make you the oblation of it!"

"I permit you that," she replied, hieratically, but with her lips curved in an indefinable smile; and, singularly, between her beautiful half-closed eyelashes, the emeralds of her eyes emitted an equivocal and disconcerting glimmer...

IV. Dilettantizing

Scarcely was she installed in the house in the Rue Vaneau than Neurocyme took her role as mistress of the house seriously; she started giving orders.

Her entry into the house intrigued the domestics greatly, for Monsieur did not have the custom of introducing "good friends" under his roof. But who could this lady be that Monsieur was treating with excessive regard, if not one of those specimens of... in brief, a "good friend."

"Come on, damn it, what do you think, Monsieur Jean?" the chef asked the *valet de chambre*, who had been the first to approach the person that they all had now to call *Madame*. "Come on! You have the confidence of Monsieur; you must know something..."

But Monsieur Jean replied with these winged words: "That's where you're mistaken! I don't even know how Madame got in here. At any rate, it's certain that she didn't come through the door, since the doorman didn't see her go past. That's all I can tell you, Monsieur Tissot."

The chef had an astonishment for which he seemed to be taking his belly as a witness, on which he was drumming with great solemnity. "Strange!" he murmured. "Very strange!"

"And take note, Monsieur Tissot, that our garden has no hidden door."

"Strange, Monsieur Jean, strange," reiterated the other, driving in his navel.

"All the more strange that Madame has arrived without a decent wardrobe. When I first saw her, on the famous day when the doctor put the other good woman to sleep, she was wearing a theatrical costume, and the next day, Monsieur sent me to the dressmaker, the lingerie-maker, the milliner and all the way to Montmartre to the shoemaker."

"She's an actress, then?" said the chef, with an expression of unfathomable scorn.

Grandiosely, Monsieur Jean opined: "One might believe so, from her manners. Even so, how to explain that she arrived here without a dress, and especially without underwear? Ordinarily, Monsieur Tissot, those ladies scarcely lack that sort of thing..."

Monsieur Tissot deigned to smile: a resigned, almost blasé smile. "Indeed." Then, swiftly, he asked: "And what kind of costume was she wearing, Monsieur Jean?"

"Oh, something very peculiar. Have you seen *Aida* performed, Monsieur Tissot?"

"I should think so. Since our old Bertrand became the concierge of a professor at the Collège de France, he's been showering me with theater tickets. *Aida* was put on at the Opéra, if I remember rightly...there was a Moorish princess in it.,..."

"Same as in *L'Africaine*—you've got it. Well, *Madame* since she's *Madame* henceforth, was wearing a costume just like that *Aida*, white, with lots of pleats and no corset—in brief, the vestment of chic people in Africa in olden times."

"Yes, yes, before the conquest of Algeria. So, it's necessary to believe that she's a singer, Monsieur Jean?"

"Um! She reeks more of the Comédie-Française, Monsieur Tissot, the Comédie."

The chef made a sudden movement of respect. "What if she's an associate, on occasion?"

"Her arrival is all the more stupefying. Think, Monsieur Tissot—not even after a performance...and the doorman didn't see a thing!"

"She can't have fallen from the sky, though!"

"Perhaps she's fallen from somewhere else," said Monsieur Jean, lowering his voice.

"Really? What do you mean by that?"

"Really. I mean that, for some time, Monsieur has been devoting himself, with the doctor, to diabolically mysterious things. After what I've seen in the laboratory at Bellevue...do you remember what I told you at the time?"

"I remember. However, just between us, an intelligent man like you...you can't believe in the existence of spirits?"

"Me, Monsieur Tissot, I only believe that a louis is twenty francs. It doesn't alter the fact that since Madame's arrival, the other individual, the medium, as they call her, is as good as dead."

"Get away!"

"Ask Alfred, who helped me take her up to her room. She seems to be asleep, so they claim—but in the meantime, she doesn't wake up..." Monsieur Jean started, and interrupted himself. "Right! There she goes, ringing for me again."

And he responded to the summons from his new "master."

The new master! Decidedly, Neurocyme was obliging the personnel to an unusual activity. Turbulent and capricious, she was turning the house upside-down with her delicate orders. At her slightest gesture, Tissot, the doorman, and especially Jean, spun like tops.

The day after her installation, she had begun composing her wardrobe. *Ring-a-ding*, all day long there had been an invasion of couturiers and lingerie-makers, a procession of milliners and jewelers, the latter carrying their sample-cases like holy sacraments. Soon, tormented by the ardent desire to transform the house, she summoned the upholsterer, the cabinet-maker, the antique-dealer, continually having some item of furniture or tapestry moved, wanting the pedestal of that bust to be changed, or that painting revarnished...

Today, agitating in her right hand a pale iris with which she was gently perfuming her hair, the other arm leaning on the jasper of a side-table and supporting her charming and willful chin, in a semi-sphinx-like attitude, she said to the valet: "Jean, we're having a dinner party tomorrow, and we're going, in that regard, to attempt a few innovations. I'm counting on the aid of your zeal..." Then she added, but with irony: "...And your intelligence."

Although very annoyed, deep down, by the idea of a change—another one!—to his calm and mild habitude, Jean replied, immovably and with absolute respect: "Madame does me too much honor. Madame can count on me."

"Good. You'll procure us the perfumes of which this is the list, and you'll make sure that some of them—these—are burned during the meal. The others are to be projected later over the heads of the guests, by mans of special vaporizers. Those instruments, as well as the perfume-burners, will arrive this evening. You can study their functioning at your ease. Oh, from hour to hour it will be necessary to vary the lighting; the electrician will dispose a set of lamps of difference colors and teach you how to manipulate them—nothing simpler! You'll carry out the changes in illumination personally."

"Yes, Madame," stammered the valet, feeling utterly dazed. Pulling himself together heroically, however, he repeated: "Nothing simpler."

"As for the plants and flowers," Neurocyme went on, implacably, "I'll choose them myself and show you how they ought to be placed in due course. It's necessary that the drawing room combines the charm of a hothouse and the splendor of a palace. Finally, as this fête will be followed by many others, we're promoting you to butler and making you responsible for training the staff for our new projects. Henceforth, you'll wear colored livery, trousers and a jacket with shoulder-knots, with a powdered wig on reception evenings."

"Madame is too kind," Jean stammered, disturbed because vanity and sloth were engaged in a violent struggle within him.

There was a pause, Neurocyme seemed to reflect momentarily. The pale iris palpitated briefly in front of her eyes.

"We'll begin to arrange the décor this afternoon; I'll explain to you then in detail what I expect of you," she murmured.

And the pale iris oscillated gently, indicating the door. "Go on, Jean."

The valet made his spine describe the most reverential of curves.

In the vestibule, with a hint of pride swiftly muffled by an indefinable anxiety, he muttered: "Now I'm the chief mechanic..."

Left alone, Neurocyme, momentarily pensive, plucked the petals from the iris on the jasper of the side-table. Then, rising to her feet, she began to pace back and forth. She paused, and then continued pacing—and while going back and forth, she smiled.

One of her first curiosities, one of her very first requests, had been to see "Parisian society." Enogat had hastened to grant that wish. To give his friend an impression that was both excellent and vivid, and in order also to give himself an intense satisfaction of self-esteem, he thought of gathering around the elemental transformed into a woman the most transcendent and the most typical minds in his entourage: those he admitted to his own intimacy.

It was then that Neurocyme had resolved to compose a sensational costume and prepare an original décor; she intended to prove to the illustrious company that was about to assemble before her eyes that she did not cede anything in the matter of transcendence, and that her arrival was a veritable event.

One day sufficed for her to improvise the décor: a few old fabrics with fresco tones or hieratic embroideries, and obligatory plants with ornamental flowers whose shades, subtly combined, constituted the most singular and the most tasteful of orchestrations.

As for her costume, that was no less piquant and unusual. Dissatisfied with the costume delivered by the couturier, whose skill could not surpass the social ideal, Neurocyme had draped her corsage and her skirt herself before the astounded seamstress.

"This a little higher, you see, and this lower..."

By imprinting to the principal pleats an ingenious direction, she had spontaneously created a series of light, harmonious rhythms, and plays of light with a strange, adorable and sure effect. In five minutes, her amused intuition had accomplished what the most learned professionals had sought in vain for several days. And the seamstress, a young woman from Batignolles, judging that operation of applied esthetics with typical suburban charity, was convinced that her new client was an "old hand" in tacking, needlework and oversewing.

A joy of ingenuous vanity, a hope of seeing and knowing, enlivened Neurocyme's cheeks with a crimson flush, while sharpening her pretty eyes.

Everything was ready.

In inviting his faithful, of course, Enogat had announced to them that he would introduce them to a foreigner of the rarest culture, a sparkling image to make all Hayem's Gustave Moreaus pale,[15] and a knowledgeable adept to astonish Annie Besant, Albert Jhouney and Marc Haven, Barlet and Thorion, and Papus himself. That is why no one was lacking at the roll-call. And even better, they all arrived on time...

There were twelve—one might say *the* twelve—not including Callidulus.

The richest and most worldly of the familiars of the house in the Rue Vaneau, Hubert Prétexta, had frequented the homes of Barbey, Renan and Goncourt, and had taken away in the adornments of his frock-cost a little of the illustrious dust that velveted the solemn furnished room in the Rue Rousselet, the high-ceilinged study of the Collège de France and the noble Grenier in Auteuil. Furthermore, he was still in communication with all the literary, pictural, sculptural and musical celebrities of yesterday, today and tomorrow. He had traveled. Without having gone to the devil, he knew all the celebrated galleries of France and Belgium, and all the museums of Europe recommended by Baedeker. He had collected all kinds of things: autographs, coins, clasps. Perhaps, one day, he would collect musical instruments and postage stamps. In the mean-

---

[15] The most famous of the numerous paintings by Gustave Moreau acquired by the collector Charles Hatem was "L'Apparition," one of the painter's several depictions of Salome.

time, he possessed a first class library and an assembly of paintings and engravings that was not banal without too many obscenities. His health, that of a robust quinquagenarian who was also an observer of the laws of hygiene, prevented him from becoming blasé. He was, therefore, like those healthy fruits that slowly become overripe without falling from the tree, and without losing any of their form and color. Satisfied with life, and satisfied most of all with himself, he spread around him a kind of radiance of amiability, and gladly rendered service to young polygraphs who brought him their pamphlets and the divine poets who dedicated their verses to him.

Old Monsieur de Nyzor, an amateur Orientalist, and young Minégoujon, very knowledgeable in Sanskrit, occupied their leisure honorably in modernizing Buddhism, the former as a benevolent moralist, the later as an evolutionist philosopher, with the aim of facilitating its digestion by artists and men of the world. The Bois de Chaville was the sacred wood of their apostolate.

The gentle Ladislas—don't get involved!—too much the man of letters to please professional philosophers and certainly too philosophical not to be merely a man of letters, had come after a long butterfly flight through metaphysics to settle on Tolstoyism, to which his oriental ancestry predisposed him somewhat. As classical, too, as a Ciceronian of the Italian Renaissance, the Slav, who only swore by Mozart, after having renounced the Wagnerian religion and Mallarméan prosody, was classical and polyglot and savant like no one else, a gentle apostle of subtle ignorance!

A prince of egotists, the clever Albin Bérénès had carved himself a reputation as a master-writer, and almost a political man, in spite of several failed candidacies, by playing at ethics and sociology, with the coquetries of an angora goat and the gossip of a chronicler; lyrical in Stendhalism jests, an ironist of quivering ardor, he was attracted by bloody and funeral sensualities. Tiepolo, Il Sodoma and the decadents of great painting spoke to him more vividly than the primitives; in that he was impulsive, but never a snob.

But the poet Sabas, an inexhaustible talker and Swinburnean drinker, expended himself so extensively in esthetic discussions that everyone had been waiting for ten years for his first volume of verse...

The literary—and literate—critic Carolus Romanitus, an inflammable and paradoxical skeptic, attempted reflections of drapery in the Median robe of Anatole France, but in workmanlike fashion; the mere word Romanticism was sufficient to exasperate him, and that intense logician perceived Romanticism everywhere.

Another skeptic, Henry Negans, an ornate intelligence—but a painter—aimed at Renanism in his art criticism and literature in his painting. Quasimodo, precipitating the hero of *Notre Dame de Paris* from the height of the fantastic towers, did not have a more discreetly teasing flick than that mordant and polished salonnier, who sonnetized at times in the Breton moonlight, before the heath and the sea, without losing his finesse. Negans had an ear as keen as Romanitas' was hard; nevertheless, in spite of their respective infirmities, the two skeptics opposed Attic harmony to all the decadent breezes that the good Voltairean Abbé Morellet had already sensed in Monsieur de Chateaubriand.[16]

Two novelists enabled the spirit of the eighteenth century to live again in their works. One, Bernard Fauve, a descendant of solemn Epicureans who powdered their philosophical or martial catogans for the salon of Helvetius—a secret chamberlain of voluptuous synods—defended all sensualities with a sanguine, indomitable ardor. The other, René Tardeval, the heir of gallant story-tellers, the great grandson of Thomas Pogge and second cousin of Pinot-Duclos, paraded an indulgent, even amused, psychology over human weaknesses. Oth-

---

[16] The Encyclopedist André Morellet was famously nicknamed "Abbé Mordsles" [Father Bites'em] by Voltaire because of his mordant wit.

erwise, nothing could be more different than those two men brought together by the same literate convictions, the former singing storms and sunlight, forests and courtesans, filibusters and corsairs in a prose as purple as his cheeks, the other more elegant and mat, hiding a little blue flower, a virginal gift, beneath the risqué bitterness of his dandyism.

Another sentimentalist: the music critic Vivian, a normalian with the soul of a poet, exactly like the Mendelssohn of *Fingal's Cave* and *The Dream*—knowing clearly, feeling delicately, was always careful to translate sensations artistically, dreaming of beautiful images as soon as he savored an orchestra and evocative prints as soon as he stepped into a museum. He vibrated at everything, expressing nervous, unprecedented, profound joys. The mere names, linked on a poster, of Tristan and Isolde, plunged him into an atmosphere of dreams, a bath of poetry. And in the afternoons of Holy Week when he listened to sacred music in shadowy chapels, he relived the ancient days of Nuremberg and the Church of Saint Catherine; he thought himself a Walther to the invisible Eva.[17]

The polygraph Saint-Dolent, on the contrary, tidied up, went out and, in vain, released all his eclecticism even in exotic regions; an incurable spleen spoiled everything for him. The slightest attempt at "art nouveau" furnished him with a pretext for copying—infinitely talented copying, moreover—and he exploited the dilettantism, the puffery and snobbery of his peers with the conscientious and morose mastery of a poodle-clipper.

Curious minds, developed in hothouses, experienced in the fencing of words, all those refined individuals only disposed of an infinitesimal sum of benevolence, and it was rather difficult to obtain mercy in their eyes. However, the charm that Neurocyme emitted had conquered them all in a matter of minutes. Doubtless, the women that they encoun-

---

[17] Walther and Eva are the central characters in Richard Wagner's opera *Die Meistersinger von Nürnberg*.

tered in their ordinary circle talked like schoolmistresses or whores, and this one astonished them with her knowledge, seduced them with the strange subtlety of her repartee and by the very grace of her silences...

"She's an American off the latest transatlantic liner," Tardeval opined to some of his colleagues gathered around Callidulus, while Prétextat, Monsieur de Nyzor and Ladislas were madrigalizing around Neurocyme's dress.

The brazen voice of Albin Bénérès rang out: "America has a boat on the banks of the Tage, then, which are among the most ardent and saddest things in the world..."

"No, no, she gives the impression, rather, of an English-woman brought up in Hindustan," protested Bernard Fauve, vaguely. "Isn't that so, Doctor?"

"You think so?" replied Callidulus with a mocking smile.

"She's not a Slavic student," though, retorted the son of solemn Epicureans.

"Nor some Irish mystic, sister to Yseult, second cousin to the fays of Broceliande," added Vivian, his dark eyes full of electricity.

Callidulus joked, winking: "How do you recognize all that? What if that intellectual child were simply a Belgian schoolmistress?"

"Come on, Doctor," said Tardeval, "You're not going to let us flounder any longer. You know that enigmatic beauty, and doubtless better than anyone, since she's one of your adepts. Just two brief questions. Firstly *who*?"

"And then?" said Callidulus.

"*Where from?*"

Like an actor certain of his effect, the doctor "took a moment" and then, in a detached fashion, uttered the few words: "She's an Egyptian."

There was a momentary astonishment. Tardeval seemed to collect himself. Bérénès shook his fine Augustan head. Over in the other group, Neurocyme's dress sparkled.

"Bah! Born of Europeans, then, your Egyptian!" snapped Negans, suddenly.

"Undoubtedly," continued Callidulus, obligingly. "And a daughter, grand-daughter and great-grand-daughter of initiates, my good friend."

Bérénès continued shaking his head.

"An Egyptian!" Tardeval declared. "Ah! That explains her air of the sphinx!"

"Ah!" murmured Vivian. "The mystery of correspondences!"

Ah! the doctor thought, privately. *The naivety of men!*

At that moment the traditional announcement rang out, and the guests went into the dining room, where the flames of a tender nacarat light lit suns in the crystal. Silky fabrics from the Orient and Venice, striated with phosphorescences, dissimulated the former décor of severe wood-paneling, and brought a warm, light and relaxed joy to the large room. A few tufts of dracenas, pandanus, and slender arborescent ferns served as niches for Chinese and Moorish perfume-burners, which took turns to charge the atmosphere with rare and heady scents.

"You've arrived, Madame, in a unique period for visiting the hearth of modern civilization, said Prétextat, when the conversations that had been engaged were resumed. "We're in an astonishing phase of transformation; never, perhaps, since the sixteenth century, have so many essential ideas been more ardently agitated."

"Really?" said Neurocyme, showing radiant teeth.

"Certainly, literary or scientific, there isn't a single veritable intellectual who isn't preparing prestigious tomorrows."

"You see me delighted by that, and I'd be grateful to you for acquainting me with some of the superior minds who are preparing the new era about which there is so much talk."

"There are several of them by your sides, Madame, and our friends Callidulus, Ladislas, Nyzor and Bérénès will take pleasure in explaining their experiments and theories to you."

"Madame, being an adept, is by no means unacquainted with the theory of occultism," Callidulus hastened to declare. "It is undoubtedly the only one that presents a powerful syn-

thesis of the impulses of all souls. What is good in philosophies and socilologies, occultism embraces and vivifies by its
tradition."

"What, you also hold to the *culture of self*?" queried
Tardeval, ironically ingenuous, caressing his lovely beard.[18]

"Didn't you know that? What is the asceticism followed
by our candidates for initiation, the asceticism bequeathed by
the esoteric centers of India and Egypt, if not a *culture of self*?
It's not only our excellent friend Bérénès who has borrowed
that culture, it's all the reformers of all times, save for the socialists—who only count in politics, don't they...?"

"Permit me, dear Magus," Bérénès interjected, "to point
out to you that I haven't borrowed my theory of autoculture
from your doctrine, of which, like everyone else, I only know
the broad outlines, and nothing more."

"Far be it from me, Bérénès, to think of contesting the
paternity of a method as original as it is opportune, under the
eye of Barbarians. I merely wanted to indicate that nothing can
be discovered that we do not already possess."

Nyzor coughed, and gravely placed his finger on his
glass. "Yes," he affirmed. And, lifting his finger, he pronounced self-importantly: "Thanks to the treasures poured
over your Occident by the sanctuaries of ancient India."

"Thanks above all to the riches accumulated in the land
of Osiris," said Callidulus.

"Without the Brahmins, what would the pontiffs of Ra
and Thoth have been?" insisted Monsieur de Nyzor.

"And without the Magi of Tello,[19] some historians sustain, what would the Brahmins have been?" said Neurocyme,

---

[18] When the present story was written, the notion of the "culture of self" was primarily associated in Parisian literary cir-
cles with a trilogy of novels by Maurice Barrès collectively
known as *Le Culte de moi* [The Cult of the Self] published in
1888-91, the obvious model of Bénérès.

[19] Tello, a site in the region of Mesopotamia that was once the
Kingdom of Sumer, was extensively excavated in the last two

her torso straight and immobile. Half-closing her eyes, however, and tightening her nostrils a little, she suddenly changed the direction of the conversation: "That's taking us a little far into the region that our ancestors called, I believe, the night of time. What if we were to return to the age of snobs?"

In his quality as ancestor, Nyzor employed faded locutions. That is why he said: "Beautiful lady, I share your opinion entirely."

Bernard Fauve and René Tardeval looked at Nyzor, and then looked at one another with a kind of ironic fixity.

"The admirable thing about innovation," Neurocyme continued, "is that it is merely the unfamiliar and rejuvenating costume of a concept twenty or thirty times centenarian. Thinking humankind is nibbling away at an ancient patrimony, and, that that renders the sacrosanct idea of progress, such as it is conceived by certain contemporary gourmets, more than a little anemic. Of all the means of generation, what are, in sum, those that most extol the present moment?"

"The development of individual energy, Madame," replied Bérénès. "And our loyal friends the doctors of esotericism won't hold it against me, I hope, if I add that our individualist renaissance owes its inspiration, in large measure, to educators from the other side of the Channel and not to occultists, whose existence our sociologists don't even suspect."

"Their theories, unfortunately for the country and the whole world, show that clearly!" Callidulus riposted. "As for England, it has been labored by hermetic lodges for a century."

"And by theosophists," added Monsieur Nyzor, almost aggressively. "People tend too much, nowadays, to lose the memory of the depositories of the Hindu tradition."

"Is the culture of individual energy so necessary to the vitality of a race, then?" asked Vivian, whom an almost unhealthy nervousness predisposed to nirvana. "Can a few indi-

decades of the19th century after its discovery in 1877 by Ernest Choquin de Sarzec.

viduals ensure the happiness of all? And why, pray, attach so much importance to the self, when appeasing nature solicits us to forget it? All of my philosophy is summarized in the *Invocation of Faust to Nature* in the hymn of the great Goethe exalted by our Berlioz. You've said, Bérénès, 'let us love the trees!'—and are not the trees our surest friends?"

The individualist Bérénès opened his eyes wide at that speech. "Nature? Come on, Vivian, you're joking!" he exclaimed. Look, one day, from the height of a terrace, I was watching a swimmer lost far below in the yellow-tinted and rapid waves of a river, a poor fellow, struggling, entirely similar to a lobster-claw opening and closing. Brave little being, how touching it was to see him working away, stubbornly and all alone, like an animal! Love nature! Forget ourselves in her? Get away! There's no prince or genius who doesn't row with his four limbs and swim with all his heart if he falls in the water."

Bérénès emptied his glass slowly and added: "Only the self exists."

But Monsieur de Nyzor raised his little finger and, emphasizing his syllables, said: "Ephemeral existence! What is that self, summoned to be annihilated in the Great All? A grain of dust, an atom cast by the wind into the Ocean. Oh, if only men followed the doctrine left by Cakia-Mouni!"

"If it's mummification before decease that you extol, dear master," said Prétextat, permit me to observe, with an ill-dissimulated pleasure that you scarcely preach by example. Your hale and charming old age rather evokes the practice of Ionian principles than those of Buddhist renunciation."

Nyzor seemed unmoved by the sarcasm. "That proves that renunciation is very poorly understood, even by our most delicate minds," he said, palpating his cravat. "The priests and the sectarians have falsified the meaning of the doctrine of Gautama. The quintessence of that doctrine is that we ought to blossom, like a lotus flower. If we are, down here, nothing but a perfume, let us at least savor the aroma and saturate our neighbor with it generously."

"Man is a prism endowed with sensibility and subject to illusion," declared Tardeval. "What is existence worth when one takes it seriously?"

"Enough, at least, for one to be preoccupied with its enjoyment," riposted Bernard Fauve, gluttonously. And as that young man, aggressive and violent behind closed doors, suffered the timidity of a little boarder at Sacré-Coeur as soon as he found three people, he suddenly fell silent and blushed; his gaze had met Neurocyme's emeralds.

Ladislas took advantage of that silence to wax Tolstoyan: "Enjoyment? Possession? Understanding? As many sources of evil. It's necessary that the rich renounce their fortune and the literate forget their science. "Animalize yourselves!"

Vivian smiled. Indignation returned the power of speech to Bernard Fauve.

"Enough Pascal and enough Tolstoy," he stammered, as crimson as an apoplectic. "The theories of that Slav end in apathy and abjection. Man is only ever saved by pride, the motor of heroism and fecund endeavors; no one has ever accomplished anything grandiose except by obeying egotism and sensuality, the indispensable stimulants. Nietzscheanism, then, instead of morphine! Let's break all the shackles of our will as soon as possible. Following the example of our ancestors the Celtic conquerors, let us be free men, proud and active—let us be males!"

With these words, pronounced in a voice that was almost veiled, but in an energetic tone, the impetuous novelist, taking possession of a cork that was idling near his plate, twisted it with a ferocious gesture.

Then, contemplating that ridiculous and melancholy fragment of cork, Romanitas, whose smiles were exquisite ironies, replied: "The soul of a Viking lives again in you, dear knight—but although pride, egotism and sensuality are excellent potions of individual energy, they cannot be sufficient to constitute a system of social organization. I appeal to the thinker you are: to regenerate a country like France, it's important to decentralize drastically, and then to Romanize the provinces."

The main thing is first to lead our unfortunate country to Buddhism," repeated Monsieur de Nyzor.

"Pardon me," asked Neurocyme, amused by that crossfire, "but which? That of Tibet, that of Ceylon, that of Japan or that of the Musée Guimet?"

"Ours, Madame," replied Minégoujon, gravely, who, being no longer twenty years old but not yet forty, dared not say *mine*. "Modern Buddhism, the philosophy of which responds to present needs admirably."

"To be sure, only a spiritual philosophy can dematerialize France," said Callidulus, naively, in the process of draining his glass, "but your philosophy, dear friend, so lucidly explained elsewhere, is not exactly a sister to ours, the great synthesis!"

"Pooh! Philosophy, dear doctor, certainly, that's something," put in Sabas, with estheticism, "but since it never explains the mystery, which is the only interesting thing, isn't it reduced to a mind-game to prove the virtuosity of the intellect? What can philosophy be without art, pray? Descartes, Hegel, Schelling, Kant, Fichte, Spencer—as many smoky night-lights by comparison with the sunlit Plato! The synthesis par excellence, where does one find it better contained, and more radiant, and more Olympian, than in Art? Oh, yes, Wagner, Mallarmé, Gustave Moreau! The Pre-Raphaelites and Ruskin! The Primitives and Gauguin! It's Art that leads the world, it's the Apollo Musagetes, the Phoebus, the god whose bow is silver, which transfigures everything, souls and things, the microcosm and the stellar worlds!"

"The religion of art! That's able to conciliate the most divergent concepts! Which of us can't take communion in the *Vita Nuova*, the ineffable Gioconda and your ninth, O Beethoven!"

"Sabas and Vivian lack precision," Enogat whispered in Ladislas' ear.

"My dear Monsieur," replied the Slav, with a smile of his own, "I've always thought that if philosophers had put more clarity into the exposition of their systems, we would have entirely ceased to be able to understand them, for the contradictions between one page and the next would appear manifestly. So..."

"Yes, yes, let's cherish art!" Bernard Fauve superimposed on that aside, his glabrous face no longer reflecting anything but a slight anticipation of dawn. "It's by means of art that a race restores its strength and beauty. From Phidias to Goethe, the sculptor of the Graces to the author of Faust, from antique nobility to the august ruins in which the shade of Helen and the genius of memories is reborn, it's by means of art that moral health flourishes again. And the grandeur of a nation depends uniquely on its degree of plastic beauty."

Negans was a hunchback; he objected: "The quality of its mind appears to me to suffer. When a nation counts numerous mandarins, partisans of free examinations, it's very great."

"And perhaps also very ignorant, alas," said Enogat, "if those mandarins understand nothing of the esthetic education of woman."

"Well countered," exclaimed Neurocyme, politely. "It's in vain that legislators and sociologists strive to elude the problem of feminism. From that solution, all other reforms flow."

"The archetype of reformers," Sabas said, "is Orpheus. He charmed the beasts, women and stones; his lyre was worth more than all grimoires. Art is the supreme magic, the eternal miracle."

"Bravo! More! Long live Vivian!"

"Occultism," Callidulus acquiesced, "the father of symbolism, has never forgotten art. It combines it with science in its vast synthesis; the numerous decorations of the temples of ancient Egypt proclaim as much. Occultism inspired Dante, Shakespeare, Goethe..."

"Art and philosophy are also reconciled in a very French genius, and with what marvelous light!" exclaimed Negans.

63

"In order for the world to become better, isn't it sufficient for it to be Renanist?"

"So be it!" replied Ladislas. "But perhaps, to begin with, it would be appropriate to give the world the means to be satisfied and blissfully optimistic of which Renan disposed."

"Let men conquer them!" formulated Bernard Fauve, in a grim voice that emotion caused to vibrate. "The future belongs to the strong!" And he massacred another cork.

Neurocyme stood up. Enogat, then Monsieur de Nyzor, and then all the guests, imitated Neurocyme. Only Saint-Dolent remained seated, his expression absorbed and pensive.

"Friend," Sabas informed him, charitably, "everything is consumed..."

They went into the drawing room, transformed into a floral palace. No one recognized it. There was a moment of general bewilderment.

"Oh, the gardens with singing syllables, Melzi, Sommariva, Guilia, the Borromees," exclaimed Bérénès. "It's admirable!"

And, her head slightly tilted over one shoulder, parading her half-closed eyes over *her* sumptuous décor, so rare, Neurocyme smiled briefly.

At the base of walls ornamented by genuinely ancient tapestries, the candor of arums and jasmine was combined with the grace of amaryllis. The yellow allegro of laburnum and the versatile pinks of hibiscus tempered the melancholy of elegant tamarisk. The rubescent pride of salvias rendered more odorous the purity of lilies and the humility of syringas. The rhododendrons combined their suave carmine with the pastel tones of a few begonias; azaleas, camellias and poppies performed their varicolored scales like precious virtuosos. The velvety foliage of coleus displayed blues and pinks between the ultramarine zinzolin of passiflora and the warm russet patches of calceolaria; the intoxicating daturas were resplendent, like opals circled by coral, between the passionate notes founded by forceful tritomas. The liliaceous bells of yuccas were silhouettes slimly beside idyllic lilacs and majestic eucalyptus. In the corners, hyaline pink honeysuckle, languid mauve wisteria and sanguinely ardent begonias hid the pedestals of old statues. And nobly, in the middle of the room, circling a spurting fountain—and ringed themselves by aspidistras and acanthia, between which vibrated the amethyst of irises with the topaz and ruby of tulips—agaves, clivias and himantophyllums raised their flagpoles, on which lemon yellows, milky whites and fiery reds palpitated as they shed their petals...

The background tones, the hues of the foliage and the play of the candles and chandeliers, everything had been combined in such a manner as to give full value to the flowers, to create, with their snow and gems, symphonies of adorable, prestigious and unusual coloration.

"Certainly, yes, it's admirable," said Romanitas, drawing closer to Bérénès. "It's even better than your Borromees, than Grenada, your Grenada, under delightfully embroidered parasols, one of the softest pillows in the world for a well-made head! Bérénès, I'll tell you: here is festooned the enclosure of a loving heart..."

Without replying, Bérénès pointed at Saint-Dolent, who wanted to say something. Indeed, Saint-Dolent spoke. He said: "The English have found nothing more esthetic."

"The blood of broken hearts seethes in these crimson chalices," murmured Tardeval, whose sentimentality sometimes became transparent after a good dinner.

In ecstasy, Vivian dreamed aloud: "The soul of the Fays lives again in these petals born of the dawn's kiss!"

But Negans clicked his middle finger and thumb—which was, in him, a sign of real impatience. He did not admit, in fact, that a cerebral individual should exhibit the slightest emotion. In a bittersweet voice, he sniggered: "Bah! It's the chromatic circle of Chevreul anticipated by Leonardo, applied by a nurseryman-florist who happened to read Charles Henry one evening."[20]

Elsewhere, the dithyrambs rang out. In one corner, amid the scarlet insolence of salvias, Saint-Dolent tuned his sad mandolin, while, dissimulated by the eucalyptus, the vaporizers suddenly went into action; the guests felt their faces caressed by a perfume and the freshness of a dew.

A few small groups had formed. Here, Bernard Fauve and René Tardeval were conversing in low voices, with grand gestures. There, planted directly under the cypresses, Prétextat and Bérénès were talking about the Escorial or the Generalife. Monsieur de Nyzor was searching in vain for a mirror in order to adjust his cravat. Soon, however, a circle formed around Neurocyme, and speeches overlapped, light and spangled.

Social renovation was forgotten. People were chattering about literature or babbling about sculpture. "Dalou, pooh!" Saint-Marceaux, ha ha! Oh, Rodin! And Bartholomé! And Vallgren! And Dampt!" They clucked about theater. The lighting passed from sky-blue to tea-rose.

Ecstatic, Vivian sighed: "Oh, that luminous modulation that seems to pass from blue minor to pink major, like a dawn! What a subtle and soft transition, which causes musical echoes to awaken in me! Do you remember the delightful dusk that the posthumous *Briseis* of Chabrier opens to our senses? The voluptuous chorus of mariners, young friends of Hylas:[21]

---

[20] When the chemist Michel Eugène Chevreul (1786-1889) was appointed as director of the Gobelins dye work, he produced a famous circular chromatic diagram in the 1850s representing "complementary colors." Charles Henry (1859-1926) was a esthetic theorist closely associated with the Impressionists, whose ideas were a powerful influence on Neo-Impressionism; his works made extensive reference to Chevreul's diagram and its associated theories of harmony and contrast.

[21] Emmanuel Chabrier's posthumously-produced opera *Briséïs, ou Les amants de Corinthe* (1897), with a libretto by

The light ship has taken flight
Toward the gulf of the pearl isles!

"And when the blond galley appears, the modulation of the D flat into E major! It's that, precisely, that is singing again within me when my eyes interpret that exquisite metamorphosis of color. How unfortunate are positive individuals who never distinguish hues, the Daltonians of the intelligence who never understand subtle analogies or mysterious correspondences, who never divine with the poet that 'perfumes, colors and sounds respond to one another!'"

The considerations that followed led Sabas to defend sensualism. Via metaphors and digressions he ended up exposing his ideas on amour, which amused Neurocyme and constrained her to show her teeth several times, which were marvelous, and to flutter her eyelashes, which were very long and silky.

While a pale mauve light inundated the drawing-room, Prétextat, desirous of conciliating the contrary opinions, renewed, in gallant terms, the eulogy of eclecticism. A second irroration of perfumes completed the pacification of minds. Sabas continued the work of Prétextat by mans of lyrical variations on syncretism, with the consequence that, when the time for retreat came, everyone had been spelling out, for a long time, discreet erudition or memories of travel with an amenity of reminiscent of the great century.

"Oh, the miraculous fête organized at the London Guildhall!" evoked Saint-Dolent, picturesque and sincerely moved. "What a procession and what a spectacle! What ingenuity in the choice and taste of costumes, and what sumptuousness! A splendor to which each workshop had contributed, for its quota, a hundred thousand francs in our money, the principal per-

---

Catulle Mendès and Ephraïm Mikhael, is based on Goethe's classic fantasy *Die Braut von Korinth* [The Bride of Corinth]. Hylas is the name of the principal male character.

sonages represented by the celebrities of English art: Walter Crane, for example, in the broad robe of Albrecht Dürer; Douglas Cockerel as the divine comedian Dante; White, the famous painter White, as a doge, a genuine doge, one would have sworn! And the daughters and wives of the painters, Mesdames, as you say here, Ernest Hébert, Jacques Blanche, Raffaëlli, Miss Reynolds and Miss Parnell, appeared in Carpaccio costumes, with attitudes inspired by the Primitives! And the grandiose spectacle offered at the Town Hall, with the kind permission of the Lord Mayor, the sheriffs and aldermen. What an understanding, what an admirable union, what an abnegation of personality!"

The electric lamps then radiated the seven prismatic tones, and Neurocyme seemed to be enveloped in a rainbow.

Callidulus having given the signal for departure, Monsieur de Nyzor murmured, very *Lauzun*:[22] "What an aromal memory we shall take away from the soirée, beautiful lady!"

"Take away a concrete memory as well," replied Neurocyme.

They all bowed, whereupon she immediately designed an incantatory gesture over her head, and flowers snowed upon the enraptured assembly.

"Are you a spirit?" asked Romanitas, aiming his keen eyes at the ceiling in the hope of discovering the "trick."

"Occultists can do all that spirits can, and even more," Callidulus articulated, victoriously. "You see there, Messieurs, an example of practical magic, mere child's play." He insisted: "A joke."

He was insisting too much to be entirely sincere: an external, artificial assurance. And after a moment considering the floret that he had just caught in mid-air, her murmured,

---

[22] The reference is to Antoine Nompar de Caumont, Duc de Lauzun (1632-1723), a gaudy and turbulent member of Louis XIV's court, named by Barbey d'Aurevilly as an achetypal dandy *avant la lettre*.

perplexed: "These are bromelia petals, and they seem perfectly real... Bizarre, bizarre!"

Outside, Vivian leaned over Tardeval's shoulder, his eyes shining in the gloom.

"Have you noticed our dear Enogat?" he asked. "He seems very enamored of that astonishing foreigner. Anyway, I can understand that! She would have enchanted Merlin himself..."

"And Burne-Jones too!" riposted the novelist, smiling in the supple ebony of his bard, determined to remain skeptical regarding the floral downpour of the finale.

Turning to Negans, who was hopping in the street like a gnome he asked: "What do you think?"

"I think," the hunchback hissed, "that that little woman is cleverer than Robert-Houdin."

Then he disappeared into the night, which was warm and florid with stars.

V. Enemy Brothers

The following week, Neurocyme organized a dinner for writers. Enogat thought of bringing together, at a Platonic banquet, a procession of incontestably aureoled individuals: Sully-Prudhomme, Brunetière, Loti, Huysmans, José-Maria de Hérédia, Jules Lemaître, Paul Bourget, Frédéric Mistral. The last-named would come from Maillane. At the enunciation of the names, however, the curious beauty pursed her lips in a small grimace of significant charm.

"I know them already," she said. "I know them all, dear friend. Do you think, then, that the autochthons of the astral are as ignorant as French rentiers? Do you suppose that in the company of souls of disincarnate litterateurs, we talk about rain and good weather, the latest sports and ministerial crises? I've had the honor of approaching Baudelaire, Hello, Flaubert, Villiers de l'Isle-Adam, Verlaine—and that suave Mallarmé has told me a great many stories..."

With a gesture that was familiar to him she leaned her elbow on the arm of an armchair, her chin in her hand and a lily on her knees.

"Oh, precious child," Enogat stammered, "how ravishing you are!"

"Oh, dear friend," replied the elemental, "How...terrestrial you are, in spite of your initiation! Yes, I know by heart their *Vaines tendresses*, their *Aziyadé*, their *Trophées*, their *Mariage blanc*, and their *Mensonges*, and it would be much easier than it would be interesting for me to discuss with Monsieur Mistral the bifurcation of French into the *langue d'oil* and the *langue d'oc*, with Monsieur Brunetière the bankruptcy of science or the superiority of the Latin genius, or with Monsieur Huysmans the incorruptible splendor of the mystical, only appropriate to console the old habitués of restaurants of fallacious roast beef and illusory chops cooked in the oven..."

70

"Ideal woman!"

"But I know them all, your literary stars, the overrated and the authentic, the adolescent and the decrepit; I know them as if I had leafed through their seven shelves, from Faguet and Jean Jullien to Margueritte, from Haraucourt and Rostand to Paul Hervieu, via Curel, Lavedan, Buchor and Lucien Descaves. I could quote the songs of Gabriel Vicaire and Jean Lahor, a sonnet by Fernand Mazade, quatrains with alternating, internal or plain rhymes by Albert Samain, Chantavoine, Raymond de La Tailhède and…Monsieur le Comte Robert de Montesquiou-Fezensac."

"Him too?"

"Him to." She smiled, as if indulgently, and, half-closing her eyes, respired the lily. Then, slowly, she went on: "No, I'm not going to involve myself with those who have made their names, nor with any of those that the newspapers feature from time to time. It's the celebrities of tomorrow, my friend, and even those of next week that I'd like to contemplate. Certain conversations with Ephraim Mikhaël have given me an appetite to know the poets and writers of prose who have…new ideas. That's how you put it, I believe?"

"I believe so…"

"Having very few relations in the future literary world, Enogat de Sothermès had to ask Sabas, Tardeval, Romanitas and Fauve to invite on his behalf the young writers who had an odor of promise. Tardeval and Fauve took responsibility for novelists, the other two for poets. None of the four succeeded brilliantly. Only their particular friends accepted the invitation.

They were, as regards prose writers: the blond novelist Raymond de Valgourd, one of the rare impenitent symbolists; Occitanel, a doctor of law, bureaucrat, and spirited dialogue-composer in library dramas; Néaucante, the sententious apostle of sentiment and life, who liked to pour out harmonious and vague words; and Sombredire, a pale and encylopedic head, a thinker thirsty for the new, a paradoxical, nervous and dreamy intelligence. On the side of the poets there was: Marc Lepentit, a Pompeiian half-breed, a disciple floating between

Abbé Delille and Banville, an excellent fellow although a verifier; Yves Berny, of whom the Muse dreamed, it seems, in the shade of Provençal olive-groves, in quasi-classical garb; and Edmé Marteau, a symbolist like Valgourd, of the very last minute, and all the more smitten with the doctrine because the Romanists mistreated it.

Well, undoubtedly, Neurocyme had a keen desire to converse with the principal and various initiators of so-called "new poetics," but Henry le Régalien was traveling in America with his wide, an exquisite poetess and the daughter of a great poet; the subtle Velin-Griffé was buried in his château in the Loire, pensively watching the flight of birds "striping the gray-blue sky denuded by the storm" through his high windows; Gustave Salomettan never went out before midnight to skirmishes where the press "howls its bellowing of a sovereign cow"; Stewart-Béryl was only unfaithful to railways and transatlantic steamers in order to emparadise himself blissfully in the middle of the romantic forest of Fontainebleau, in a house of sweet solitude, in the company of Aimée, who knew "how to make the rose bloom on the window-sill"; and Canéas could not resolve himself to quit, even for one evening, the Vachette, his Helicon.

What about the others? The others—my God, none of the other foreseen authors wanted to expose themselves to contact with antipathetic or antagonistic colleagues in the homes of profane individuals devoid of utility, since even the gossip columnists never breathed a word about their dinners. Neurocyme had, therefore, to content herself with the half-dozen specimens supplied. She did so with a good grace that touched virtue.

As soon as the guests had all arrived, she addressed a few homages to them, which they received with an imperturbable serenity and ease, too accomplished not to be contrived. Afterwards, very skillfully, she extracted their impressions of recent books and the two or three recent dramatic works that merited remembering. It was a marvelous pretext for the young men to display their erudition, so they hastened to take advantage of it during any interval between the soup and the sumptuous distribution of dessert. They were, moreover, admirable in agility and suppleness, avoiding with supreme tact casting reflections on the physiognomy of the competing neighbor, plunging into inoffensive generalities as soon as a phrase took esthetic wing.

For her part, Neurocyme refrained from troubling that literary cackle. So many prudent evasions, adroit changes of subject and deliberate mistakes interested and amused her. In any case, Tardeval had advised her to wait for the coda of the meal to demand their sovereign principles of art from those enemy brothers, whom the absorption of a vast and succulent menu ought to incline to benevolence.

"So it's still as in the time of the Huret investigation?" the elemental had interrogated.[23]

"Still," Tardeval had replied. "At present, Dame Malice has obtained the freedom of the city."

At dessert, laden with unctuous patisserie and ambrosia cream, all the literary "personalities" gathered under Enogat's multicolored chandelier seemed humanized; their ideas and images, projected with a delightful animation, did not contain any explosive or seed of a quarrel. Valgourd was sustaining to Néaucante that there was pantheism in certain verses of the monk Notker Balbulus. Widening his lovely gazelle-like eyes, his mouth pursed and his hair in the style of Massenet, but

---

[23] In 1891 the journalist Jules Huret, working for *L'Écho de Paris*, began an extensive "Enquête sur l'évolution littéraire" [Investigation of Literary Evolution] interviewing 64 writers and asking deliberately provocative questions, attempting to set Naturalists against Symbolists on the one hand and neo-Naturalists on the other, thus stirring up or mythologizing many of the conflicts supposedly raging in the period, which the present chapter seeks to illustrate further. Huret explicitly represented the literary marketplace as a battleground whose participants were engaged in a Darwinian struggle for existence.

nevertheless thicker than those of the rhapsodist of *Les Coccinelles*, Yves Berny was confiding his ideas on astrology to Enogat. His eyes bulging and lips moist, Marc Lepetit, who seemed to have been fed since early childhood on antique poetry and was as zealous a Latinist as Déroulède, was reciting numerous elegant translations of Horace to Sabas, who was telling him the Eddas between odes. Occitanel was explaining the mind of Lucretius to Romanitas by means of his Etruscan origin. Marteau was revealing the plan of a poem that would sing all the rancor of intellectuals against military service, which Bernard Fauve approved, between a couple of citations of Saint-Simon and Casanova. Sombredire, finally, with sparks in his blue Lorrainean eyes and convulsive nostrils, was commenting on Ibsen, Bjornsen, Jacobsen, Strindberg and Herman Bang in company with Neurocyme, who was showing herself no less sensible to the court that Tardeval was paying to her. The brief portrait of Bang, in particular, piqued the curiosity of the elemental;[24] she listened, half-smiling and half-earnest.

"In truth," revealed Sombredire, "the best-known of Bang's ancestors was his grandfather, a physician in Jutland, who left him two thousand francs exactly. Young Bang went into the theater as a ham, then a newspaper that went bust, then another where he battled against all his few ideas. Since then, a reporter like Chinchole, a novelist like Abel Hermant, a lecturer like Lintilhac, and editor like Francis Laur, he's tried many things. He even ran a café-concert in Norway, where the daughters of pastors were engaged. In that era he affected to let his hair fall all the way to his eyes, powdering it like a demoiselle, as tight in his garments as if he were wearing a corset. Suddenly, he races to a wig-maker, runs to an English

---

[24] Neurocyme's particular interest in the works of the Danish novelist Herman Bang (1857-1912) might be thought to relate to his preoccupation with unfulfilled passion and isolated women rather than the inaccurate biographical sketch offered by Sombredire.

tailor. He has himself shaven. He changes is appearance. He mutates. He's a gentleman of letters, clad and coiffed like a member of the Jockey Club. He's Count Herman Bang. One of these days he'll be the Margrave of S..."

"How nice!" chirped Neurocyme. Then she turned to Tardeval.

The setting of the previous gathering had been renewed, of course, but the "cerebrals" of literature were only slightly interested in lighting and colors. When the erudite company was installed in the drawing room, however, the marvelous arrangement of flowers impressed them for five minutes; verses sprang from all mouths.

A poseur in his Borgiaque posture, but sincerely moved by the music of the strophe, the livid Sabas pronounced:

> *And you make the bleeding whiteness of lilies*
> *Which, rolling on seas of sighs that it skims,*
> *Through the blue incense of pale horizons,*
> *Rises dreamily toward the weeping moon!* [25]

Raymond de Valgourd, attracted by the yellow petals, proclaimed, with folded arms:

> *Your flowers of honey have the color of golden sands...*[26]

And, directly before the symphonies in red:

> *The flamboyant flowering of the crimson of gladioli!* [27]

murmured Marteau, in the attitude of someone who has just seen lightning strike; while Romanitas, who was already not looking at anything except Neurocyme, collected a classical memory from the depths of his mind:

---

[25] These lines are from Stéphane Mallarmé's "Les Fleurs."

[26] From Henri de Régnier's "Tel qu'en songe."

[27] From José-Maria de Hérédia's "Les Trophées."

Quales rosae fulgent inter sua lilia mixtae...[28]

A pause. Yves Berny aspired the aromas and, with the gesture of a choirboy swinging the thurible, modulated:

Placid perfumes exhaled by corollas
Rise like incense from immeasurable altars.

In a sententious tone Néaucante suggested:

Collect today the roses of life! [29]

which induced Lepetit to proclaim, gaily, that he wanted to live henceforth:

Under the blossom that hangs from the bough.[30]

Did Enogat want to show that he was worthy of taking part in that poetic concert? The fact is that he cried:

The lily, iris of azure and the pink azalea
Mingle their perfumes in light tourneys,

And Neurocyme, proud of imitating him in that, at least, cooed with the softness of a dove:

My heart is the rose of May
Whose humble perfumed effluvia
Embalm the most distant aerie...[31]

---

[28] "Like roses that gleam among lilies"—from Ovid's *Amores*.
[29] From a sonnet by Pierre de Ronsard
[30] From Ariel's song in Shakepeare's *The Tempest*.
[31] From Adrien Remacle's novel *La Passante* (1892).

"What!" exclaimed Lepetit, whose mulatto features lit up with an Ionian smile. "You know *La Passante*?"

"It's an initiate work," she replied.

"The fortunate idea of offering, in the same décor, that which art has of the most exquisite and nature of the most gracious! *That go the primrose way to the everlasting bonfire*," concluded Occitanel, who possessed Shakespeare textually.[32]

"Ah! To return to nature, the source of powerful inspirations," declared Romanitas, with lyricism.

"The Isis from whom all the veils are never lifted!" proclaimed Sabas, nevertheless making the gesture of lifting them.

"The fecund Maya!" continued Sombredire, coldly ironic, who took advantage of the situation to unburden himself of a possibly-mystificatory citation:

O mother who creates, in your bosom just and strong,
Calices swinging the future phial,
Of great flowers with balsamic Death
For the weary poet etiolated by life! [33]

"Have we gazed at nature enough?" Occitanel said, more literary than contrite.

"No, *you* certainly haven't gazed at her enough, all of you, *our elders*," proffered Berny, with a juvenile conviction. When one thinks that Canéas mistook beetroots for salad!"

"And his astonishment when Henri Gronde revealed the asphodel to him in the woods of Crespières!" added Marteau, who was far from equaling Alphonse Karr in the science of flowers.

"Which of you has not been a trifle Canéas, my dear seigneurs?" Berny put in, reconstituting, unwittingly—which was all the more flavorsome—a pose of Fréderic Lemaître.

---

[32] Occitanel's quotation (from *Macbeth* Act 2, scene 3) is given in English in the original.
[33] Mallarmé again.

"Nature, Hegel says, is nothing but the affected idea of an exterior form." And Valgourd, having articulated that aphorism with a disdainful wink, went to sit down before a Pompeiian Hermes, into the contemplation of which he sank.

A curtain in the drawing-room had just been draw aside, allowing a glimpse of a sparkle of fresh polychromatic beverages. Neurocyme thought the moment propitious to go into action, and, her elbow at her hips, joining her hands, she asked in a negligent tone: "Of what, in sum, does this naturism consist that people are trying to render fashionable?"

"Of a vague and ringing pantheism fit for democratic electors," replied Romanitas, while he picked up a kirsch sorbet. "It's the invention of an inoffensive ephebe, the magnanimous Saint-Michel de Vol-au-Vent."

"To create veridical heroes and attain the epic, such is the aim of his school—for, after the example of the ancients, he plays the magister," mocked Berny, in the verve of criticism. "In its thirst for grandiloquence, naturism will neglect individuals for archetypes, and place the later in the sole décor appropriate to them: the eternal sites. Thus, the work of art becomes a monography of Eternity. Barnum couldn't have thought of that!"

Romanitas, finishing his sorbet, continued: "The founder of that doctrine, more ethical than esthetic, if he can be believed, considers that the mission of the present-day poet is to render humanity its heroic beauty, to repair the bonds uniting it with the world and cast bright light on man's place in nature."

"His place," Occitanel went on, "is quite simply that of God. '*God has vanished from the world*,' proclaims the good Saint-Michel, whom an indigestion of mysticism has led to the cesspit of great Pan. 'The Earth, plants, metals and human toil replace him; those are the objects of our worship.' In reality, it's the cult of the self, presented in that fashion in order not to shock the neighbor."

"This Vol-au-Vent," said Neurocyme, appears to me be stronger than the late Joséphin."

"I think so," replied Tardeval. "The hirsute Sâr was only a derisory diminutive of a mage. Saint-Michel is Amour himself, with a capital A, for he is a Poet, with a capita P. Now the Poet, according to the naturist dogma, is identified with Amour."

"The naturist Poet also has for his mission that of illuminating the roads," said Sombredire slyly, in his turn. "It is his prerogative to lead each soul to 'the places of its destiny' and to reveal 'angelic treasures' to him."

"It's a psychopomp that *enlightens*," said Tardeval to Neurocyme, whose indulgent nod of the head made it manifest that she understood the idiom of the boulevard.

"As for those 'treasures,'" Sombredire went on, "they consist of an axiom borrowed from the serpent of Eden: 'Humans are gods who do not know it,' So, Master Saint-Michel de Vol-au-Vent, who knows himself intimately, looks God in the face, as one of his disciples, dazed by good will, puts it."

"Mock auto-deification as much as you like," said Néaucante then, breaking a silence, "Taint theories of art of a juvenile exaggeration, so be it again—but recognize at least that Saint-Michel represents a force that isn't despicable. He's not a man, he's an idea."[34]

"Bah!" riposted Marteau. "Hasn't that already been said of Signorino, that aede who proclaimed himself a prophet, promised to change the face of the world and replied to a lukewarm colleague: *May the azure pardon you*?"

"Yes, but he was a southerner to the extent of exuberance, to the extent..."

"Admit that he wasn't a true southerner," complained the proud Occitanel, with panache in this voice.

---

[34] This treatment of the school of *naturisme* founded and promoted by Saint-Georges de Bouhélier (1876-1947) might seem excessive today, when the poet and the movement are virtually forgotten, but in 1900 he and it would have looked like plausible candidates for future celebrity.

"This time, dear friend," cried Romanitas, "we're entirely in accord. Good minds too often confuse the Latin with the Gascon."

Neurocyme was beginning to be amused. Resolved to set fire to the powder-keg, she launched the spark joyfully with an insidious interrogation: "And the symbolism of which there's so much talk—what's that, exactly?"

"Madame," replied Romanitas, "It's the incessantly-renewed illusion, like idealism."

At that moment Berny was "offering himself" a second glass of punch. Punch was a beverage he loved sincerely. However, he stopped drinking in order to confirm that symbolism was definitely defunct.

Raymond de Valgourd, extracted from his contemplation, protested vehemently. "Oho! You'd like to think so, brave Berny. Symbolism dead! But it is, precisely, that which does not die, for it's the quivering idea, living in all forms. In art as in nature, everything can be a symbol, since everything has a hidden meaning."

"Obermann didn't say otherwise," murmured the erudite Romanitas.[35]

"Very good," replied Néaucante loudly, entering the lists, "but that meaning, it isn't the human mind that gives it; it's an abstract entity, the Infinite, that is behind things. The Symbolists are too lacking in philosophy."

"Eh! Should art be a metaphysics?" growled Sabas, straightening himself as if against an outrage. "Of Verlaine and Sully-Prudhomme, which is the artist? The only philosophy a poet needs is found in the principle emitted by a master: 'Every soul is a melody that it's a matter of comparing, and

---

[35] The reference is to the Byronic protagonist of the novel *Oberman* (1804; revised as *Obermann* in 1833) by Étienne Pivert de Senacour (1770-1846), highly praised by leading members of the Romantic movement but subsequently somewhat neglected.

for that, everyone has his flute or viol.' Symbolism? Heavens, it's the soul of matter. Without symbolism, no more poetry."

"La Fontaine wasn't a poet, then?" growled Lepetit. "and Racine?"

"La Fontaine is a special case," replied Sabas, unmoved.

"Like Villon," sniggered the poet with the Moorish head.

"As for Racine, his verses are embellished with symbols."

"We know that your divinatory gifts and your talent for exegesis permit you to find them even in Nicolas Boileau," the mulatto continued, adjusting his spectacles, "but all the symbols that you could cite to us, from Dante to Baudelaire, don't prove—far from it—that their authors conceived symbolist works. Those symbols, the adornment of poems, don't constitute the weave; they are, Sabas, the fruit of inspiration, not the result of a method."

"And that's what overturns your theory," concluded Néaucante, with conviction.

"Are you sure of knowing everything the Symbolists have wanted to realize?" asked Sabas, his hands solemn. "Symbolism, as we understand it," he said, in a slow and cadenced voice, "does not destroy life, it transfigures it; it only represents it in its aspects of beauty. Oh, you're strangely unjust toward symbolism! But it has been the regenerator of an epoch rotted by debased literature! By opposing its evocations and its dreams to coarse materialism, it has constrained the minds of a nation, which were scarcely thinking any more, to remember the existence of art. It has purified the literary domain of the filth deposited by the Augeas of the novel. If filthy sensualism has had its day, if Naturalism is no longer possible, it's to Symbolism that we owe it, and without it, you couldn't exist, and you'll return to it in spite of yourselves, after having realized the nullity of your sentimentalism."

"You've pronounced a word on which it's appropriate to reach an understanding before taking the discussion any further," riposted Néaucante. "As for symbolism, we recognize that it's the necessary form of great art at all times; it's in the capacity of the formula of a school that we reject it, that school having proven its impotence."

"Truly, Néaucante," said Valgourd, "it would seem, listening to you, that Symbolism has only been incarnated by valetudinarans. Without taking sides, consider the initiators, consider the other original authors, and you'll be obliged to recognize that they had the vision of the absolute."

"Of the absolute?" Sabas repeated.

"Yes," replied Néaucante, "but they confused that absolute with the metaphysical infinite grasped by their intelligence; they thought themselves capable of constructing the synthesis with ideas..."

"And they have constructed it!" Sabas cried. "Ideas, we have piled them up. We have built immense, sumptuous palaces with them!"

"Sumptuous, granted—immense, no!" said Néaucante. And after a pause: "Look, your mistake was, precisely, not having got beyond ideas. That's what prevented you from arriving at natural symbols, the only ones valuable in art.

"And how, then, do you claim that you've reached them?"

"By means of sentiment."

An ironic murmur greeted that declaration. The drawing room seemed to have been invaded by a storm wind.

"Only sentiment," Néaucante went on, "gives an esthetic sense of the real and the ideal. Sentiment is the internal absolute that possesses the secret of all the relations of worlds exterior to thought and sensation. Veritable art is a symbolism of the heart."

"Ah!" cried Neurocyme. "I like that! But then, you're all symbolists; only a simple question of words separates you."

"What human being isn't a symbolist?" replied Romanitas, with the mocking gravity of a rhetor of the time of Quintilian and a certain amenity of the worst insolence. "Who, in forming thoughts, doesn't have recourse to signs in order to communicate them?"

Marvelously, Occitanel appeared conciliatory, and miraculously, he pronounced in a tone than was almost calm: "There are, evidently, a few points on which we always come together, while conserving our principles in their integrity. And that's the ideal situation; in everything, individualism. Thus are obtained powerful and resplendent synergies."

Then, glad to make a few of her guests "pose," Neurocyme intervened. "Would it be too demanding if I asked you to synthesize your principles in a formula? I'd so like to know them better!"

"Oh, for myself," Néaucante replied, "I can say to you, with Novalis: 'My entire principle is in my intimate sentiment of life.'"

"Art, I believe with Vigny, is 'the chosen truth,' life expressed esthetically," said Occitanel. "Art, as Emerson puts it, is summarized in the perpetual effort toward the expression of the spirit of things."

Sombredire turned up his feline moustache. "To a great extent," he insinuated, "for the most part, art is, as Barrès says, *lectulus florulus*, a little bed of repose and softness, all flowery. It consists, then, of collecting beautiful baubles from poets and writing doggerel in preparing to become a vaudevillian..."

There as a moment of vague malaise; and as the silence extended, Sombredire went on: "I just named Barrès; I'll cite him again. Perhaps the work ought to tend to the conservation and aggrandisement of your self, in registering, with an ironic tact—as the philosophy of the deracinated counsels—all the contrasts that often exist between our ideas and the conditions of your manifestation."

"That's skepticism!" said Neurocyme.

"Madame, it's skepticism in quest of the truth," replied Sombredire, in a serious tone, but with a humorous glint in his eye.

Then, in his blank but firm voice, Bernard Fauve articulated: "Art is the national patrimony that it is appropriate to conserve in its splendor. Let us lay waste to the political institutions, but let us respect nevertheless the tradition of the race. Let us protect the language, the divine language of our forefathers, against Barbarian invasions. Oh, let us shout down, above all, the epigones of Shakespeare. That Maeterlinck is odious, odious. Don't you think so?"

"Let's be classical and independent!" launched the vibrant voice of young Berny, whose gazelle-like eyes were sparkling.

"So, as many individualists, as many opinions," Neurocyme concluded.

"Except for the Roman school, where Canéas maintains an implacable unity, there's glorious anarchy everywhere," relied Berny, rubbing his hands.

"And do the numerous individualities of your groups bring the incense of their homages to some unique genius?"

Berny exclaimed: "We all believe in Verlaine

When your closed mouth as ceased its song
Verlaine, in our verses you shall sing again! [36]

"And yet, you don't all admit that his art is the typical form?"

"Certainly not," said Romanitas. "Verlaine's poetry is exquisite, but, as a poetry of collision and prodigy, it can't serve as a type."

"Oh! Oh!" protested Saba, raising his eagle-like profile.

"If you doubt it, I'll refer you to his *Poetic Art*:

Let your verses be the good adventure
Scattered in the crisp morning wind...

"Is that an opinion concordant with the tradition of our race? The immense merit of Canéas is to have renewed that tradition..."

---

[36] From *Le Verger doré* by Yvanhoé Rambosson.

"Eh! Canéas is only a singer, a palikare enamored of sequins," Sabas interjected, with the gesture of turning a somersault.[37]

Romanitas riposted: "That palikare is a man, and remembers it. His verses, you have said yourself, dear esthete, are 'thought sentiments.'"

"Indeed! Was it not a man, and the most human of all, poor Lélian, that you so aptly named a Christian poet with the legs of a faun?"

Néaucante intervened. "You're both right," he accorded, graciously.

Her head delicately tilted, Neurocyme had a smile delightful to see, a trifle brazen, and without looking at anyone in particular or addressing anyone directly, she asked: "What do you think of Mallarmé, then"

"He's a noble intelligence," Sabas replied.

"Pooh!" declared Lepetit, in a suddenly mordant voice, "he is, in a word, a failure."

"In his mouth, that affirmation might seem a compliment," Tardeval murmured to Fauve.

"Look at him carefully," said the latter. "Is that not the head of Othello adapted by Jean Aicard? He'll end up as a dramaturge for the popular Odéon of the Château-d'Eau..."

"Or a singer in a cabaret on the Butte."

"In the genre of Jehan Rictus!"

"More like Montoya."

Although Tardeval and Fauve had been talking in whispers, the anti-Mallarmist had heard them. They understood that by the singular glance that he cast at them, and they burst out laughing. On reflection, intimately sure of a far more august fate, and in any case a poet devoid of bile, Lepetit laughed louder than them.

---

[37] A palikare is a Greek militiaman, whose supposedly-typical costume was one of the most popular affectations of Parisian masked balls.

"Mallarmé will remain," said Néaucante, in the meantime, "an accomplished type of the hierophant of letters. That will be his grandeur and his weakness. Certainly, it's under his influence that so many young writers are enclosing themselves in ivory powers. We intend, on the contrary, to aspire life with full lungs, mingle with the action, even participate in social life."

The worthy Enogat started in alarm, and opened his eyes wide asking: "Good for the plastic arts—'apotelesic,' as the peripateticians put it, who assign them a utilitarian goal—but are we, then, going to enter an era of civic poetry and electoral literature?"

"Not at all," replied Berny. "Our ambition is higher and nobler. We intend to bring about an instauration by means of our works..."

"Make them, those works," interjected Sombredire. "But you must be beginning to suspect that it will be difficult, and that talent won't be sufficient. Oh, it's hard, the métier of letters, and you can deck yourselves with courage and patience, for advancement therein takes a long time. In sum, the only possible base, in that estate as in others, is a personal fortune permitting one to wait for benefits and to write uniquely according to one's taste, or a marriage permitting substitution for lack of fortune. And in reality, the greater number tend to that solution. The instability of salaries and the iniquitous division of benefits ends up making the literary career one of the most frustrating. Its advantages are brilliant, exterior and vain, its labor is great and ingrate, its profits meager. And one senses that in all that there is a strange, mysterious error. *Literature is not a career*. The error is mistaking it for one. Literature is a vocation and a mission."

"It is an aristocracy," said Saba, looking at Neurocyme.

"No, no more an aristocracy than an elegant amusement or a métier," Sombredire retorted. "Beyond the amateurs, the dilettantes and the posers of literature, the gift of writing is a grave, profound obligation, which very strict moral duties and requires a constant surveillance of oneself, in order that the

86

life of the writer is coherent with his thoughts and his books. For writers of real vocation and race, the role of the man of letters is revealed to be considerable and akin to a mission, a devotion of oneself to an abstract and ideal goal. The profits follow, if they will and if they can; if poverty is the result, that does not matter anymore. A writer must consider himself invested with a redoubtable responsibility, from which he cannot remove himself, which will shackle him for his entire life. He is obliged to be doubly irreproachable, for himself as for others."

Thus spoke Sombredire. And he added, coldly ironic; "Excuse me, my dear Berny; I interrupted you momentarily. What do you intend to found with your works?"

"The era of social reforms," the other replied, dryly.

"That which Le Play evokes," said Occitanel, ever passionate for sociology. "Messieurs, since you have such good intentions, I advise you to read Le Play; he's the most human of economists. And read Tarde; he's the most thoughtful of sociologists."

"Also read Saint-Yves d'Alveydre," hazard Enogat, slightly bewildered in the midst of these successive tourneys.

"And Saint-Martin," recommended Marteau, "Claude de Saint-Martin; the solution to all our social problems can be found in his works."

Enogat leaned toward Neurocyme. "Our friend is affiliated to a Martinist lodge," he confided to her in a whisper.

"We'll read all those authors, although we've already read too many books, and we'll do better than them, I dare to hope," Berny declared, with an untiring Jovian self-confidence. "It's above all in humanity and in nature that we want to learn to read, and it's in showing people how one ought to be free that we'll render society better."

"If people were less rebellious to the beautiful," Sabas sustained, "it would be sufficient, in order to solve the social problem, to create a theater in which verses were recited to the profit of the unfortunate."

But Berny smiled at that project, which he qualified as "young." His hands were agitating, and he hastened to expose the theories of aristocratic anarchism by means of comparisons and hypotyposes that amused the elemental.

After having given herself the impish pleasure on several occasions of putting the fine theoretician in contradiction with himself, the humorist fluttered her eyelashes, patted her golden red hair, and suggested joyfully, in a quiet voice: "Your theories appear to me to be in discord with your person, Seigneur Berny. You're the victim of a nervous overexcitation; your anarchism has no other cause than the abuse of hashish.

"But Madame," replied the juvenile aede, quite astonished, "what makes you think that?"

"My divinatory gifts complete what the physiognomy indicates to me," the elemental replied.

Enogat, serious and almost compassionate, said "Alas, one cannot hide anything from Madame.

Berny, however, preferred to suppose that Sabas was indiscreet, and promised himself to reveal to Neurocyme, as soon as a favorable occasion presented itself, that the Borgiaque esthete maintained an illicit commerce with the salamanders of alcohol.

While Berny ruminated that dark project, Néaucante pleaded the cause of scientific politics, Romanitas exalted his dear federalism, and Fauve argued the necessity of capitalist despotism. And while Lepetit pensively sought to remember a quatrain that he had slipped into the hand of a pretty Greek girl he had met on an omnibus. Occitanel, who had not ceased to batter in the breach the theories of all his colleagues, thundered against any attempt at oppression and concluded with an ardent appeal for synergy via amour.

At that moment, the lights of the drawing room were irradiating it with multicolored fires: silver and gold, ruby and turquoise, cobalt and copper, emerald and amethyst, all metals and all gems in fusion. The corollas, the foliage and the drapes, the black suits, the faces and the fingers caught fire, beribboned, fringed and dappled. Masked with red, yellow, violet, green, amaranth and all the blues of the firmament and the sea. The surprise, however, was of short duration.

"Why, a symphony by Besnard," said Sombredire.

And Marteau, whose beardless face seemed divided between azure and sinople, and that impertinence of flame, exclaimed: "It's the image of the nations of tomorrow, all united in one light!"

"Personally, I would have called it lighting for harlequins, your symphony of universal harmony," trumpeted Occitanel.

"Because your individualism prevents you from entering into communion with the soul of crowds," riposted Berny, impetuously.

"And they've pulled René Ghil's leg," muttered Valgourd, with haughty commiseration.

"Let's go live in the United States in the future, then," snapped Lepetit, his lip curled. "If they give us the Future Eve, she'll recompense with a smile the verses dedicated to her."

Sabas and Valgourd withdrew almost immediately. Neurocyme tried in vain to restore harmony; the argument resumed, more violently, under all the colors of the rainbow. Attacked and harassed by all his colleagues, Occitanel faced up to them with the volubility of a cricket and the force of a hurricane. Néaucante, who was not possessed of facile elocution, soon renounced trying to interject a syllable. Berny, and then Marteau, dispersed by those periodic charges, were removed from the combat in their turn.

At two o'clock in the morning, when the guests left, the little Velasquez with the proud manner was still talking, in a southern accent that dominated all the others. The imperious Occitanel cited Leroy-Beaulieu as he kissed Neurocyme's hand, recommended her to read Tarde as he pirouetted on his heels, resumed his thesis on the perron, continued it in the street, and when his last adversaries left him at the Carrefour de la Croix-Rouge, they, and not he—O marvel!—were exhausted.

VI. Of Various People and the painter Léonidas,
Prince of Ideo-Naturists

After that soirée of elevated conflict, Neurocyme, even more curious to know the celebrities who had refused Enogat's invitation, decided to go to them. Tardeval and Sabas prepared her for the interviews and, as gallant knights, accompanied her.

Her first visit was to the *Revue Noire*, where she was awaited passionately. The director of that periodical had, in fact, gathered for the occasion all his most "future era" collaborators—those who transposed anarchism for the use of people in society. Each of them talked about his articles, and was as brilliant and lunar as a magnesium flare.

Blond and pink, Moïse Lachance sustained, in imagistic terms, that the Semites alone, those civilizers par excellence, those supreme solidarists, those prestigious assimilators, could realize the new palingenesis.

"So," said Neurocyme, "you're only awaiting the Jewish Messiah."

"The young Aryans haven't yet understood the role that the writer of today ought to play," replied Salomettan gravely, "in the literary zone, and in the political sphere..."

"Make an exception for me," put in Paulève, without false modesty. "I have a few reasons to believe that, having understood the present, I'm ready to prepare tomorrows."

The sumptuous fantasies of Monsieur Paulève interested Neurocyme greatly. That is why, after having contemplated the beautiful searching eyes of that eminent young master momentarily, she asked him, melodiously: "Do you think, Monsieur, that the book will be a sufficient instrument to accomplish the social transfiguration of which so many writers are dreaming?"

"No, I don't think so; the book prepares; the functionary achieves."

Neurocyme could not hide her astonishment. "The functionary?"

"Yes, Madame. Think about it. Certainly, it's only a minister, an administrator, a governor or a prefect who can accomplish great things. And first of all, to resolve the social question in Europe, and in France above all, it's important to colonize. Salvation lies there. Evacuate the surplus of our cities to Africa and Oceania, everywhere there is ground to break, soil to conquer from forests or marshes. Appoint me as governor of a colony, and allow me to apply my theory, and the bankers of Israel would be mutated into Medicis, and the populace would no longer bring anyone into the world by Étienne Marcels or René Caillés."

There was a brief silence; and suddenly, without transition, "You've studied spiritism, haven't you?" Neurocyme said, with apparent seriousness.

Paulève leaned back in his armchair, which was bamboo with knots ringed by a layer of gold. With his hands crossed on his left knee, he replied, in a grave and eloquent voice: "At one time, I devoted myself feverishly to spiritist writings. I obtained extremely curious results, which I counted on relating in five or six novels, on which I began work; but I was obliged to cease my research."

A gesture from the elemental asked why.

"In the wake of certain experiments, I suffered; the blood flowed to my head and swelled my ears. I never stopped fainting. The meninges became dolorously inflamed. The cervical vertebrae cracked in the neck. Here"—he waved his index finger nervously over the top of his head—"my entire life seemed to be flowing away through two or three holes. And in the street, every passer-by who brushed me took away my strength, as if he were a magnet capable of attracting it. I was obliged to make all my journeys by carriage, not wanting to fall to the sidewalk, helpless."

Neurocyme sketched a movement of alarm. Afterwards, rising to her feet, she took her leave of those "messieurs" of the *Revue*. Outside, the air seemed soft and light.

She was walking beside Tardeval. "You know," she said to him, "he's someone not banal, that Paulève."

"Undoubtedly."

"He's an authoritarian socialist, that anarchist," Neurocyme added.

They fell silent. They arrived at the *Amadis de Gaule*.

There, Raymond de Valgourd and Bernard Fauve introduced the beautiful curiosity-seeker to the virtuosos of paradox, the princes of critical erudition and a few preparers of the new times, as correct as diplomats. Soon, Neurocyme's questions prompted discussions, as learned as they were eloquent, on the works of all nations and all ages. There was an orgy of theses, unexpected analogies, rare citations and authoritative statements. Although the debates were rapidly animated by digressions of a metaphysical or political order, and a few allusions to burning issues, those writers did not depart from a verbal dignity and an august manner.

"One senses here some perfume of the Hôtel Pimodan,"[38] said Bernard Fauve, escorting the elemental out. "Don't you think so, Madame?"

"Oh," Neurocyme replied, "those Messieurs are 'very strong,' as your ladies say: scholarly, eloquent, ingenious, true sons of Prometheus. They have found the art of civilizing philosophemes and giving literature an armor simultaneously solid, supple and shiny, like the starch of which the laundresses of Albion are said to hold the secret."

She had a smile in her eyes. "Where are we going now?" she asked Tardeval.

"To Lagoupille's."

Lagoupille was reputed—and still is—to be one of the most authoritative universitarian minds in the world of letters:

---

[38] The Hôtel Pimodan on the Quai d'Anjou was where Charles Baudelaire, Théophile Gautier and other members of the "Club des Haschischins" experimented with psychotropic drugs under the tutelage of the psychologist Joseph Moreau de Tours in the 1840s.

a very interesting model of the pawn who has used his cerebellum and elbows a great deal. Some method and enormously urbane, that Lagoupille, and youthful in age if not in soul, you see.

He was waiting for his visitors, surrounded by several of his friends, in the attitude of a man habituated to rubbing shoulders at the Pont-du-Change. He talked like a professor of humanities standing for parliament, striving to attenuate his arrogance.

"My principles," he said, in substance "are: adhere to modern science; have faith in holy Science and no-less-holy Democracy; love the people and the Fatherland."

"Isn't that the program of Freemasonry?" interrogated Tardeval, in whose mouth an Aristophanean smile was flourishing.

"It might be," replied the young master-pawn, dryly. "It is, at any rate, that of the University, the sole focal point of intellectualism capable of forming virile generations, artists and devotees of the religion of progress, the only true one and the only one possible henceforth."

"No more churches then?"

"The Church," he said, mistaking the question, "it is necessary to kill."

"In the person of its princes," endorsed one of his associates, a tall, stiff, angular and inquisitorial individual whom the young and almost illustrious pawn had introduced under a name that reeked slightly of the auto-da-fé: Carbonnade. "Yes, its princes! And assuredly, the superior interests of humanity and charity—and of altruism, I want to say—demand that sacrifice, which, in any case, wouldn't sadden anyone."

"Except the victims," snapped Tardeval.

An hour later, Neurocyme said to Enogat, when they were alone: "It's singular; that Carbonnade has the voice of poor Edouard Dubus.[39] Have you noticed that?"

"It's true," the dilettante replied. "But how do you know that?"

"I've heard the soul of Dubus reciting verses in the astral to the souls of Gérard de Nerval and Jules Laforgue."

Four or five days went by.

One evening, the elemental had herself taken to the Vachette by the obliging Romanitas. There, to the right, as Olympian as a god can be who wears a moustache, Canéas, surrounded by his faithful disciples, was enthroned before a marble table, which, in spite of cyathes of a vulgar style, assumed the gravity of an altar, Romanitas having made the introductions, Neurocyme began with a los to Ronsard that won her the master's benevolence.[40]

"It's was just in time that we arrived," he declared, superb and indulgent. "What decadence since Racine!"

After which the favorite disciple, Plessis-Piquet—whose face presented the particularity of being shaved at the temples—pronounced the eulogy of the members of the cenacle, and, by way of peroration, compared the beautiful stranger to the Queen of Sheba coming to interrogate the wisdom of King Solomon.

----

[39] The Symbolist poet Édouard Dubus (1864-1895), one of the co-founders of the *Mercure de France*, was a drug-addict whose died of an overdose in a public toilet.

[40] "Los" is an obsolete term referring to a hymn of praise. In order to follow this slightly gnomic passage it is useful to bear in mind that by 1900 Jean Moréas, the author of the Symbolist Manifesto, had moved on to form the *école romane* [Roman School] with Charles Maurras, Raymond de la Tailhède, Maurice du Plessys and other disciples, which also became the base of the right-wing political group that eventually became Action Française.

Then the cenacle took Neurocyme to Les Halles, where no one any longer talked about anything except the splendor of the Pleiad and the virtues of onion soup.

It remained to see a poet, Adolphe Agreste, the ex-symbolist converted to the cult of nature and anarchism. He was resident, alas, in a distant village, reminiscent of Ferté-sous-Thule. Nevertheless, Romanitas offered himself again as an introducer; and they left one morning, with Enogat, whom these interviews which somewhat undilettantish minds were, however, beginning to fill with melancholy.

"Comrade" Agreste praised, between two character assassinations of Mallarmé and Henri Le Régalien, the pleasures of the rustic life, the necessity of hygiene and mental equilibrium; then he intoned an ode in prose of Kropotkinian lyricism, which concluded with the pure and simple overthrow of present society.

"Transform it, this society? Oh la la! That's utopian. This bourgeois society that sweats gold! What is scientific is to build another; and for that it's necessary to make a *tabula rasa* of everything that exists: the sole means of having a necessary emplacement and sufficient materials."

"Are you quite certain, then, of modeling the society of your dreams?" asked Enogat, courteously.

The other replied: "Let's destroy first. And when everything is reduced to ruins...at least the world will be picturesque!"

Enogat did not insist. But on the return journey, looking at Neurocyme, he said: "Well, how do you find them, our writers?"

"I would have preferred them discussing esthetics or the language, I admit, battling for free verse, preoccupied with transforming the novel and the theater," said the beauty, her eyes half-closed. "At least, on those questions, they'd be competent. But in sociology? Poor Fantasios fallen from their roof into the Académie des Sciences![41] They don't know anything about economists, biologists and sociologists, and are ignorant of social life itself. Before the cases of the conflict between capital and labor they're all a little like Canéas before beetroots. *The fecund illusion lives in their…*oh well, that's what sells!"

And she laughed. On seeing her laugh, Enogat cheered up somewhat. And a few more days went by.

Negans had been asked to reveal to Neurocyme the artists of the latest wave, and that of the next. Unfortunately, the role of cicerone through the studios and the cenacles had nothing that could please him.

Might as well parade some Corinne of the sub-prefecture though the Jardin des Plantes, he thought. *If some have received from Heaven a physiognomy that predisposes them to that kind of amusement, I believe I'm not of their number.*

He therefore deployed the eloquence cultivated during long evenings in the brasserie to persuade Neurocyme to renounce her project.

"In general, Madame," he said, "artists are only interesting in their works, and those of today are certainly no exception, being almost all rustics, employees of the customs, undertakers or old rogues still faithful to the 'japes' of their twentieth year..."

"I can divine those street-urchins," the elemental put in.

"Sincere compliments. You're better informed, beautiful friend, than a reporter from the New York *Herald*. But what you don't know is that the present street-urchins of the palette or the chisel are far from having the intelligence that Gavarni sketched, and their glibness, as bourgeois as the rest, almost always ring false. As for the 'artists' whom one can introduce to ladies"—Negans took on a particular intonation in order to spell out that phrase—"they're insupportable pedants, as tedious as parvenus with pot-bellies or courtesans with flat feet."

---

[41] Fantasio is the eponymous hero of an 1872 comic opera by Offenbach based on a play by Alfred de Musset.

"Let's leave those to the ordinary public. Is there not, among the others, some curious mind, open to innovation, with whom one can talk about esthetics?"

"Esthetics! If you think they know what that is! Ha! Their esthetics consists of walking on their feet in order to make snobs think that they paint with their toenails, and juggling with a few terms—Mystery! Beyond! Symbol! Idealism!—in order to delight the client, and pass turnips off as golden apples from the old garden of the Hesperides. An ideal, them? Yes they have one: sell dear, as dear as possible..."

"If it were only a matter of showing you two or three curiosities, Madame, we might risk the adventure; it wouldn't surpass human strength. But the cenacles that contain some rare phenomenon count an overwhelming number of individuals as banal as stuffed kangaroos. You might as well sit down at a simple political banquet, presided by a municipal councilor in a sash, with toasts in verse over dessert to Monsieur Carjat and prosopopeias to Monsieur Jaurès. The cenacle is no longer a chapel, it's a club. We live—as you certainly know, for I perceive that you know everything—under the regime of coteries. The extra-lucid sociologists demonstrate that it's to parliamentarism that we owe that. Very inconvenient for Art, that regime, but famous for the professionals. Nowadays, after two years in the studio, and even before then, one can be consecrated as a master. It's sufficient to draw, to the scorn of certain laws, like a drunkard's walk. The paradoxal periodicals all have one young man, or often two, one of whom is sometimes mature, or overripe, who like nothing better than to declare as genius the scribblings of loonies."

"That's a vile word."

"All right, let's say 'mediums,' Madame. And all these mediums...all these clubists, I mean, would scandalize you by their ignorance in making works of art, and by their sportsmanlike concepts. Neither among those of the latest trireme, nor those of the galleys in formation can I see a group or an individual to whom to introduce you. There's no conversation possible with an artist. One flatters him or one listens benevolently to his nonsense. Those people have scarcely more intellectuality than dancers, and they're less interesting, even setting questions of athletics apart."

"Indeed! You scarcely cherish..."

"At least don't think I'm exaggerating! I'm emphasizing the contours of the portrait, but I'm not extrapolating them. By pedestalizing the social importance of artists, after having stupidly swallowed it, we have made those prideful big babies into unsociable beings. They've acquired the conceit of the midwife and the actor, the arrogance of a bureaucratic deputy chief, or one of those electors who comes to vote between two pauses at the tavern. Everything offends their star-like susceptibility, everything wounds their tyrannical prejudices. At all times, under any sky, the artist only practices an excessive modesty, but to be a contemporary artist is an elixir of vanity. Besides which, so many sons of Joseph Prudhomme, Tribulat Bonhomet and Monsieur Homard now devote themselves to painting. They can try to clean their souls, but something always remains of the ancestral strain, as you can imagine."

"And among those who have no boat, you can't cite me one original character—not one?"

"Oh, among those..."

And Negans, allowing his shiny Triboulet gaze to wander over the ceiling, pretended to search the abysm of his memory.[42]

"If necessary, you can search the old frigates," Neurocyme persisted.

"No, no, it's futile! Let's not trouble the sleep of the bonzes. I can see what you need among the isolates..."

"In fact, they ought to have more individuality than the arrivistes."

"More pride above all, but so candid, so unconscious...the one that I've decided to exhibit to you isn't far from believing that he gives birth to an Athene every time he sneezes."

---

[42] Triboulet was court jester to Louis XII and François I.

Neurocyme smiled. Then, momentarily, she seemed to mediate, and, furrowing her beautiful somber golden eyebrows slightly, she said: "That psychological indication reveals the exterior man to me. He has a sturdy figure, a mat complexion, steady eyes and brilliant and bloodshot as carbuncles—and he wears a pointed beard like General Boulanger, doesn't he, Monsieur Negans? His head, symmetrically constructed, presented a slight square forehead, fleshy and furrowed, thick eyebrows, a rather small mouth, white teeth, a straight, short nose, his flattened hair and flourishing beard are burnt Sienna in hue. Is that almost exact?"

"Exactly. Ah, Madame, how did you guess?"

"Very easily. Your words indicated the artist's principal astral signatures. He's doubtless a rather pronounced Jupiter-Solarian type."

"So be it; at any rate, this Jupiter-Solarian excels in decorating his speech with more or less singular ideas."

"Truly?"

"At least he's collected a certain number of baroques notions, and when he chances to accept a sane one, it's to transform it bizarrely, for he cultivates hyperbole with the dilection of a Dutch tulip-enthusiast."

"Better to cultivate hyperbole than the commonplace. When can we obtain an audience with this master?"

"Tomorrow, I hope," replied the art-critics. "To that end, I'll send him a telegram."

As he made as if to leave, Neurocyme asked: "And his name? You haven't told me his name."

"Léonidas."

"Is he a Greek?"

"He's not even from our Midi; nevertheless, he has the state of mind of a son of Tarascon raised in Alexandria in the days of Porphyry."

Nothing at any rate, was complex enough for the handsome and eloquent Léonidas, who delighted in veiling the simplest things with disconcerting symbols. By dint of searching the slightest trivia for meaning and double meanings, he had arrived at conceiving misinterpretation as the most perfect expression of the truth. An argument had no value for him if it was not presented in a rare form or in an ambiguous manner. And he was convinced that a master of his importance ought only to offer himself to profane gazes under Aulic aspects and imperious attitudes, but as he lacked the gift of doubling the self, his mannerisms only caused amazement. As for the "chic" and magnificence of his costumes, they depended on the good will and *savoir-faire* of the latest tailor who had allowed himself to be taken in hand by the master,

Negans having announced the visit of an Egyptian lady, an eminent occultist and transcendental esthete, Léonidas had put on his tunic of solemn days, once entirely white, holding the middle ground between a chemise and a dressing-gown, which shrank him slightly, but gave him a vague appearance of a flamingo.

By virtue of a series of contingencies seemingly fortuitous, the mysterious law of concordances had led the painter Léonidas to fix his residence in the Passage des Thermopyles. The principles of his art, however, bore no resemblance to those of Jacques-Louis David. He had given himself the mission of not painting anything that did not translate the supernatural or evoke subtle associations of ideas, perhaps convinced—with him one never knew—that he was thus collaborating with the amelioration of humankind. He dreamed of figures revelatory of the invisible and compositions presenting philosophical syntheses. That was what he hastened to explain to Neurocyme with long sidelong glances, fatal attitudes and a great luxury of metaphorical details.

"I'm seeking," he concluded, "to reconcile the real and the unreal, the alpha and the omega, the sensible and the suprasensible. The soul of glorious ancestors lives in me"—here a fist on the hip and a tenebrous leer—"and it's their work, Madame, that I'm intent on continuing, completing it by means of scientific discoveries and rendering it more eloquent by means of nuances. Oh, the nuances, that's terrible; everything is in the nuances. By them alone can the idea of today—

my ideas—be expressed. There's another sphinx to create; that's what will translate the most intimate aspirations of our contemporaries, their condition in the face of the Beyond, their anxiety before he social transformation that is in process. That's what I'm seeking to render by means of the harmonization of the animal form and the human form: the eternal symbol of matter and mind, which, moreover, it's no longer necessary to represent as fatally locked in conflict, but, on the contrary, in perfect conciliation."

"And it's a single beast that's going to express all that?" asked Negans, in a corncrake voice, his arms in the air, aping alarm.

"Negans, my dear, you're astonishing," said the big flamingo, slightly nonplussed, but with an inclination of the head that affected disdain and a taut smile that attempted to be merciful. Then, turning to Neurocyme and enveloping her with his most splendidly fatal gaze, he added: "That's Parisians for you, Madame. "I'll wager that people understood life quite differently under Ramses."

"Good! Do you think that Madame dates from the erection of the Ramesseum?"

"Negans," said Neurocyme, "You have an aggressive attitude today. I'm convinced that our dear master will obtain a very good result from the project to which he's just made us party. What can one not enclose in a symbolic work when one has a mind open to the supernatural? In any case, is it not finer to tend always to transform matter as a prophetess, as a revelatrix of ideas?"

Léonidas stuck out his chest and, throwing his head back, but without taking his eyes off his visitor, he gargled: "There! Ah, Madame, you have understood me. I'm a revelator of ideas, and I'm convinced that the work of art is the best of the modes of education, socially as well as mentally."

"Oh, of course...," murmured Negans, with one finger up his nose.

"You doubt it, man of all skepticisms. Well, look and judge. Here it is."

And Léonidas swiveled an easel supporting a canvas covered with numerous characters. "This," he said, "is Harmony and Beauty preparing the era of Anarchism."

His interlocutors immediately uttered a significant "Ah!" And immediately thereafter, Neurocyme added to that "Ah!" an "Oh!"

"Harmony and Beauty"!" exclaimed Negans, closing his left eye.

"By what correlation?" hazarded Enogat, extending his right arm.

"I'll make you an exegesis of the work," Léonidas replied, satisfied with the effect produced. And in a voice simultaneously splendid and sticky, he commenced the explanation: "The draped woman to the left of the scene informing a group of ephebes, while young maidens offer her flowers"—a tender wink at Neurocyme—"is Harmony."

"Damn! I would have wagered that it was Loie Fuller in repose," yapped Negans, with a certain conviction.

"Why is that?" asked the flamingo.

"Because of the multiple shades of her drapery."

"They're the colors of the rainbow, and I'm content with that find. What more luminous symbol is there of harmony?"

"The idea is, in fact, luminous," snorted Negans, with an insolent seriousness.

But the elemental exclaimed: "Say that it's genius! And why, Monsieur Léonidas, is Harmony distributing to the ephebes the flowers that the maidens are offering to her?"

"That signifies: Love nature; all joys are in her. Dispose your gardens tastefully, and your souls will be beautiful poems, exquisite symphonies. Cultivate the flowers; interrogate them, and you will know Harmony, and she will be established within you."

"Very good. Understood. Pull the petals off the daisies," said Negans.

"Now, let's pass over to the right," Léonidas continued. "You see that other draped woman who is perorating in the middle of a crowd; that woman"—a thunderbolt-gaze at

Neurocyme—"is Beauty. She is recognizable by her splendid complexion, to begin with, and afterwards, by her almost complete nudity. Notice that I've given her a body as beautiful as it is antique. And she is finally recognizable by the eye profiled in her diadem. It's thus that our Poussin conceived her."

"That eye intrigued me," Negans declared. "I wondered, at first sight, whether you might have wanted to represent, in the manner of Roty, the Prefecture of Police."[43]

"Joker!"

"Not at all. Alongside Anarchism, the Prefecture of Police; that seems to me to be indicated."

Léonidas' eyelids were vacillating madly, like those of a hero dying of amour.

"With an ample gesture," he went on, his lip curled, "Beauty is pointing with her right hand to ruins, which are those of Paris. As for her gesture, it means: 'Now that the archetypal city of all ugliness is destroyed, it is necessary to raise temples to Beauty. Now that the tenements have been reduced to rubble, it is necessary to build cottages. Lay out parks, erect triumphal arches, plant flagpoles, and you will live happily.'"

You believe those reforms to be sufficient to maintain wellbeing?" Negans asked.

"Yes, with simple tastes."

"Ah! Good. But my dear friend, your work requires a caption."

"Why? Everything I've just said, it's the attitudes and gestures of my figures that say it on the canvas. Heavens! If you understood all that a gesture can express!"

"I admit that I'm not yet strong enough..."

"It is, however, quite simple; my characters are expressive in their very simplicity. Thus, look at my Beauty's second gesture; she is putting her left hand in her heart, and radiance is emerging from that heart, which goes to touch the hearts of those around her. A child could grasp the meaning of that

---

[43] The reference is to the medallist Oscar Roty (1846-1911).

symbol. Beauty is showing the human species, synthesized by a few individuals of both sexes and various ages, that the religion of the future emanates from her heart. Let all participate in it and that will be the end of corruption and egotism; humanity returns to the Golden Age."

"And everyone can cultivate tulips without worrying about paying the rent? An admirable language, Turkish…the language of gestures, I mean!"

Seemingly very absorbed before the extraordinary canvas, however, Neurocyme slowly shook her head, and put her hands together.

"That heart," she pronounced, "which wants to attract all hearts…the idea seems to me to be very touching…"

"Radiant, dear, utterly radiant," opined the exquisite Enogat, in order to say something. And the sonority of his own voice doubtless stimulated him a little, for he turned to the great flamingo. "But my dear master," he asked, "why is Beauty looking at the woman who is surging forth gloriously in the middle of the scene, instead of looking at those she is haranguing with her gestures?"

"Because the woman that she is indicating with a gaze full of love and admiration is Anarchy, and because that completes her discourse. That gaze means: 'Now that the old society has had its day, and it is necessary for you to build a new one, found it on the love of nature and humanity.' Note that an old man is standing next to Anarchy."

"Yes," replied Negans. "One might think it was *Oedipus Rex*."

"It's Ruskin."

"What! Ruskin is the chaperon of Anarchy?"

"Yes, for Ruskin is the veritable apostle of the new era."

"Really? What about Tolstoy?"

"Tolstoy does not have the sense of beauty, not being English. He's a sentimental cobbler."

"Oh!"

"Ruskin is the only man since Plato who has had Beauty, and perhaps the only one since Longus who has loved nature with passion."

"Are you certain that Longus didn't prefer hetairas?"

"Yes, because the hetairas of those days had forms that made them symbols of nature."

Enogar had perceived that the painter had not ceased winking at Neurocyme, and as, in the course of the conversation, the winking had become livelier and freer, he dared to interrupt, albeit with civility.

"This, Messieurs, is taking us a long way from Ruskin."

"Yes, yes, let's get back to Ruskin," said Léonidas, darting a glance of supreme languor at the elemental. "His presence there signifies: 'Love nature, and you will love one another; and, nothing any longer troubling concord, the era of Anarchy will commence,' Look closely at my Anarchy. I'm quite content with her forms." Another languorous glance at Neurocyme. "Sky and sea! That drapery gave me difficulties! It was terrible. Finally, I draw your attention to her buckler, in which the federation of the peoples of the two hemisphere is symbolized, not maladroitly, by those groups, each individual of which incarnates a nation, and to her helmet, where the principal planets of our solar system stand out in relief, the image of the order and equilibrium that ought to reign in the future society. Look at all that and fix it in our memory. My Anarchy is Wisdom, the Athene of tomorrow."

"What! Athene the symbol of Anarchy?" protested Negans. "Until now, the latter has been considered rather as disorder and fever."

"That's not at all how I understand it, personally," pronounced Léonidas.

Negans whistled. "I congratulate you for it. But are you certain, then, of being in the anarchist spirit?"

"I'm certain of being with nature, which is sufficient for me," the flamingo replied, his eyes blank. "Nature is the image of Anarchy, and that is why the latter appears to me as the reign of Harmony. No more cities; only villages. No more central government; a federation of provinces, each having its customs. No more local authorities; the Commune mistress of everything. Finally, no more oppressive capital; everyone constrained to work. As for artists, it's just that the Commune maintains them, for they are the priests and educators entirely appropriate to the new society. They could be given, for that, an income of twenty thousand livres."

"Each?"

"Of course. In exchange the artists would deliver all their works to the commune, as much for decoration of public or private edifices as for the education of citizens."

"But that's socialism, all that, and the most authoritarian!"

"It's my Anarchy—that of Léonidas," said Léonidas.

Neurocyme, who could see a quarrel coming, hastened to pour floods of eulogies over the master whose talent, so unexpected and so subtle, excelled in presenting the greatest problems in lively, and even rejoicing, forms. She said all that with a charming seriousness, and very slowly, in order that the flattering syllables would caress the enraptured ears of the great flamingo for longer. Then, suddenly addressing Enogat, she twittered: "Oh, my dear friend, "I'm sure that an intelligence like yours must savor this ideistic and truly supraterrestial work very profoundly."

The dilettante, who had been invaded by a torpor, started, smiled and stammered: "Yes, indeed... undoubtedly... certainly. But my idea is initiatic art—I mean an art that would translate the esotericism of the Sepher Yetzirah, the Zo'har and the book of Hermes. Do you think that might be possible, my dear master?"

"Do I think so! But that's exactly what I'm seeking" Léonidas exclaimed, stretching himself with the indolent grace of a bayadere. "To initiate by the image, of which one is far from knowing all the virtues, to reveal the Beyond via nature, work magic in painting; I'm convinced that occultism is indispensable to the happiness of peoples."

"What! You're a candidate mage now!" sniggered Negans. "Well, if you succeed in reconciling the authoritarianism of the cabalistic Rosy Cross with that of Anarchism..."

"Everything is reconciled in occultism," said Neurocyme, with a grave smile. "And you'll be convinced of it, Monsieur, when you know the thirty-two roads to Wisdom."

"What! One alone isn't sufficient?"

Drawing away somewhat from stubborn persiflage, however, the elemental said to Léonidas: "Dear Master, I'm delighted to have made your acquaintance, and I'll say *au revoir*, for I'm absolutely determined to possess some work of yours. We'll talk about it soon."

"For the present, Madame," replied the dear master, detaching a sketch from the wall, "permit me to offer you, in memory of this unforgettable visit, this little drawing...it's quite superior."

"I can't thank you enough, truly, for, in spite of my esthetic incompetence, I know that you're making me a princely gift. I can read in your astral, in fact, that you're called to a sublime destiny."

"In truth, I had an intuition of it," Léonidas replied, his eyes ablaze. "I'm the only man of the present time to be preoccupied with manifesting the Infinite by means of a sovereign and beautiful art, Madame..."

And more than one wink: an ultimate wink! It was passionate and morose, slow and lively, splendid and tenebrous; it was synthetic! The flamingo showed his guests out, swaying his hips. Neurocyme thought he was dancing.

She appeared, however, quite satisfied with her visit to the noble and aristocratic anarchist Léonidas, whose familiarity and verve had really amused her. She had only pitied him briefly, supposing that he had a lesion of the optic nerve, a kind of St. Vitus' dance of the retina.

"I like him, that interpreter of the inexpressible," she declared.

Very much a woman, although an elemental, she thought at first of commissioning him to paint her portrait, and the idea of seeing her in a legendary costume in a magical décor seemed attractive momentarily. Having looked at herself in a mirror, however, she reflected that the flamingo was too idealistic to make her resemblance, and as she did not think it possible to embellish her, she quickly changed her plan.

"What if we charge him, my dear friend, with decorating the house?" she suggested to Enogat.

"This house?" he replied, somewhat stupefied. "But, ravishing friend, why?"

"Firstly because, veritably, it lacks frescoes. Secondly, because a series of very original compositions would make it unique in Paris."

And immediately, he gave in.

"It's true, dear, it would be new. And in any case, it's sufficient that the project seduces you. How do you see that decoration? Have you some dream in mind already?"

"Yes, a scene of initiation in ancient Egypt...the promenade of the astral body of an adept in interplanetary space. But all that is still confused. And then, can a paining render such effects? The best thing, I believe, dear friend, would be to consult Léonidas."

The great flamingo, invited to dinner, inspected the various rooms of the house and declared that their Louis XIV style rendered any mural decoration conceived in a modern sentiment impossible.

"It's as if you were to put Madame in the hat and shawl of one of our great-grandmothers. If there's no harmony between the fresco and the ambience, bonsoir unity! And as, without unity, no decoration is possible, *bonsoir* decoration."

"What can one decently put on these walls, then, in your opinion?" asked Enogat, almost heart-broken.

"Seventeenth century tapestries."

"Décor in the style of Le Brun?" said Enogat, pulling a face.

"What if we left this old dwelling instead, which would be simpler and wiser," proposed the elemental, with a sigh so soft that the dilettante's heart opened up, suddenly ablaze and burning.

"That's true!" Enogat exclaimed, without having any precise notion of what he was articulating. "Yes, nothing attaches me to this place. Why not look elsewhere? Or rather, no...oh, yes, not at all! What a good idea! Why not have a house built?"

"A very modern house," proclaimed Neurocyme.

"A very symbolic house," Léonidas specified, "manifesting, in its plan and its elevation, the laws of the quaternary and the ternary, like the pyramids."

"With rooms and bedrooms prepared to receive ideist frescoes," added Enogat.

"In those conditions, I'll take responsibility for making you masterpieces," Léonidas affirmed, in a paroxysm of enthusiasm.

But no wink—not the slightest wink! He had obtained from Neurocyme all that he expected, even more than he had hoped. He had finished winking—for her. And she was certainly not wrong to think that joy had "cured" him. A little later, going away in the dark, if he still "made eyes," it was at the stars above.

"Oh, you shall have a dwelling worthy of you, dear," Enogat modulated to Neurocyme, very tenderly, as soon as they were alone.

A plot of land was found immediately, in the Avenue de Wagram. By contrast, the choice of architect necessitated a careful and laborious enquiry. Where could the original and subtle artist required be found? Enogat would have liked Monsieur Vaudremer, Monsieur Menot, Monsieur Pascal or Monsieur Daumet, because they were, at least, members of the Institut; but Negans claimed that the messieurs in question were good, at the most, for constructing temples. With that, Léonidas, his thumbs in the armholes of his waistcoat, vaguely proposed Mr. Waterhouse, Mr. Fordham, Mr. Webb or Mr.

Shaw, sustaining that architecture was only any longer understood in England. Callidulus, whose connections extended over the two worlds, promised to make a search for the rare bird in all the capitals of Europe and the two Americas. It might take a while...

In the meantime, nevertheless, Léonidas piled up sketch after sketch. Then, one day, he invited Neurocyme and Enogat to come and see, in his studio, the plans for the decoration of the future house. As he had declared himself a partisan of initiatic art, he had been left completely free in the choice of subject.

Thus, his arms deployed like the wings of an albatross in flight, he said: "This is how I see the thing. Firstly, the decoration will form a unity. Each fresco will be a fact of an ensemble, an in that fashion, the house will gain in magnificence. There are ten compositions, as many as the sephiroths."

"Genius!"

"The first composition that will strike the eyes, when one penetrates your home, represents nature lamenting over the universal boorishness of the epoch, and appealing for a savior Orpheus. Nature is symbolized by a group of draped women, each of them representing some typical aspect of the microcosm—the mountain, the forest, the sea, etcetera. As décor, an autumnal dusk, with a sulfurous sky and a carpet of dead leaves, entirely impressive. The second fresco will show us the reincarnation of Orpheus. On the terrestrial plane, mages watching life gradually penetrate its material envelope; on the astral plane, elementals and astral bodies showing one another that spectacle; on the divine plane, where the symbols indicate the movement of the Soul of the world, a great resplendent light; it is the superior spirit of Orpheus that a flood of light in attaching to his sensible body."

"A masterstroke!" approved Enogat. "It's absolutely the sublime art of which I dreamed."

Léonidas was not wearing braces—they are so unesthetic! Gripping the belt of his trousers in both hands, he hitched them up with an elegant languor. He declaimed:

"Among the mages, I intend to place a portrait of Madame, as well as yours Monsieur."

"Ah, a delicate attention!" saluted the flattered dilettante, while the elemental thanked him with a mundane smile.

"In the third composition, Orpheus is beginning his work of regeneration. He is destroying the Bourse, and while the elementals are overturning walls and columns, cabalists, employing the method of the fakirs, are making trees, flowers and plants grow over the ruins. Here, I believe it would be interesting to represent Dr. Callidulus making lilies bloom."

"Delightful! That will be delightful!"

"Oh, what is the theme of the following fresco? What do this redoubtable light and these spurting flames signify?

"It's the Chambre des Députés blowing up. I'm counting a great deal on that violent and sumptuous effect, quite new in mural decoration. Puvis de Chavannes wouldn't have dared that, nor Gustave Moreau, that master goldsmith of miniatures and water colors…in his fortunate moments."

"And this, another scene of destruction?"

"Yes, Orpheus burning the Trocadéro and toppling the Eiffel Tower."

"Perfect."

"In the sixth composition, Orpheus is diverting the course of the Seine, still with the help of elementals, in order to purify the site of the demolished Hôtel de Ville. They are, you see, as many labors of Hercules. In the seventh, Orpheus is returning Ville-d'Avray to the state in which the divine Corot, that Mozart of the palette, left it. In the eighth, he is charming, by means of his eloquence and is fluidic radiation, the barbarians of the times. There, I have chosen as décor the Tuileries, and I have put in the first rank of the crowd the most ferocious beings of our society: rentiers, landowners, industrialists and editors, who are shedding tears as they empty their wallets on the altar of altruism, while—notice the lovely decoration of the little monument—influential artists embrace one another and decree the end of abominable juries. The evil jurors themselves are converting, abdicating and voting their downfall. It's the fourth of August of letters and the arts. Everywhere, affection reigns; everywhere, the most energetically noble resolutions are flourishing. One could believe that they were hearing the finale of some gigantic symphony..."

"It's attaining the grandiose by means of the picturesque. What a crescendo! That's true mastery! Oh, yes; that's good!"

"You've said it," Léonidas approved, with admirable condescension. And he resumed his "inexpressible" pose.

"The ninth motif," he continued, majestically, represents the Observatoire, where, before the united scholarly bodies, Orpheus is communicating with the inhabitants of the planet Mars. The latter are giving him a legislation, which the disciples are transcribing immediately—hence the surprise and profound joy of the assembly."

"It's doubtless because of that marvel that those two individuals in the central group are falling into one another's arms?"

"Yes, that's Hervé Faye hugging Camille Flammarion to his breast. Not far away, Pierre Janssen is contemplating them emotionally."

"Utterly exquisite!"

"Finally, the last scene: Humanity is celebrating its salvation with a grand fête that is unfurling through the Champ-de-Mars, transformed into a flower-garden. The cordial and pompous atmosphere of old is reborn. Orpheus is culminating on a throne, surrounded by the masters of occultism. In the air, the souls of disincarnate adepts form choirs. Up above, the sign of the absolute, the universal pentacle of Martinism, is shining like a sun."

"Incomparable!" Enogat declared. "Ineffable, dear master! Nicolas Flamel could not have done better!"

"It leaves the works of James Tissot far behind."

"Certainly, in order not to understand, after examining these frescoes, that Orpheus symbolizes occultism, it would be necessary to be..."

"Monsieur Chincholle," said Neurocyme.

112

"Monsieur Bouguereau," said Léonidas.[44]

Then they remained silent and pensive for a moment. Dusk was falling tinting the studio with the entire adorable gamut of mauve. It was the hour when Sabas and the other Symbolist lions came to drink.

Suddenly, raising her frail white hand toward the sketches, Neurocyme pronounced, musically: "My dear master, the conception of such a work makes you ours. Oh, henceforth you belong to us. It only remains for you to receive the initiation."

Then the flamingo made an Olympian movement of the head; and they went to dinner.

---

[44] The references are to the journalist Charles Chincholle (1843-1902) and the academic painter William-Adolphe Bouguereau (1825-1905); the latter was reviled by the impressionists as the archetype of the salon painter.

*VII. In which it appears that the pleasures of elementals
are not without bitterness*

However, the original and savant, strange and subtle architect had not been found.

Neurocyme, who was burning to be admired in unforgettable décors, resolved to improvise a few receptions, the sumptuousness of which all Paris would praise. And truly, was it not necessary to quit the house in the Rue Vaneau with a bang? On the other hand, understanding very well that she would lose her hieratic quality and her exoticism in banal city garments, she no longer wanted to show herself at home except in costumes that were historic or ideally fantastic. Now, in order not to contrast with her entourage, it was necessary, was it not, ingeniously to oblige her guests to dress like her?

That decision made, Neurocyme had no difficulty—a simple soft gaze and a suggestive quiver of the lips sufficed—in immediately obtaining the consent of Enogat, whose dilettantism, in any case, could only take pleasure in such amusements.

They decided to organize four fêtes, by way of a trial. The first one would be held in an Egyptian palace of the time of the Ramessides, the next in the palace of Assurbanipal, the third in the dwelling of Plato and the last in the manor of Laure de Noves. The door would be realized by means of frameworks covered with painted canvases, draperies and accessories copied from museum originals. The guests would be required to dress in accordance with authentic documents. Servants in accoutrements no less exact would complete the illusion.

Léonidas drew the sketches of the scenery and designed the majority of the costumes. The execution of both was confided to the professionals who work incessantly to render theaters ingenious. A few weeks sufficed for them to deliver the elements of the great Egyptian fête.

It was all simply magical.

The décor represented a sequence of painted bas-reliefs superimposed in several tiers and surmounted by a frieze covered in hieroglyphics. Four enormous columns with campaniform capitals, furrowed by painted ornaments, supported a ceiling decorated with meanders intermingled with rosettes and flocks of birds. In the middle of the ceiling gaped a square opening; the chandelier occupied its center, but hidden by a thick blue-tinted canopy. Through four false windows fitted into the walls to the left and the right, further rays of electric light were projected, giving the impression of silvery moonbeams.

Neurocyme was the costume of a queen: a long straight robe. The perruque of a goddess composed a natural diadem. Around her wrists and ankles shone gilded rings and bracelets of turquoises and pearls in lapis lazuli, cornelian and green feldspar. A golden chain, from which was suspended a scarab embedded in blue glass, heightened with gold, unfurled around her neck. On her bosom, a broad necklace was displayed similar to the one worn by Queen Ahotpou, a *wesekh* with nine tiers, decorated with two clasps carved in the shape of hawk's heads, and a pectoral illustrated with a mystical scene: the soul between Amon and Ra.

More than that ornamentation, which was a little overladen with gold, however, the delightfully simple vestment, which enveloped her without veiling her, brought out her native majesty, in allowing the fluid and firm contours of her body to be fully divined, giving it a grace by which more than one person was secretly troubled. When she passed before the electric light, something mysterious emanated from that animate statue, which inspired an indefinable sentiment, quite different from amour and even desire...

Enogat, for his part, was decked out as Ramses III, greatly inconvenienced by his helmet, but as happy nevertheless as a child playing at being a sovereign. From time to time he frowned, or caused his nostrils to quiver with a shrug after the fashion of Mount-Sully. Down below, Romanitas, Tardeval,

Fauve and Marc Lepetit were dressed up as warriors, Sabas as a poet, Berny a young embalmer. Beneath a *pschent*, Vivian evoked Étienne Méhul's Joseph. Further away, clad in a flesh-colored leotard, Albin Bénérès was creating the effects of torso and legs of a scribe, but not crouching, while Callidulus, in the tunic of a high-priest of Amon-Ra, was striving to appear simultaneously amiable and magnificent.

Thanks to Léonidas, who had undertaken to reproduce historical verity in his designs with pre-Raphaelite scrupulousness, all the guests were "in character"; and as the majority of the costumes reproduced different individuals of similar decoration, one could have believed—without the moustache of one and the monocle of another—that the bas-reliefs of the temple of Medinet Habu had come to life.

All the Egyptologists had been asked, by way of an illustrated papyrus, to honor the evocative fête with their presence, and Prétextat, who knew Monsieur Maspero, had maneuvered diplomatically to get him to make representations to his colleagues. The illustrious master had come as a priest of Osiris, Monsieur Prisse d'Avennes as a priest of Thoth, and a few other specialists had agreed to accompany them. Those messieurs were more amused than at sessions of the Institut, and did not withdraw until an advanced hour, after having witnessed the concert, which presented nothing Egyptian except one ancient hymn rendered into French by Sabas with music by Vivian.

At two o'clock in the morning, a supper bought the guests together around tables with lions' feet, on which olive-green amphorae were grouped picturesquely. On the table where Neurocyme's place was set, an admirable copy of the vase of Queen Titi had been placed.

Enogat was radiant when Callidulus came over, moist with delight. "Oh, by Trismegistus! What a marvelous soirée, friend Sothermès! What a good idea to invite the Egyptologists! I've been able to talk to them as I desired, those messieurs who never come to our courses—never! I've been able to explain the esotericism of hieroglyphs to them, and even touch on a few words of the hermetic university. Another hour, Sothermès, and I'd have been commenting on the emerald table."

Ramses III, ecstatic, nodded his helmet gently.

"If you'd seen all three of them! Dr. Le Bon contracted his frontals, to change them into Roman arches; Monsieur Prisse d'Avennes took notes feverishly; as for Monsieur Maspero, he was stupefied, my dear, petrified!"

Those were the last words of that first fête.

The second was no less magnificent, and had no less success.

The Assyrian palace, with its decorations of painted sculptures, its ardently-colored wall-hangings and carpets, filled the guests with admiring stupor. The bas-beliefs, the painting of the walls, the seats and everything else had all been reproduced in accordance with the vestiges of Nimrod and Kuyunjik. The painted canvas ceiling imitated a vault with an opening in the center in the form of a cylindrical sleeve, and it was through that alone that light arrived. The archivolt of the door of honor was decorated with bricks whose enamel represented sacrificer djinn.

At first, Neurocyme had promised to appear as "nurturing Ishtar" in the glory of her nudity, but, begged by the anguished Enogat to renounce that project, it was in a robe enlivened with rich embroideries and coiffed in a stephane, in which the pentacle of universal force gleamed, that the capricious beauty offered herself to the eyes of her admirers. Thus, with a jewel on the forehead, bracelets around the wrists and ankles, a star with eight rays at the neck and, over her bosom, the legendary septuple adornment, she was the archetype of the idol. Assyrians, suddenly resuscitated, would have flattened themselves on the ground before her mysteriously smiling majesty.

Sothermès wore the ceremonial costume of Assurbanipal, Callidulus that of the pontiffs of Bel-Marduk. Léonidas, his beard carefully braided and wings on his shoulder-blades, applied himself with an altogether oriental gravity to figuring

117

a jinni. A few paces away, Bernard Fauve displayed, not without pride, the heroic garb of Isdubar, the Mesopotamian Hercules; Saint-Dolent exhibited himself as a chief of archers, Tardeval as a cavalier with a long coat of mail, and Negans as a eunuch.

Prétextat had bought Melchior de Vogüé, who, beneath his beautiful embroidered robe, his mantle with glorious fringes and his unicorn miter, was sumptuously reminiscent of Sennacherib. The illustrious archeologist took, after Neurocyme, the honors of the soirée, not to say the night.

The servants declared those pleasures imbecile. They were shocked, and ashamed, to be wearing costumes of long ago. They had been dressed in an old style, and that attire, rich and sparkling as it was, seemed an assault on their dignity as flunkeys born after the Revolution. In the servants' parlor, they could not look at one another without feeling sickened or furious. The blushing chef opined that everyone gave the impression of carnival masks. A valet who was embarrassed at having to appear with naked arms in front of ladies, dared to wish aloud for the advent of socialism, and Monsieur Jean declared that if he continued much longer the vile métier of an actor he would be forced to render his livery to Monsieur...

The displeasure and disdain of the servants notwithstanding, rumor of the success of the two fêtes having spread throughout Paris, many important people, including several diplomats, a few former ministers and the seven novelists in fashion went as far as veritable baseness in order to obtain the favor of participating in the following ones.

Neurocyme who sighed unremittingly after further flatteries, wanted Enogat to satisfy the cream of the solicitors, with the result that to the evening of the third reception, the house of Socrates was too small. Toward midnight, everyone was stifling somewhat; the women took off their calyptras. Numerous guests went home, including Messieurs Lucien Magne, Maxime Collignon and Edmond Pottier, whose gallantly classical attire and bas-relief manner had existed flattering enthusiasm. Others, for whom the spectacle of beautiful living statues was not worth as much as a cigar, spread out into the garden, where the night was mild, and, chlamydes thrown over their shoulders like military capes, they smoked like factory chimneys. But the women, young and not so young, remained heroically in the drawing room, because there was dancing.

"The Hellenes loved and practiced the dance," Neurocyme had said, so, it was necessary to dance.

The French waltz had pleased Neurocyme immediately. Soon, she was crazy about it—to the extent that she forgot the harmony of her costume and compromised it with untiring whirls. She had adopted the open peplos, clasped at the shoulders, the tunic with innumerable pleats, and the lampadion coiffure that swayed when Athenian women walked in the open air. Léonidas had to spend no less than two hours draping her "adequately." After a few waltzes, alas, nothing subsisted of that patient, sagacious and graceful arrangement. The elemental, who had had, at the beginning of the evening, the grand style of a friend of Pericles, ended up by resembling, at supper time, some maenad returned from the Bal des Quat'z'arts.

One could have said as much of the other dancers, all of whom were in an imitative disarray. The most genteel had made an improbable souquenille of their talaris tunic, and a vulgar bath-robe of their himation. Those whose hair was imprisoned in kekryphales seemed more unkempt than the rest. While swilling champagne in that antique attire, the guests gave a definite impression of a troop of chorus-line dancers celebrating a hundredth performance.

As for the regular guests of the house, they retained, to some extent, the tone of elegant Athenians. Prétextat as Socrates, Yves Berny as Euripides, Bérénès as Alcibiades, Tomanitas as Agathon and Tardeval as Isocrates remained surrounded. A rather judicious critic, who had had his hour of renown but about whom less was said the more he wrote, Théodore Prisca, was wandering hither and yon as old Lysias; and people pointed curiously at Messieurs Paul Deschanel as a

119

mime, Cassagnac as a discobolus, René Bérenger as an archon, and Thureau and Dangin as menechmes.[45]

In sum, waltzing apart, Neurocyme had not been delighted by the movement of that fête. She obtained a splendid revenge at the Medieval evening, when, in the costume of Laure de Noves,[46] she presided over a court of amour, clad in white silk, girdled with golden cloth, ornamented with masterpieces in lace.

> *Whiter than carved ivory,*
> *Whiter than heaped snow,*[47]

as Sabas murmured, she seemed an apparition.

The other ladies seemed out of place, in costumes modeled on ancient miniatures, which did not correspond to their forms nor heir sentiment of dress. The men undoubtedly looked better in ancestral character. Even so, those simpletons thought themselves obliged to strike theatrical poses, which modernized them in a ridiculous manner. Even Marc Lepetit, very "well-rounded" in the attire of Arnaud de Marveil, was awkward in his mannerisms of a contemporary poet.

"He's Richepin," opined Fauve.

"No, Jean Rameau," corrected Tardeval.

In sum, the best of what there was, along with Neurocyme, was the décor, the interior of a Provençal manor, which would have drawn clamors of joy from Jean-Baptiste Lassus. For want of that illustrious figure, Messieurs Anatole de Baudot, Édouard Corroyer, Scellier de Gisors and Lecoy de

---

[45] The division of the name of the historian Paul Thureau-Dangin is a joke—*menechmes* are twins.

[46] Very little is known about Laure de Noves (1310-1348) except that she was the wife of Hugues de Sade, ancestor of the notorious Marquis, but she was widely rumored to have been the Laure with whom the poet Petrarch was platonically obsessed.

[47] The lines are from an ode by Ronsard.

la Marche, clad as feudal lords, recognized that everything was perfectly "in the style." That was also the opinion of the various *cigaliers* and Felibrigians present, the notorious Benjamin Constant, the ardent Xavier de Ricard, the noisy Clovis Hugues and the worthy Maurice Faure.

Prisca, by dint of stratagems almost equivalent to those of the late Ulysses, had succeeded in attracting Joris-Karl Huysmans, promising him an ample crop of human documents. The father of Durtal had donned, for the occasion, the gray-brown habit of a pilgrim: a Tannhaüser returned from Rome. The writers who were pullulating at the fête, had no sooner recognized him than they had taken possession of him, to the great discontent of the feminine audience. Alas, after a quarter of an hour of that critique in passionate culinary colors of which he has the gastralgic secret, Joris-Karl Huysmans declared that Neurocyme smelled of burning and headed for the door.

"Pooh!" he said to Prisca, who tried to retain him by praising the archeological reconstitution that he had before his eyes. "A Middle Ages that lacks miracles is a coulibiac without onions, a macaroni without parmesan, a plum pudding devoid of ginger and gin."

"But she does work miracles, the alabaster mistress of the house. My dear friend, she's a Circé..."

"Really? Well, let her transform into intellectuals the stew of cretins that is simmering in her larder. That, Prisca, is the best use she can make of her gifts as a thaumaturge. The best!"

And he disappeared toward the pacifying cloisters of Ligugé.

Sothermès would have sworn that those fêtes had amused Neurocyme prodigiously, so his amazement was immense when his friend declared that she did not want to give any more of them.

None at all! But why? Had she not accorded her approval to the program elaborated the previous week? He had offered to resuscitate the Persia of Artaxerxes and the elemental had manifested an ardent desire to make, on that occasion, the acquaintance of Madame Dieulafoy. Were reconstitutions of the India of King Asoka, the Rome of Romulus, the Rome of Augustus, the Byzantium of Constantine, the Bagdad of Haroun-al-Raschid and the Grenada of Boabdil not to come thereafter? What pretexts for prestigious settings and fulgurant costumes! Negans glimpsed an Antioch more than Renanian. And would it not be very amusing to contemplate Callidulus as a bonze, Nyzor as a senator, Prétextat as Basileus, Occitanel as a caliph and Léonidas in any costume at all, provided that he was paid? If necessary, besides, they could add spice to the soirée by hiring a few artistes from nearby theaters as extras. Mademoiselle Laparcerie, as a Byzantine princess, could have declaimed verses by Sabas; Coquelin cadet, as a fakir, could have recited a monologue by Tardeval; Antoine and his troupe could have performed the principal scenes of Occitanel's Moorish play; and the lovely Meyriane Héglon, as a vestal, could have played some ethereal music by Vivian at the same time.

But the elemental shook her pretty head. Those attractions no longer spoke to her.

For some time already, Signora Chevalier, the remarkable medium, had been becoming anemic in her persistent sleep, and Neurocyme was feeling the effects of that unhealthy condition. As a consequence of being overexcited in the preceding fêtes, staying up late and dancing too much, she had become singularly irritable.

There was also something else. By enlarging the circle of her guests and admitting women, Neurocyme had struck herself the deadliest blow. By virtue of a supreme coquetry she had wanted an entourage of rivals, in order to compete with them in wit and grace, certain of outshining them with her distinction and finesse, her science and her beauty. Had she gained a few admirers more by that? It is true that Georges d'Esparbès had addressed prose to her and Henri de Régnier verse, Edmond Rostand roses and Comte Robert de Montesquiou hortensias...but she had created implacable enemies, who enveloped her henceforth in an atmosphere of scandalous gossip, and worked in perfect unison to ruin her elegant prestige. And Neurocyme knew about those perfidious rumors.

Oh, doubtless she sensed that, whatever was insinuated and whatever was said, she would remain the Muse and the Queen, and yet...and yet, even if the most prestigious homages continued to converge on her person, would not those messieurs become, if not more liberal, at least more familiar? That infamy, familiarity! Were the poets not beginning to treat her, under the...lyre, as a pretty woman? That horror, a pretty woman!

Neurocyme had reflected, and she had understood that, in order for her glory not to pale, it was necessary for her to go away without further delay. After a certain time of absence, it would be easy for her to reconquer her prestige. In any case, knowing her public, she would take the measures necessary to create the obedient, adoring court that she desired.

To Enogat's questions, therefore, she replied, melancholy at first but soon nervous: "These fêtes, although very artistic, would bore me if they were prolonged, dear friend, because of the people they group around us and the deplorable psychic atmosphere that emanates from them. I begged you to acquaint me with Parisian society; now that I am no longer ignorant in that regard, I ask you, please, to take me away from it—far away from it."

"What! I'm far from wanting to defend Parisian society, whose lack of literary culture I reproach in particular, but let us recognize however, certain qualities therein..."

"What qualities?"

Sothermès thought for a moment, and then risked: "Elegance."

"I would greatly prefer less elegance and more character, dear friend."

Ingenuously, the dilettante admitted: "It's cream of the crop that I've shown you—the elite, dear Neurocyme, of the city-brain."

"A very sick brain," then. All the milieux that I've traversed are full of crackpots, degenerates and neurotics. I was warned on high: Paris is very superficial. Truly, I didn't believe its elite could be so..."

"It certainly is, my dear," said Enogat, with tender conviction.

"The best things there are in this city are the ladies' suppliers. By giving reasonable advice one's milliner and appropriate emoluments to one's dressmaker, a person of good taste can end up with an acceptable wardrobe. Let's make purchases, my good friend, many purchases, and let's rapidly quit, without regret, what your Forain ferociously labels the "pleasant country."[48]

"But..."

"No buts; let's flee, for everything sickens me here: the gallantry of your gentlemen, the verve of your chroniclers, the wheezing of your poets, the quests of your artists, the theories of your ideologues, the posters of your Muchas—everything, including your honest ladies. Go on, my friend—I suppose that traveling doesn't displease you?"

Certainly not! And I'm ready to go around the world with you," Enogat conceded, not without resignation. "But then, dear, what will become of our project for the ideal house?"

"Let's postpone its realization until later; perhaps we'll unearth our architect on the way!"

And for which shores do you want to set sail?" asked the dilettante with an abandoned smile. "What would you say to a pilgrimage to the cities of art, beginning in Italy? It would be so pleasant to forget oneself in Florence, that paradise of memories... Florence, eh?"

"Pooh! A night-light in history. I need a land where some civilization is resplendent and dazzling."

---

[48] The painter Jean-Louis Forain (1852-1931), who contributed many illustrations to satirical magazines, was notorious for his biting wit.

"Dazzling? In that case, let's see...Greece?" the dilettante pronounced, timidly, whose infinite benevolence was not crushed by so much ill-humor."

"No thanks! Old Hellas is encumbered with politicians, and those pedants dishonor everything. When I think that trams circulate in Athens, that a smoky railway train would take us to the foot of the Acropolis...!"

Not without some sagacity, Enogat observed: "Those, dear friend, are petty miseries that you'll find everywhere."

"Not in the ruins of Thebes of the hundred gates, nor in the desert! Let's depart for Egypt," said Neurocyme, standing up, as pink as if she had been running.

VIII. In which important revelations are made

The preparations for departure commenced immediately. Neurocyme wanted to take an automobile in order to travel at her ease from necropolis to necropolis, in the sand and the sun; but the most improved vehicles afflicted her by virtue of the ugliness of their form, all resembling carriages from which some facetious enchanter had removed the horses So she had a desire, quickly repressed, to throw her arms around Léonidas' neck when the young man with the furrowed brow offered to design a harmonious model for her.

"It won't be too dear."

Having said that, the master ideo-naturist stuck out his chest, swung his hips, and ran off to set to work. He produced a black-and-white sketch in a couple of days, in with a chariot in the form of a swan was silhouetted. But a scale model constructed in accordance with the sketch made a deplorable effect. The swan, condemned to roll on firm ground, was entirely lacking in grace and style; is looked like a cross between a child's toy and a carnival float.

"What if you were to try a sphinx?" Neurocyme suggested.

"For an automobile designed to travel in Egypt, that symbol does indeed seem to me to be indicated," added Sothermès.

The sphinx deceived their hopes. It was impossible to modify its forms without robbing it of all character. Unless a cavity could be fitted into its flanks and the automobile hidden within it, there was nothing to be done with it. Léonidas judged it preferable to create another monster, in the body of which a constructor could easily placed its engine of locomotion, and he thought of a dragon. The head high and menacing, the fabulous animal was gathering its strength, ready to launch forth. Its mobile wings served as doors; its paws, bristling with terrible claw, partly hid the wheels.

Once finished, the monster-automobile appeared a little heavy, but in sum, it was decorative, and even Bayreuthian. The task of rendering it interesting was completed by giving it a bronze appearance, by means of a skillful patina. Finally, it functioned in a satisfactory manner, and if it had been possible to evacuate the smoke through its maw instead of via the tail, it would doubtless have charmed Parisians and terrified the Fellahs.

While these works were being carried out, Enogat de Sothermès had revealed to Callidulus the new state of his soul. Passion was growing within him with such force, and he as subject to disturbances so strange that he was resolved, he declared, to espouse Neurocyme.

On hearing that news, the excellent doctor started.

"Does the secret doctrine teach that there's some inconvenience in a mortal being united with an incarnate elemental?" asked the dilettante, with a pang of anguish.

"It is mute with regard to that circumstance, because it was never foreseen by our glorious masters; but given what it teaches us about the beings that populate the beyond, any adept would advise you to be prudent. Remember that it's a *force* with which you'd be allying yourself. If you don't dominate it, it will dominate you, and then to what perils would you not be exposed? Do you think yourself capable of imposing your will on that elemental become woman?"

"I sense that I love her like a madman."

"Oh, now we're in trouble! Poor friend, why have you allowed yourself to be invaded in this fashion?"

"That's easy for you to say, Callidulus."

"Does it at least reciprocate—does *she* reciprocate, I mean—your love?"

"I don't know."

"It's necessary to know. If Neurocyme remains indifferent to your sentiments, you'll have no purchase on her, and in that case, it's better to return her to the astral."

"Never!" cried the distressed dilettante, his arms raised toward the ceiling.

"Dear friend, I beg you, react against your senses; it's by that means that we hold the elementals, for they correspond to our sanguine globules, which carry, as they do, animating force."

"Eh! How can I react against this fire that is devouring me?"

"Multiply your will tenfold! It's absolutely necessary that Neurocyme be like a hypnotized subject in your hands."

"Once she's my wife, will she not submit more easily to my ascendancy?"

"I have the keen regret of replying to you that you're beginning to talk as if you were in a play by Molière, my dear friend Sothermès. Will-power, damn it! Have will-power! Will is the sense of the intellectual man, the genius Claude de Saint-Martin has said. Come on, courage! Give me your hands, in order that I can communicate a little of my fluid to you. Be a man...no, be an adept, Enogat!"

And after a vehement pressure of the phalanges, the excellent Callidulus withdrew tranquilly, as is appropriate to someone conscious of having fulfilled his mission.

"Damn the treasures of the occult sciences!" groaned Enogat, left alone. "I'd give all the secrets of magic for the love of that woman; for, after all, it's no more astral than yours. She's a woman at present."

As soon as his trouble had diminished in violence he went to Neurocyme, firmly resolved to gamble his destiny. Doubtless he had promised himself to be eloquent and original, to put into his words a rhythm like the one that the casual and solar Léonidas imparted to his clavicles, his vertebrae and his sacrum. But emotion betrayed him, and it was in an ill-assured, colorless voice, that he exclaimed in a comical fashion:

"Dear friend, I need to talk to you!"

"Eh? What pallor, very amiable seigneur! What's happened to you?"

"A force more powerful than my will, Neurocyme, curbs me at your feet. As soon as my eyes had perceived you, I con-

128

fessed my love for your ineffable person. Since then…my God, since then, I've applied myself with supreme care and a tenderness that I would have liked to be even more enveloping to prove that love to you. Are you convinced, now, that I love you, Neurocyme?"

She moved her head in a sign of affirmation. She even said: "Certainly, and that's why I take you for the best and most intellectual of mystic lovers."

"Ought I to believe, by those words, that I am not entirely indifferent to you?" the dilettante hazarded.

"Be assured that my affection for you is acquired."

"Neurocyme! Can it be? Then you would consent to…to our souls being in perfect communion?"

But she simulated the most ingenuous surprise. "Enogat, are our souls not living in that already?"

Quivering, he drew nearer to her. He murmured: "I mean…if I were to ask you to unite more narrowly your…destiny with mine?"

"What union could be narrower than ours?"

That sentence was spoken with such perfect candor that he felt a cold sweat bathe him suddenly. Oh, what if the elemental had nothing of a woman but the form? Did her heart beat only for the secret doctrine? Or might she be more ignorant than the most honest young women of our time…?

"Neurocyme," Enogat de Sothermès went on, after a pause, "you know more things than our masters—but do you know what passion is?"

"Passion?" For a moment, Neurocyme seemed to be searching. "Passion…?"

Trembling, Enogat waited, his fingers joined, his head slightly bowed "Passion…?" And suddenly, the elemental replied, gravely: "It's a dynamogeny."

"Very good. But have you ever experienced, Neurocyme, the effects of the interior fire that it engenders: that incomprehensible furnace that seems to be devouring a soul, and yet brings it to life."

"What excitement! In faith, my friend, you have a fever. Harmony no longer resides in you."

"That's the work of passion. Listen to me. Listen, my dear, only you can cure me. Would you like to become my wife?"

"Your wife?"

"Is the affection that you have admitted for me great enough, dear, for you to consent to reconstitute with me the primordial *sympneuma*...in sum, to become my spouse?"

"I love you too, dear Enogat," she cooed, smiling and fluttering her eyelashes."

"Oh, you put me in ecstasy!"

"Wait, dear enthusiast! I love you enough to dematerialize myself if I would, as a woman, harm your terrestrial well-being and your ascent toward the luminous summits."

"Oh! What are you daring to suppose?"

"Before replying to your request, I ought to submit you to a few questions. Have you reflected sufficiently on the difference between our two natures? You know where I come from, and you're beginning to glimpse, I think, the adept that I am; I can inform your hierophants and surpass your archimages in prodigies. Now, it's forbidden for us to link our life with a mortal whose knowledge doesn't equal ours, and the initiation you've receive is so little. You're so far, so very far, from glimpsing the truth! Callidulus knows nothing, and his friends no more."

"Truly?"

"Have you seen them accomplish any prodigy?"

"Oh, I don't contend that they go as far as thaumaturgy. Callidulus, however, in give you a body..."

"Callidulus has nothing to do with my own materialization; I alone did everything. It wasn't your incantations that attracted me; I incarnated myself of my own free will, taking advantage of the means that your desire offered me."

"What am I learning?"

"Your pretended occultists live on erroneous theories; the true doctrine of which the ignorant have no suspicion, that of Solomon and Apollonius, and esoteric Isis, I can unveil to your eyes. But it's necessary to reject your aberrations. Between your former initiators and me, my friend, it's necessary to choose."

"Oh, Neurocyme! Can I hesitate? Isn't it you that I love, rainbow of my soul? But tell me right way, will this new initiation take very long?"

"No, for the love that blazes within you will facilitate my task. Soon, dear Enogat, you'll possess my science and my power; you'll receive the title of Sanskrta, and then, nothing will any longer oppose my belonging to you in the complete, radiant and human manner, Enogat, that you desire."

"Neurocyme! Exquisite Fay!" he pronounced, trying to capture her in his arms.

But she stood up, mysteriously solemn.

"'My heart owes its mystic blossoming to you,' you said to me when I arrived down here, and you have offered me that heart. Will you consent to my keeping it forever? Are you giving yourself entirely to me? Speak."

"Oh, yes, recklessly and joyfully!"

"Your initiatrix will be your magess, then, when the time comes. Sign the pact...there."

She gave him her hand to kiss.

If, less amorous, he had had lips less burning, he would have been surprised by the coldness of that hand; and if, less blinded by dynamogeny, he had seen what a wicked joy was sparkling in the emerald eyes of his darling, he would have cried out in fear...

But he perceived those things so little that in the wake of that conversation he recovered the calm that he sensed to be urgent in order to await the arrival of the wellbeing, so sweet, that he coveted; and he did not even have any shame in being so weak, so abandoned and so petty. Hope and tranquility now, and soon, happiness! The engagement to which he had subscribed did not raise the slightest anxiety in his mind. Incapable of resisting his passion, fascinated by Neurocyme, Sothermès accepted his abnormal life lightly. He had shown

131

himself to be ready, and he remained ready, for anything, in order not to lose the object of his enveloping desires.

Having ceased to believe in the excellent Callidulus, he refrained from rendering him an account of his sovereign conversation with the elemental. Moreover, when Callidulus enquired, not without affection, on the eve of the departure for Egypt, as to the state of his disciple's soul, that disciple, who was one no longer, lied to him disdainfully.

"All my being is singing hymns of delight; I'm beloved, my dear doctor."

"So much the better!" relied Callidulus, dissimulating a grimace, distressed only to be called doctor, like Berger, Doyen, Potain and anyone at all. "So much the better...you've recovered your will, then?"

"I've never felt as strong, doctor. I eat well, I..."

"My sincere congratulations, be glad," Callidulus interrupted, with an immense bitterness. "Above all, don't weaken, now."

"No. I'm attracted to Neurocyme more by her psychic value, in sum, than her beauty, and I intend to continue, with her aid, my studies in occultism."

Callidulus frowned. He rapidly concealed his chagrin mixed with anger, however. "Oh, dear friend, permit me one last piece of advice," he insinuated, artfully. "Mistrust the science of an elemental, even kamamanasic. And if, truly, this one is to become your wife, make yourself, from now on, its educator."

"However, you supposed previously that it...she...that that elemental knew unparalleled secrets; you asked it for revelations as soon as it...as soon as she materialized. Did her words not lead you to believe, immediately, that we were dealing with the astral body of a traveling adept?"

"Hmm! My ideas have been modified since then. Neurocyme had promised to enable us to penetrate many arcana, but she has never ceased to elude my questions. Every time I've reminded her of her promises, she has replied that I was not yet sufficiently prepared. I've concluded that her science does not surpass that of Fabre d'Olivet, or Éliphas Lévi, or..."

"Why prejudge thus?"

"In any case, my friendship for you imposes on me the duty of indicating to you an aphorism that that summarizes the observations of our venerated masters: 'If it is good that an adept studies with his companion, it would be bad for him to go to her school.' It's the Mage that ought to model the Magess."

"Have no fear! Amour is the best of masters of modeling. Pygmalion..."

"Love, then, dear friend Sothermès; savor the sweetest joys. It would be very agreeable to me, have no doubt, to be kept up to date with your studies."

Callidulus left the house in the Rue Vaneau shaking his head, as he had the habit of doing in critical circumstances. He sensed that the soul of his disciple no longer belonged to him; and, in spite of the latter's victorious air, he only had a mediocre confidence in his union with the elemental.

"Pooh! That union...it might, at least, interest me in the capacity of an experiment."

And the excellent doctor promised himself to follow its phases with the greatest attention.

As he was hastening toward Belleville with his hands behind his back, Neurocyme, having made Eloa absorb an analeptic philter, recovered her strength and her good humor.

Jean, to whom Enogat accorded all his confidence, was charged with watching over the medium during his masters' absence, and giving her, at weekly intervals, the beverage that maintained her slumber and her life.

All the necessary acquisitions, and even a few superfluous needs, having been made, the couple quit Paris, not without much gaiety. Well, they were going first to the cemetery—Egypt was entirely that!

"Our wedding voyage!" Neurocyme had murmured, as they took possession of their sleeping-car. "A celebratory voyage *before* the wedding! Confess, dilettante, that that's not banal!"

A poetic reflection and the most charming augury: Enogat de Sothermès clapped his hands, laughing. He even started whistling an unpublished tune. He was so certain of finding, at the end of his journey, the sovereign felicity, that he yielded to almost-plebeian joys.

As far as Marseille, there was no incident. Neurocyme had never been so radiant, so full of verve, since the evening when, as Laure de Noves...

And naively, since he was veritably infatuated, her dear seigneur attributed that expansion to amour. He was flattered by that, in a profound manner.

In truth, however, the sentiments and sensations of that strange and delightful creature were not of the mild sort that the dazzled dilettante supposed. For the first time in her terrestrial life, the elemental found herself in a railway carriage. To be carried along at full steam amused her. The express reminded her, vaguely, of her flights through ethereal space.

The ship did not please her as much; she was scarcely installed than her enjoyment faded. From the height of the deck, she explained, morosely, one could not perceive adequately the progress they were making: a judicious remark, no doubt, but insufficient to justify such a somber mood.

In reality, the sea influenced that nervous being extraordinarily, and her surliness came from that. Everything seemed to her to be banal, lamentable and insupportable. Without the shipboard routine, which sometimes gave her a few small distractions, she would never have ceased to exhale bitter criticisms. In addition, at intervals, troubadouresquely inclined before her, Enogat intoned verses that he believed to be appropriate:

> *The husband sang to the wife:*
> *O princess of Archangels,*
> *O sister, pensive and jealous*
> *Of my strange memories!*

"What memories, dear friend?" asked Neurocyme, in a faint voice, stretching her graceful arms.

But "the husband" quickly resumed, emphasizing his tenderness:

Wife with pale golden hair
Reading in the depths of a palace
The arcana of the mighty God
And the secret canticles!

"Whose are they, those verses?" interrogated "the wife?"
"Albert Jhouney's."[49]
"They're very beautiful."
Then "The husband," almost with ecstasy:

The blue and divine boat
Without a tiller or oars
Travels to the goal it divines
And flies through the waves.

Alas, one cannot always be reciting verses. Enogat's poetic provision was, moreover, limited. He did not want to use it up all at once; and ennui had begun to grip Neurocyme again when they arrived within sight of Alexandria.

"Finally!" she cried, on disembarking. "I can breathe. How annoying the life on board is. That forced promiscuity with…terrestrials!"

Enogat smiled, thinking to himself: *Evidently, she lacks the sense of sociability. Bah! What does it matter to me? As long as she loves me! Oh, I'm a fortunate mortal.*

---

[49] Albert Jhouney was the form of his name sometimes adopted by the poet and occultist Albert Jounet (1863-1926), whose first collection of poems, *L'Étoile sainte* (1884) contains the poem from which these lines are taken.

When evening came, Neurocyme declared that they would leave Alexandria the following day. Since the day when the "pact" had been concluded, she no longer indicated her desire; she affirmed it; she gave orders. Monsieur de Sothermès was a fortunate mortal.

In order to enjoy the landscape more, they resolved to travel to Thebes along the Nile.

"Nothing amuses me or impresses me more than what is new to me," Neurocyme declared. "A journey on the river, of which I've heard mention on high, appears to me to be divine."

After having hired two Arab servants, one of whom claimed to be able to serve as a guide, they took passage on the steam-boat of a merchant who was going all the way to Khartoum. Scarcely had they embarked than they sought to excite one another by exhuming historical memories, and discussing the mysteries of the religions of ancient Egypt. In spite of their efforts they had a disappointment; the waves of the river had just withdrawn; there was, as far as the eye could see, a muddy, black soil in which pitiful palms had the air of living on dry bread without water. Undoubtedly, when the sun set, everything was magically transformed for a few minutes; the mud became a vibrant lake with gilded reflections, and all the rocks resembled colossal carbuncles—but could the two travelers be moved by such spectacles? Could they truly comprehend the immense and suave harmonies of the breeze brushing the boat, the roses of the sky mingling with the palpitating irises of the river-banks? And could not the pale, fragile and delicate coloration that smiled on the horizon after the descent of the star have affected them more if, like their dear Ramessides, they had been mummified?

They appeared to come to life again when they arrived in sight of Medinet Habu. Neurocyme wanted to lodge under the tent, and insisted on choosing the camp-site herself. The Arab servants went to the nearby village to obtain a fellah and donkeys, and he little caravan headed toward he great temple of Ramses III. The state of the ground not permitting the employment of the automobile, Enogat and his companion—dressed as an explorer and joyful exhibiting herself in trousers—had taken two charming donkeys for mounts; the others were carrying their baggage.

As it was too late to visit the vestiges of the temple of Medinet Habu that day, Neurocyme took the direction of the Ramesseum and about half-way, she launched her retinue westwards, far from the road. There were several abandoned quarries there, one of which was quite spacious, and dissimulated by the projections of the neighboring terrain. They set up camp there.

"We'll be marvelously placed here, equally close to the Ramesseum and Medinet Habu, eh, Enogat! No danger of tourists or other nuisances coming to disturb us!"

"On the contrary, dear, don't you fear that jackals…?"

"You still don't know the power of my fluid. There's no wild beast that can resist the emanations of od that my fingers project when I exteriorize my energy. Oh, if Reichenbach were among us, what beautiful experiments I could permit him to make!"[50]

"Exquisite Fay! You delight me. Every day, I discover some new quality in you."

"You'll see many others. In the meantime, strive to become a practical companion. Come on, dear friend, shake yourself up! We're no longer in the Rue Vaneau. Our men have a great deal to do, and already Osiris is going to bed. Help me to unload one of the donkeys, or it will be midnight before the tent is set up."

It came from Paris, that tent; it was vast and improved, so it took rather a long time to set it up, and no less time to furnish it.

That first journey in the sun had exhausted them. As soon the elemental had given the signal for retreat with a movement of her chin, they were on their bunks, separated by

---

[50] Karl von Reichenbach (1788-1869), the popularizer of the notion of "odic force."

a modest arrangement of curtains. The servants lay down with the donkeys.

Until daylight, there was a great silence.

Awake at first light, Neurocyme summoned her disciple and took him, still somnolent, to contemplate the two colossi of Amenhotep III.

Neurocyme had inaugurated her work as an initiatrix during their short voyage on the Nile. She resumed her explanations of the secret doctrine, and the prodigies accomplished by the adept of Tyana furnished the theme of a copious lesson. She had only just finished when they arrived at the pink granite colossi.

"Dear," said Enogat then, "you are so well able to lift me from the terrestrial plane that as soon as I fall back to it, nothing appears beautiful to me except you. I confess to you that these two great machines have no effect on me. Frankly, we had better than this in the drawing room. That was worth Rodin's *Balzac*, and yet…this isn't worth his *Eve*.

"Be careful, you're going to blaspheme. If these blocks say nothing to you, look around them."

But…there's nothing but lamentable ruins!"

"These ruins already existed in the time of Apollonius. What thoughts that ought to inspire in us! Apollonius of Tyana came to dream before them!"

The sun was beginning to get hot. Enogat sponged his brow. After that he enquired: "Tell me, dear, you who know everything, have adepts ever been numerous down here? Did they ever, in the Thebes that stood here, constitute a body and a force?"

"Not at all. No more under the Ramessides than under the dynasties of your Palais Bourbon were they well-grouped: a few isolates, that's all. If it had been otherwise, Egypt would never have been subjected to the foreign yoke."

"What Monsieur Schuré relates, then…"[51]

---

[51] Édouard Schuré (1841-1929) was an ardent Wagnerian before becoming one of the most prominent popularizers of the

"Monsieur Schuré is making a mockery of the doctrine, and it has repaid him, so peace to his Wagnerian vagueness. Will it please you if I invoke, one of these nights, the soul of an ancient priest of this very place? You would thus be documented in a sure manner."

"Certainly that would please me. Dear daughter of Viviane, how adorable you are! On this pedestal, where Apollonius might perhaps have sat his thaumaturgical person down, permit me to embrace you!"

"How terrestrial you still and always are!" said Neurocyme, mercifully yielding her fingertips to the dilettante.

"But I certainly hope that kisses are exchanged on high...or down here?" he murmured, accepting that advance token with full lips.

"Amour is an eternal felicity; so, when one is in love, it is also necessary to be able to wait," said the beloved, gravely—and, as if judging that the hand-kiss had gone on too long, she stepped back.

"I'm doing my best to put on a brave face beneath the symbolic elm," Sothermès stammered. "But for want of any other compensation, may I not know whether, from the viewpoint of amour, that which is above is as what is below?"

"The time has not yet me to broach such a theme, graver than you seem to think. Let yourself be guided in full confidence."

He replied, rather lightly: "I obey, dear, hoping that you will not take me too late in the direction of lunch. This morning excursion has given me the appetite of Gérôme."

They resumed the road to the tent, were they found a rather copious meal. Restored, they devoted the afternoon to visiting the great temple of Medinet Habu.

They case a simple glance at the bas-reliefs; that heroifamiliar imagery amused them; it would soon have appeared tiresome to them if they had studied it in detail. After an hour

occult revival, famous for his scholarly fantasy *Les Grands initiés* (1889; tr. as *The Great Initiates*).

of touring the ruins, they sat down in the shade on a stone, and Sothermès started to light a cigarette—but Neurocyme retained his arm.

"My friend," she said, with the intonation that she adopted from time to time, almost as often as Madame Segond-Weber did the other evening,[52] "Don't smoke, I beg you. Enogat de Sothermès, you are presently on the road of the adeptate; certain abstinences are becoming necessary."

"What! Really? It's important to renounce tobacco?"

"It's important! The action of maintaining with one's breath a fire that serves no luminous purpose ought to be left to hylic men. Pythagoras never smoked."

"For good reason," insinuated Sothermès, his mouth morose.

"Do you think, then, that he was ignorant of America?" said the elemental, in an offended tone.

"Until this moment I would have bet on it."

"Undeceive yourself. The adepts of your antiquity knew all the continents of the globe, and more than one sent his astral body in exploration to the banks of the Mississippi and the summits of the Cordilleras. They would only have had to give an order to the elementals to have tobacco brought."

"I'll put my cigarette back in the case and try not to maintain non-luminous fires any longer."

"Non-magical. Especially here. To smoke here would be unworthy. Our brothers have meditated before these walls, Enogat."

"Our brothers! What you told me on that subject this morning keeps running through my head. Would you care to proffer a few more words on the first initiators?"

---

[52] When the present story was written, the actress Caroline-Eugénie Segond-Weber had recently appeared at the Comédie-Française playing the Queen in Gaston Schéfer's *Le Roi* (premièred 1899).

"So be it. Hermes-Thoth was the initiator, the first agathodaemon of the supreme Hierarchy; it is him that some modern kabbalists call Adam-Kadmon."

"And Krishna?"

"That one only ever existed in the overheated imagination of Fabre d'Olivet."

"And Plato?"

"Plato was never any more than a poet rubbed with philosophy: a Victor Cousin of antiquity, with talent."

"What graces I owe to you, dear Fay! And that tradition of Hermes-Thoth, the Alexandrians received as a deposit?"

"Not at all. They only knew fragments from those who had failed the initiatory examinations. Apollonius only formed one disciple, Haroum, who received the order to go and live among the Arabs, the people chosen to transmit the doctrine to Occidental Europe. It was that disciple who, before leaving Ephesus, wrote the Sepher Yetizrah and the Zo'har."

"That's singular—I never heard talk of that Haroum..."

"I can believe it! Your Kabbalists don't even know his name; and yet, he's the author of the Kabbalah!"

"The Kabbalah that my brothers imagine to be so ancient! What ironies there are in life!"

"Yes, dear friend, that so-called ancestor of books was composed at the end of the first century of your present era, because the Hermetic tradition was then lost in Egypt, and the false doctrine of the Gnostics was gaining ground. Thebes, having ceased to be the city of the sun, and humans increasingly wallowing in darkness, it was necessary to leave a written summary of the true secret doctrine, which was drawn up in such a way that, without a key, its true meaning could not be grasped. That is why modern occultists give it, after the Alexandrines, an absurdly erroneous interpretation."

"What—the Gnostics did not have Apollonius for a forefather?"

"Never! It was in order to have their system accepted and to ruin their competitors in pseudo-esotericism that they laid claim to that illustrious name. Simon, Cerinthus, Basilides,

Valentinus, Carpocrates, Cerdo, Marcion and Saturninus were the Calliduluses of their time, theoreticians without science, magi without enlightenment, and they it was who deteriorated the doctrine and transformed it into the *Cuisinière Bourgeoise* of occultism. It was one of their instruments who produced the false Hermetic books. You know now, Enogat, what it is necessary to think of those divagations."

"What are you telling me? What about Apuleius?"

"Pooh! A snob who wanted to play the mage."

"What a pity! But then...Porphyry, Iamblichus, Annobius, Firmicus Maternus, Rufinus..."

"Pierus, Ungerus, Proclus...the Louis Figuiers of metaphysics, my dear friend."

"And Hypatia—oh, I tremble, Neurocyme—did she proceed from those messieurs?"

"Alas, that...lady did proceed from them. An insupportable bluestocking, in any case. You can't imagine, dear friend, the poseur, the schoolmistress that she was!"

"Something is weeping within me!"

"I remember having attended one of her lectures. Well, shall I confess it to you? I prefer those of La Bodinière or the Mathurins, or the ladies of the Fronde..."[53]

"Oh, my illusions...my heart...my head! But, to get back to the adept sent to the Arabs, did he succeed in his enterprise?"

"Certainly. He did not take long to discover minds worthy to receive the truth, and soon afterwards, by means of the disciples of those sages, the doctrine penetrated into Spain, from which it spread, during the Middle Ages as far as the Germanic lands."

"Did Hugues des Payens receive it?"[54]

---

[53] The three names cited are those of popular Parisian theatres.

[54] Hugues de Payens (died 1136) was the co-founder and first Grand Master of the Knights Templar

"No, Hugues was only a soldier politician, a kind of General Boulanger, but without Naquet and with a more hieratic ambition."

"And Rosenkreutz?"

"A good fellow, that one, but not very strong, at least in philosophy, since he accepted, blindly, the pseudo-hermeticism emerged from the Simonian matras. As for his Rosicrucians, mediocre alchemists, they gaped before the mysteries like the obtuse Scudo before *Tannhaüser* in 1861."[55]

"And Claude Saint-Martin?"

"A marvelously intuitive philosopher, but a mage, no."

"Really?"

"In truth, no more an adept than François Arouet de Voltaire."

"Nothing, henceforth, can surprise me. Cagliostro?"

"A poseur."

"Fabre d'Olivet?"

"A victim of bibliothecomania and the solitary life excessively prolonged, which is better suited to pure artists: Michelangelo, Beethoven, Ibsen. Born to write novels like Walter Scott, he went astray by taking his imaginings too seriously."

"Mesmer?"

"A Robert-Houdin of animal magnetism, good for furnishing neat refutations of physics that amused the late Ernest Bersot, director of the École Normale."

"And Swedenborg, whom I forgot?"

"A worthy pastor of souls, a candid poet of the married state, whose *Arcana coelestia* make young people dream and transmitted a little infernal laughter to the romantic Pandemonium of old Balzac. Artists, all artists!"

"And Papus? And Péladan?"

"One of those two messieurs is very intelligent..."

"In brief, dear Fay, none of those whom contemporary occultism recommend received the veritable doctrine?"

---

[55] Paul Scudo gave Wagner's *Tannhaüser* a famously bad review.

"None. The last of our brothers in Europe, Baslaï of Prague, was operating among the Medicis when he received the order to depart for Mexico."

"Since the beginning of the sixteenth century, then, no European has received the sacred deposit left by Trismegistus?"

"None has been found to be worthy. It's in America that the adepts are recruiting the most, at present. As for the sons of your Occident, they'll remain abandoned, until further orders, to skepticism, sensuality, bureaucracy and the universitarian mind. The only exception has been made in your favor."

"Thanks to your amour, dear Fay."

"No, because you've been called to play a role."

"Can it be?" Sothermès marveled.

"It can. My amour, although immense, could not lead you to the adeptate if you had not been chosen by the spirits of superior orders. A work is expected of you."

"A work? Of me? What?"

But the elemental shook her head. "I can't tell you any more today."

In vain the dilettante, proud, anxious and intoxicated by joy, hope and anguish, implored: "Just a word, for pity's sake! What?"

Neurocyme half-closed her eyes, put her index finger over her lips, and breathed: "Shh!"

IX. In which the hero flirts with elevated problems

During the night that followed that conversation, Monsieur de Sothermès was very agitated and hardly slept. The last words of his "dear" materialized before him continually in letters of fire. An exhausting obsession! What work was expected of him? And by whom?

At first, he was flattered to have "a role to play," but that intoxication soon dissipated, and he was invaded by a profound anxiety. A work, an *occult* work! Was that not going to trouble his life, disturb his projects? For after all, his aim down here was to enjoy perfect amour with Neurocyme. He did not care about anything else. Civilizing or spiritualizing, was any mission worth as much as the possession of that woman?

In thinking about *Her*, however, another, crueler doubt came to assail him. Was *She* really a woman? Neurocyme disconcerted him by means of her attitudes and replies, her dexterity in avoiding caresses, even while she affirmed her amour. What if her words concealed a manipulation? What if that more than strange being were conducting experiments with him? Perhaps she was an agathodaemon, like Hermes-Thoth in person. In that case, she...no, *it* could only love him, Enogat, like a brother.

Now, she's a sister, concluded Monsieur de Sothermès, increasingly troubled. *She's a sister...no, it's a lover that I desire. Oh, my heart, my head! After all, why shouldn't an agathodaemon be incarnate as a true woman? Doesn't Neurocyme recall, in various ways, the eternal feminine...? Evidently, this mystery will be clarified as soon as I'm an adept; all mysteries will be clarified at that moment—as long as those clarifications satisfy me! One never knows with mysteries. And between now and then...? It's very annoying. What am I saying? It's frightful! Nothing is as alarming as uncertainty.*

The sun surprised him in his reflections. Soon, however, a summons from Neurocyme made him get up, and shortly thereafter, he forgot everything. Nevertheless, he begged his "dear" to put off until the next day the excursion to the Ramesseum that they had planned for that morning.

She consented to that generously, with an amiable smile and a long gaze devoid of irony, almost warm. She even became maternal, and having prepared a philter with one of the substances brought in the guise of a traveling pharmacy, she made her disciple drink it, only imposing on the indolent sensitive a small course in occultism.

The day went by in that fashion, very calmly. A mixture gratified the amorous Enogat with a reparative slumber. At dusk he closed his eyes and slept peacefully until sunrise, as judges and street-porters sleep. That is why he found himself, on waking up again, fresh, well and ready to depart.

They took with them tins of sardines and tuna, and terrines of *foie gras*, for they had the intention, after exploring the Ramesseum, of descending into the tombs of the ancient necropolis and spending a part of the night there, if not the whole night. In accordance with her promise, the elemental was to devote herself there to the evocation of a soul.

After a march, not too long, through the valley strewn with pebbles, they arrived at the cenotaph of Ramses II. Enogat admired those vestiges with his mind's eye, through is reading. He remembered, particularly, a few pages of Gérard de Nerval, and he was trying to recall the verses of Louis Boulhet to a mummy when he had the sensation that one of the pylons, held in equilibrium by a millenary prodigy, was about to collapse suddenly on his head. He uttered a little cry of fright and drew nearer to Neurocyme, who, equally insensible to the bleak grandeur of the landscape and the gigantic proportions of the statue of Ramses, smoothed his hair gently and, pretty and tranquil, began his lesson.

"In the eyes of adepts," she explained, "temples like the Ramesseum present an image of initiatory asceticism by the arrangement of their rooms and the play of their lighting.

From the raw light of day, the image of the false clarity of the terrestrial world, one passes into the hypostyle, where, already, everything is covered in half-tones; then, after having traversed a succession of increasingly dark rooms, one finds oneself in the depths of the monument, in almost complete darkness, the symbol of the mystical light."

"Oh! Darkness, the symbol of..."

There was an irruption of a group of English tourists.

Chagrined, Neurocyme raised her arms in the air. "The enemy," she groaned. "And what an enemy! No more remains for us, dear friend, but to beat a retreat."

"Why is that?" said Enogat, shaking his nose.

She looked at him severely. Nevertheless, he was clawed by such a desire to distract himself a little, to steep himself again for a moment in the stupid but precious charms of society, that he was emboldened, and persisted: "Yes, why not engage in conversation with these imbeciles? After all, they might be interesting."

"Do you think so? Have we quit Paris to idle with the profane?"

Enogat uttered a long sigh. "An unfortunate snag, my dear. It's just that the heat is so atrocious! If we set forth again, under this sun, I confess that...in any case, our donkeys can't do any more."

"All right, we'll stay," she said, charitably. "It's necessary to have pity for the donkeys. But let's keep away from Albion, I beg you."

They retired behind a section of wall, and sat down in the shade, beside an enormous pillar. In the distance, the guide had begun to recite his explanation: "Ladies and gentlemen...," and, while two or three of the tourists followed it in their Baedekers, the others aimed their binoculars at the bas-reliefs. They conscientiously examined every page of the illustrated bulletin of Ramses II's campaign in Syria; then, coming back to a bas-relief that represented an episode of the battle fought against the Khetas on the banks of the Oronte, they gathered in a circle around a young gentleman who was brandishing an elegant volume. It was the English translation of the epic song of Pentaour, the Bornier of that formidable struggle.[56] The gentleman declaimed a few passages with thunderous vocal emphasis, and his companions saluted that homage to the Egyptian poet with frantic hurrahs.

"You read as beautifully as Irving," declared a beet-red woman, the classic type of the wife of a London clergyman.

After that, the indigenous servants accompanying the troop set out a few honorable victuals flanked by an appropriate number of comfortable bottles, and they drank, in order to recover their strength, port, stout and pale ale, with whisky.

Morose, her brows slightly furrowed, Neurocyme watched those respectable drunkards. Also frowning, Enogat regretted having forgotten Pentaour. That Briton had deprived him of a certain "effect."

"Ow!" said the lady with the dark spectacles, as imperturbable as a well-bred Englishwoman. "It's a great pity; one doesn't know everything that it's appropriate to admire. Ow! We lack a book by Ruskin on the monuments of ancient Egypt."

"I share your opinion," declared an obese baronet. "We need a *Stones of Memphis*."

"Or a *Laws of Theba*."

"This degenerate nation also needs a solid, esthetic and honest government," said an old man in his turn, sententiously. "In the interest of archeology and art, it's high time that we took effective possession of this unfortunate country. These ruins need to be maintained."

"Evidently."

"It could, in any case, be a source of considerable revenue if they knew how to take advantage of it. Just think that surrounding it with an enclosure equipped with a turnstile, a

---

[56] Pentaour was Ramses II's scribe, who recorded the battle of Kadesh for posterity. The comparison likens him to Philippe Bornier (1634-1711), who recorded the edicts of Louis XIV.

practical administration could earn, at the end of a year, enough to buy everything required for future excavations."

"Splendid," simpered a vicar's daughter.

Neurocyme could not take any more. She leaned toward Sothermès and murmured: "The savages!"

Then, calmly, her attitude serene, only her gaze imperious, she extended her right hand toward a heap of stones gilded by the sun, and, to Enogat's great alarm, an asp emerged therefrom.

"Go, dear uraeus," the elemental said to the reptile, indicting to it the part of the temple where the tourists were. "Chase that rabble away for me."

In a trice, the asp was "in the bosom of Albion," which arrival was announced by the strident cries of the ladies and gentlemen. Meanwhile, the speech-maker, scarcely livid, brought out his revolver and fired at the snake, which he missed.

"Ow!" roared the well-bred Englishwoman, imperturbably.

But someone else intervened. With a hardwood cane, he made terrible whirling movement. He struck the ground resounding blows to the right and the left of the snake, so close to the asp that it only required another millimeter and he would have flattened it—but there was always that diabolical millimeter. All that the sportsman could do was to protect the retreat, which was operated through all the exits with heroic celerity.

When the champion had disappeared himself, the elemental and her disciple sought a propitious location, and, having opened the tins, commenced their lunch. The reptile joined them and, crawling around them, ate the crumbs. As soon as it was sated, though, obedient to a sign from Neurocyme, it reared up on its tail, and swayed rhythmically, designing all kinds of graceful and unexpected spirals.

"What! You can charm snakes?" stammered Enogat, in a voice that betrayed great apprehension.

"As you can see," she said, extending her arm to the asp, which coiled around it as a bracelet.

"Be careful!" the dilettante cried.

"Have no fear," she said. "You too, friend Sothermès, will charm snakes one day."

"I don't think…"

"They're easier to direct than humans," she assured him, smiling. And she sent the asp away.

When the siesta was concluded, they set out for the necropolis, through barbaric terrain; then they passed into roads that had ceased to be maintained since the Ptolemies. They avoided the tragic Bab-el-Molouk, where the royal tombs are, because there was another band of English tourists there."

"It was already like this in the time when Strabo held the employment of Élisée Reclus," the elemental explained. "Guides, as fallacious as simple moderns, piloted Roman tourists around this royal cemetery; the patter hasn't varied much since."

Having dismounted, they glided toward the sepulchers of simple individuals, elected a place that as sheltered from indiscreet gazes and set about opening a few more tins.

Around them there were hillocks of arid ground and he openings of hypogea; on the horizon, the Libyan chain raised its collection of calcareous apophyses like a wall tumefied by some interior fire. A grim sadness floated over that singularly silent Père-Lachaise devoid of verdure.

"One could believe oneself in the empire of the gnomes here," observed the dilettante, tucking into the dinner.

"The spirits that correspond to your gnomes are, indeed, at home here."

"What, they really exist?"

"They exist. And the day is not far off, my dear, when you'll be able to see them and converse with them."

"Thanks to your kindness!"

"No, with the aid of the power that you're going to acquire, as it were, by virtue of your normal development."

"Truly?"

"When, having become a Sanskrta, your spirit knows the mysteries, you'll perceive the currents of material molecules that direct living bodies in the animal realm, the vegetable realm and the mineral realm in order to reconstitute them, and even those that emerge from those bodies and disperse them. And it's because your eyes will thus have become precious microscopes that you'll distinguish, as clearly as you see me, the spirits of the elementals, the souls of water, earth and fire. You'll then see what your ancestors called undines, sylphs, gnomes and salamanders."

At that moment the sun disappeared behind the horizon. The sky seemed to be larded with greenish gold, and while the Libyan chain was tinted an indigo violet, fields of flint cast a black carpet here and there over the yellow-gray of the sand, from which not a single tree or bush emerged, only a few clumps of grass, which the burning rays had reddened

Without lingering over such futile spectacles, however, Neurocyme said: "It's time to go down into the tomb." And as Enogat started, and then paled and weakened, she smiled. "Yes, into the tomb to whose tenant I'm going to introduce you. Come on, poor friend, take a little more of the philter I composed for you; it will give you the strength to stay awake…for it's going to be necessary to stay awake."

She poured a rather strong dose of the mysterious liquid into her disciple's cup of tea. When the dilettante had drunk it, he helped his beloved pack their minuscule baggage, and they gave the donkeys a bundle of oat-straw and a few handfuls of bran.

Enogat, who took little pleasure in these domestic tasks, uttered two or three sighs—after which, contemplating Neurocyme, he asked, languidly: "Are we going to leave the donkeys here?"

"Of course."

"You don't fear that wild beasts…"

"My friend, wild beasts always desert the places frequented by scholars and tourists. It's functionaries that replace them."

"We still have to fear the Arabs, who are meritorious thieves," Sothermès objected again.

"There's nothing to fear with me—stop it, please."

Immediately taking her cane, with a metallic conical tip, she drew a pentacle in the sand, near the donkeys; then, having traced a vast circumference around them, she pronounced a few strange words.

"That, my dear," she said, afterwards, "should ward of any danger. No one can enter the circle."

"Really?"

"Try."

Enogat stepped forward, in order to cross the mysterious enclosure. A force comparable to a violent wind threw him backwards. He tried to persist; the wind knocked him down.

"Are you convinced, skeptic?" exclaimed Neurocyme, laughing. "No one can penetrate the circle, any more than the animals it encloses can get out. If the donkeys tried to run away, they'd remain nailed to the spot—but they won't even have the desire."

"Oh," he said. "That, one can't know."

"Sleep!" she ordered the donkeys then, extending her arm toward them.

Meekly, the donkeys lay down on the ground, back to back, and, after having found a comfortable position, they let their large heads fall and closed their eyes.

"What an enchantress you are!" murmured the dilettante.

"And that's not all! I've given an order to the gnomes to frighten anyone who comes this way. Look."

Scarcely had she sketched a gesture of command than several fire follets sprang up. While delivering themselves to a studied choreography, they drew near to Monsieur de Sothermès, swirling around his legs like a swarm of flies excited by a storm. One of them, having bowed gravely, leaped on to his shoulder, capered on his nose, and disappeared above his head.

"Uh oh!" Enogat complained, stupefied. What's got into that one?"

A frank burst of laughter replied to him, and he saw all the punch-flames writhing on the ground like snakes.

"Look, dear friend, these messieurs are splitting their sides, as your boulevard wits put it."

"They're familiar, our...messieurs?"

Another gesture, and all the ironic phosphorescences were confounded with the dusk.

"Yes, very familiar, and a trifle farcical," said the elemental, with a delightful indulgence, "but such good little devils, my friend. Let's go, the moon's rising. It's the favorable hour, Enogat. You see that sepulcher, larger than the others?"

"Yes."

"That's the one. That superb tomb was built for the high priest Petamounoph."

"It's the soul of that illustrious individual that you're going to evoke?"

"Yes. I've chosen that one, firstly because it inhabits the body of an eminent scholar up to date with the latest discoveries, since he lived under the twenty-sixth dynasty, and secondly because the soul speaks French like one of our academicians—guess which one? The souls of Champollion, Marette, Chabas, Daressy and Navelle have given our Petamounoph lessons. You'll admire his syntax..."

"It's you that I admire!" he exclaimed. "With you, one goes from one surprise to another, for I never suspected that incarnate souls could speak!"

"Patience! You'll hear. You'll understand later, when you know what a soul is in itself."

"I thought we were going to communicate with the deceased by means of typtology."

"That's rich. Lecture me about spirits when you're one of them."

"Oh, my dear..."

They had arrived.

Facing them, between two walls of raw brick, an opening gaped, not very luminous. Bravely—he was now battle-hardened—Monsieur de Sothermès was about to go into it when Neurocyme held him back.

"Be careful! The stairway has no rail."

He advanced his head and did, indeed, see several steps leading into a vast courtyard open to the sky.

Together, they penetrated into a courtyard smaller than the previous one, ornamented with a portico under which a sculpted door could be distinguished.

"We're here," said Neurocyme.

Taking out of her traveling bag a small lamp in which a stick of magnesium stuck up by way of a wick, she set the white metal alight.

There was a pause; then she said: "Go in, my dear, in complete security. No unfortunate encounter is to be feared."

The night was resplendent. In the silence, more profound even than in the dusk, Enogat felt a strange emotion descending over his person, like a heavy and glacial cape.

The door gave access to a vast subterranean chamber.

"This is the antechamber," Neurocyme explained. "Once, two rows of four pillars were seen here. It's the speos of primitive mastabas, accommodated to aristocratic fashion. We're going to encounter other rooms similar to this one; the Theban hypogeum is the hypertrophy of the speos. Now we're going into corridors whose condition leaves much to be desired. Stay behind me, and be careful of false steps."

Mute and very straight, at an assured pace, she moved into a gallery as if she knew the way. For several minutes they walked thus. They emerged into a chamber with walls covered in paintings, and the Beloved stopped.

"How pale you are," she said. "Are you afraid, by chance?"

But no; Monsieur de Sothermès was definitely battle-hardened. "With you?" he protested, bracing himself. "Never! Except that I'm not used to wandering through catacombs. Will we be here long, dear friend?"

"The galleries of this hypogeum extend over a length of 266 meters, but don't worry; we aren't going all the way to the end. I'm taking you to the chamber of commemorative ceremonies."

After having traversed a further sequence of corridors, they finally arrived at the chamber of commemorations.

"We're here," Neurocyme declared, inspecting the religious scenes painted on the walls. Get your breath back for a moment, and I'll commence the evocation."

"I feel quite strong," the dilettante assured her. In fact, the philter was beginning to take effect on him. The Beloved understood that by the gleam in his eyes and their slightly hallucinated gaze, and permitted herself a furtive smile.

"You have no need of a medium for this evocation?" asked Enogat.

"Not even an ordinary subject."

"In that case, how can the astral body evoked enter into communication with a plastic mediator?"

"Know, to begin with, that it isn't only the astral body of Petamounoph that will present itself before us, but also its superior unconscious, its Buddhi and its Athma; then know that true adepts have an irresistible action on ordinary souls. At their appeal, the latter have no need of metallic points in order to condense. The scene you're about to witness won't resemble any you might have seen before. Evocations of astral shells, by means of a medium, are only good for the broken-necked occultists of your miserable boulevards."

"I'll be all eyes and ears, I assure you."

"Very good," she said. "I'll begin."

"What about the lamp?" he asked, anxiously. "Aren't you going to extinguish the lamp?"

"Enogat, Enogat, when will you stop taking me for a Callidulus?"

In a vibrant and rhythmic voice, Neurocyme commenced the evocation.

Five or six minutes went by, during which Monsieur de Sothermès, battle-hardened as he was, felt an impertinent sweat inundating his scalp, while certain convulsions of his stomach suggested to him that he was suffering from seasickness—but the idea that his "dear" might perceive that state multiplied the courage of the aspirant adept tenfold; he stiffened himself, braced himself against the wall in a corner, and, with the aid of the philter, succeeded in standing almost upright.

The last words of the evocation had scarcely finished charming the echoes when an indefinable odor spread through the chamber and a luminous form appeared to emerge from the wall that the elemental and her disciple were facing. The form saluted Neurocyme with deference.

It was the soul of Petamounoph.

It seemed to be a gaseous substance, made in the resemblance of the material body that had been its vestment down here, as resplendently yellow as a beautiful August moon. Delicate indefinable nuances, vibrant with azured gray and ultramarine, broken by tea-rose, emphasized the shape of the body of light, as well as the pleats of the robe of the same essence that covered it. The physiognomy was intelligent and noble; the eyes testified to a tranquil pride, the mouth to a diplomatic finesse—the mouth of Massenet! No age could be read in the features, fleshless and yet devoid of diaphaneity, which palpitated incessantly, like starlight.

Neurocyme has extended her right hand toward Petamounoph, and the latter had shaken that hand with an entirely modern gesture; the high priest and the Beloved exchanged a few words in the Egyptian of the Theban epoch. Then the elemental designated Monsieur de Sothermès, whose pupils were dilated, and made the introduction in French.

"Charmed to know you, Monsieur," said Petamounoph, with great courtesy. "And since you are a disciple of Her Grace"—he designated Neurocyme—"I place myself at your disposal for all the information you desire to have regarding our ancient Misr."

"Too kind, dear master," stammered the dilettante, fundamentally stupefied.

"Now the acquaintance is made, let's sit down, dear seigneurs, and chat," said Neurocyme, expansively. And, setting the example, the elemental squatted on the ground in the Oriental fashion. Petamounoph immediately imitated her.

Enogat, after having observed once again the absence of any chair or any stone appropriate to substitute for one, sat down as a good Occidental, like someone taking the fresh air on the grass in the Bois de Verrières. When he was seated, he applied himself to moving as little as possible, and, naturally, maintained a religious silence.

"Monsieur," declared Petamounoph, with the manners of a man of the world, "the majority of the discoveries of which your contemporaries are proud, we have made before them. In certain sciences, in mathematics and astronomy, for instance, we knew, in the Thebaid, more than the scholars who arrive every year from the Occident."

"In astronomy? You astonish me. Did you, by chance, dispose of instruments analogous to ours?"

"We had very advanced telescopes, which impressed Plato greatly when he came to follow the course at our university. It's thanks to that philosopher that Aristotle knew their usage, and that was what gave him the idea of constructing a 'tube'—I'm using his own expression in order to observe objects without being inconvenienced by the dispersal of their rays."

"Where, then, does Aristotle talk about that tube?"

"You have in your library a translation of the treatise *De generatione animalium*, dear friend," said Neurocyme.

"I'll take your word for it," replied Monsieur de Sothermès, bowing modestly.

"We also knew the microscope," Petamounoph continued, simply. "At the time of my death, its usage was beginning to spread into profane milieux."

"There wasn't an idler of some culture, in the civilized nations, who didn't know the microscope," put in the elemental.

The high priest continued: "You will understand without difficulty, my dear Monsieur, that scholars like ours, accustomed to the manipulation of lenses, were not unaware of the refraction of light. We also had a precise notion of the isochrony of the vibrations of the pendulum. As for steam, we could do with it—I can say this without flattering us—almost anything we wished."

"I know from Agathias that steam was not unknown in the sixth century of our era," said the dilettante, glad to be able to show that he possessed a few rare authors. "On the other hand, I didn't know that in the sixth century before our era..."

"The sixth century before your era! Oh, my dear monsieur, it was with the aid of instruments powered by steam, notably the machines called ibis, that the pyramids of Cheops, Khafre and Menkaure were built."

"Did electricity play a role in the construction of your prodigious pyramids?"

"No. Electricity was only ever employed inside temples, for bells and the telephone."

"What—you had the telephone, but not the telegraph?"

"The latter was superfluous for us; we had from our ancestors a system of psychic telegraphy infinitely more rapid. And the splendor of our nights rendered electric lighting no less unnecessary."

"Into what astonishment you're plunging me! You knew, then, almost everything that the moderns know?"

"In chemistry our knowledge was more limited. Some of our industrialists, however, manufactured alcohol and sugar, and—much more importantly—a priest named Anhouri, of the temple of Teni, had succeeded in fixing on plates, ingeniously sensitized, images of concrete reality: a system analogous to your photography, if I'm not mistaken, monsieur."

"Can it be?" said the dilettante. "You knew photography, and you didn't leave to posterity views of your temples, portraits of our celebrities, your beautiful..."

He was about to add *women*, but the high priest interrupted him, saying: "My dear monsieur, some of us fixed on special papyrus the features of our kings, our pontiffs, our...functionaries and the outlines of our various edifices, but the prints, as you put it, did not resist the action of time. None of our chemists found a truly unalterable method. We shall see, moreover, what will become of the photographs of the Brauns, Alinaris and Reutlingers in a few centuries."

"Did you know mechanics thoroughly?"

"It was a priest of Nit who wrote the first treatise on mechanics at Saïs. From pulleys to lift stones and drays to transport obelisks to mobile platforms that transported soil rapidly to the terraces of temples, so many interesting inventions! The most curious was one put into practice by a certain priest of Hathor in the temple at Denderah. Can you imagine, dear monsieur, an ingenious combination of two wheels of unequal size, and a sort of rubber prison in which air is incarcerated, between which an individual, even obese, can take his place in a saddle? Once he was able to impart movement to his machine, while maintaining his equilibrium, that individual could compete for speed with many a horse; he traversed distance with the rapidity of a lance thrown by a sure hand; beasts and rider were only one."

"Of course! That's our bicycle."

"Truly, monsieur, the Occidentals have rediscovered that small marvel?"

"I'm astonished that you haven't yet seen one on the banks of the Nile; it can't be long delayed. You pedaled, then, dear master...I mean, you used that means of locomotion?"

"No, not us, our servants. That was how they carried our messages and our orders."

A sudden suspicion made Monsieur de Sothermès blink. Might this high priest, this phosphorescent individual, be abusing the credulity of the aspirant adept? But no— Petamounoph was not Sapeck![57] Petamounoph was really Petamounoph. And rapidly, setting aside any suspicion of trickery, as a kind of sacrilege, the dilettante asked, in a tone

---

[57] "Arthur Sapeck" was the pseudonym of Eugène Bataille (1853-1891), an illustrator associated with the Hydropathes who became notorious for organizing the farcical Exposition des Arts Incoherent in 1883, whose exhibits anticipated Dada.

of veneration: "How is it that no artist has reproduced the silhouette of your servants flying along the roads in that fashion?"

"They were strictly forbidden to fix, by image or by writing, the inventions rendered public, in order that people in communication with us could not make copies of hem and try to counterfeit them," Petamounoph replied. "You would not believe, my dear monsieur, how necessary it was to mistrust the Hellenes. Those people had a genius for adaptation. We also had impression by means of molded characters; the college of Ptath had tried it under Harmhabi."

"Astounding!" exclaimed Enogat.

"And almost immediately, the college of Osiris at Pa-Ba-Ned-Da thought of launching a great daily newspaper, the *Echo of the Pyramids*.

Then Enogat said, gravely: "All history needs rewriting."

X. In which the hero continues flirting with the great problems

After having taken his leave, the soul of the high priest melted into the wall.

"A charming soul, isn't he?" said Neurocyme to her vassal, while they were going back through the long corridors.

"Charming indeed, and exquisitely candid," the dilettante replied.

"At least we're documented now as to how little humans can boast of being. You're satisfied, I think?"

"Very satisfied, and...a little surprised. How many mysteries surround us, how many mysteries!"

At that moment they crossed the threshold of the last room of bas-reliefs.

When they emerged from the hypogeum it was one o'clock in the morning.

The aspirant adept would gladly have slept on the hard ground, so tired and exhausted was he, but Neurocyme rallied him. Was it not better to tame his fatigue like a true mage, and take advantage of the nocturnal coolness to return the camp? She therefore woke the donkeys, after having erased the magic circle; then, having helped her disciple to bestride his mount, she climbed briskly into the saddle herself—after which they both set forth in the direction of Medinet Habu, guided by the fire follets.

As soon as they had arrived, Enogat threw himself on to his bunk fully dressed, and even when the sun was shining over the horizon he remained plunged in a deep slumber. He saw in a dream Octave Gréard repeating to Monsieur Lavisse what the high priest Petamounoph had just told him. Like Ulysses facing the sirens, Monsieur Lavisse blocked his ears, crying: "Come on, Gréard, this doesn't concern me. I'm a historian who knows France, the Eastern frontier, Alsace, Germany and the Kaiser, but Egypt? Go find Maspero!" That was the cry of Monsieur Lavisse, an orderly and methodical man who did not like people to talk about objects other than those of his cherished studied. And in his dream, the aspirant adept judged that Monsieur Lavisse was quite right.

However, as the sun began to sink, the elemental shook the sleeper and asked him: "Don't you want dinner, my friend?"

Then Sothermès got up and ate dinner. After a short walk, he went back to the tent and sleep reclaimed him—but the dawn found him completely rested. That is why Neurocyme took him to visit the temple of Khonsu at Karnak.

As they were examining the great obelisk in a courtyard, a certain scene of offering attracted the attention of the aspirant adept.

"The image of the priest that this obelisk presents to us," he exclaimed, reminds me of the worthy Petamounoph. "His Terran evolution is not finished, you said as we returned from visiting his soul. You haven't yet explained the meaning of those words to me."

"You were asleep," replied the elemental, cheerfully. "As for my words, their meaning is quite simple. They signify that the soul of Petamounoph has not yet quit the astral of our planet. The soul of a profane is only ready for reincarnation after a rather long stage—reasoning according to your measurement of time, at least."

"What! The soul of such a savant, dead for so many centuries, has not attained the age limit necessary to be reincarnated!"

"No, my friend."

"That soul interests me. Tell me, dear Fay who knows everything, will it remain in our astral for a long time?"

"No, its evolution will be complete in a few months."

"I'm delighted to learn that. So, in a few months, the excellent Petamounoph will be a nursling again, and we can take his new form treats and rattles..."

"Steady on, dear friend! Imagination is carrying you too far. A Terran soul isn't reincarnated on our globe; it's always sent to another planet."

"How many mysteries!"

There was a brief interval of silence. Sothermès scratched his head, as if he wanted to get rid of one of those parasitic thoughts that bite harder than lice. Suddenly, he asked: "O queen of Fays, excuse my curiosity, but…you intrigue me so much. Are you not an agathodaemon?"

Neurocyme let out a sonorous burst of laughter. Her charming eyes sparkled with malice. Without replying, she shook her head and gently tapped her foot.

"That question was burning my lips," Enogat went on, in an excited tone. "What do you expect? When I see you so passionate for the doctrine, I wonder why you condescend to remain beside me in a feminine form…"

"Oh, in trousers," she interjected, showing off her explorer's costume with an elegant gesture.

"Mock, mock, Neurocyme! But what will I become now that you have captured my heart, if you ever fly away?"

"Terrible child, have I not promised you 'my hand,' as the women of your country say?"

"That's true, dear Fay! But our life is so original…"

"You never stopped complaining, in Paris, about the banalities in which society enmeshed you. Are you in Karnak, regretting the house in the Rue Vaneau?"

"Certainly not… I only wanted to express, daughter of Viviane, that…in spite of your promise, dread sometimes comes to me regarding our future. I wonder whether I can ever succeed in fulfilling the conditions imposed…and that's a cruel anguish, you understand…"

"Dissipate it, poor friend, attack it, as Seti I charged the Bedouins of the Sinai." So saying, she pointed at one of the decorations of the exterior wall along which they were walking at that moment.

But the "poor friend" sighed.

"Come on, Enogat," she went on, "a little more courage. A sincerely smitten lover ought not to fear any obstacle. As for my personality, you'll know it when you've conquered the palm of the supreme grade. Until then, monsieur..." She formed a smile of malice and mystery. "Until then, respect my incognito."

They visited the temple of Luxor next; and for a further week they explored the region of ancient Thebes. Convinced that they had nothing more to see, and nothing any longer attracting them in Nubia, they decided to leave for Gizeh.

In that direction there was to lack of roads fit for wheeled vehicles; they could go there in short stages, by automobile. This was the moment, if ever, to use Léonidas' dragon. After having studied the disposition of the monumental tombs of Gizeh, perhaps it might be possible, with the collaboration of elementals, to penetrate into an unexplored pyramid—that of El-Lahoun, for example. That project was worthy of meditation, and they meditated it on the way.

And thus, one morning, they raised camp, bade farewell to the fellah, but kept the two Arabs. The latter were not a little amazed and anxious when they took their places in the strange carriage that galloped without horses...

The journey across country was accomplished in the most modern fashion in the world, with no more incidents than on a road in France. On departing from ancient Abydos, where they stopped for a few days to visit the temple of Seti I and the necropolis of venerable mastabas, the landscape, with its villages of earthen huts, always the same, its cultivated fields identical in aspect, and its scarcely decorative inhabitants, appeared tediously monotonous, and they traveled at top speed. The elemental thus recovered some of the emotions she had felt on the railway.

At Gizeh, a halt; there, in the land of the Pyramids, the arrival of the smoking dragon excited a vivid curiosity, and when Neurocyme got down from the vehicle, she produced a great sensation: they were a truly pyramidal curiosity and sensation. But the honest idlers—guides, camel-drivers, donkey-drivers, ladies and gentlemen—did not enjoy that entertaining double spectacle for long. A baksheesh to the Bedouin beggars, a gaze of crushing disdain for the English Tartuffes, and the elemental, having garaged the automobile and hired donkeys, set off to find a camp-site for her little troop in a less accessible location. The tent was erected, a few tins were opened, tea was made, and they went to bed.

The next day, they visited the great Sphinx. Its state of dilapidation disheartened Monsieur de Sothermès; and having clicked his tongue as a sign of disappointment, he murmured, in the attitude of Louis Lépine[58] contemplating a burned building: "What a pity that such a work can't be restored! Perhaps Saint-Marceaux, or even Bartholdi..."

"You think so?" said Neurocyme, her expression lightly ironic.

"Well," said Enogat, nonplussed. "Since it's crumbling, that god!"

The Beloved maintained silence; and, darting a last emerald glance at the immense, impassive and pug-nosed face, she led her disciple to the temple of the Sphinx.

Sothermès suddenly cried: "Why, one might think it a Protestant temple!"

"You blaspheme easily, my poor friend," Neurocyme replied, this time. "Mephistopheles would say that it's easy to see that you're French."

"But my dear Fay, there's not a single image..."

And he dilettante, troubled, exquisite and ingenuous, widened his eyes before the walls, paraded their gaze over the pillars, from the base to the architrave, examining, searching, and wondering what might give beauty to such an austere monument.

"This temple," the elemental went on, gravely, "is one of those constructed by the descendants of the red race, the last Atlanteans; they enjoyed an intellectuality too elevated to or-

---

[58] When the story was written Louis Lépine (1846-1933) was serving his second term as the Prefect of Police in Paris.

nament with images an edifice dedicated to the psychic development of beings. Their architects expressed everything in combinations of proportions, just as their metaphysicians explained everything by means of numbers."

Sothermès opened his arms wide, exclaiming: "Why didn't you tell me that right away? But tell me, dear, how the red race came to plant temples here? For, after all, Atlantis extended, did it not, in a place submerged today by a part of the Atlantic Ocean?"

"Yes, between Africa and America. This is how it happened. When Atlantis was assailed by the cataclysm that you know, the various people that inhabited it sought to flee to the continents nearest to their respective lands. A few thousand individuals succeeded in landing in Africa; others came to ground in Asia; yet others reached America."

"How is that? Did they, then dispose of excellent ships, or was Atlantis linked by some isthmus to neighboring lands? That intrigues me a great deal."

"Atlantis was surrounded by water, and the violence of the cataclysm rendered the best ships useless. The coastal populations were the first victims of the invading waves. But the Atlanteans, whose civilization was then in full bloom, practiced aviation with a rare virtuosity—for it was not the worthy Petamounoph who conceived the first flying machine—and thanks to that means a large number escaped. Oh, it was horribly hard! It was first necessary to rise above the clouds where the tempest was growling, and then maneuver, sometimes battling the wind, for league after league. Many succumbed *en route*."

"And our worthy scholars have no suspicion of it! Oh, this humankind is crawling in the darkness."

"Those Atlanteans who had been able to fly as far as Africa, where they also possessed a few colonies, settled in Egypt, because of the salubrity of the climate. The land of Misr was then inhabited by representatives of the black race. The latter, on seeing unknown men arrive from the sky, thought they were dealing with supernatural beings, and threw themselves at their feet. Having become omnipotent masters, the red men civilized the black, and then, as they lacked women—few Atlantean ladies and demoiselles had been able to accomplish the aerial journey—they interbred with the indigenes, and from that fusion the Egyptians were born. Thanks to those adepts, the reign of the Atlanteans was a true Golden Age, a period of multiple felicities, so the nation never lost the memory of it. It is that period that was named the reign of Sheshoa Hor—which is to say, servants of Hor."

"Ah! Monsieur Maspero, if only you were in his place, to hear my delightful Fay!" proffered the aspirant adept, in a transport of generous joy and magnanimous pride.

But the "delightful Fay" continued:

"The Atlanteans who landed in America found themselves confronting a population of the yellow race, once immigrants from Asia when Lemuria raised its mass between the two continents. The Atlantean bachelors were united with the yellow race, some of whom lived in the region situated between Colorado and the Mississippi and others on the shores of Lake Titicaca. That was the origin of the Toltecs, the Chichimecs and Huarochiris. Those whose wives had shared their flight settled on the banks of the Missouri and the Great Lakes, and as their descendants did not make alliances any more than they had, they did not take long to degenerate. They are the present-day Redskins."

"I'd always wondered where those people could have come from. And the Huaro…?"

"The Huarochiris fused with the Peruvians."

"Oh! Very good."

"The Chichimecs were destroyed by the Aztecs; as for the Toltecs, now dispersed in Mexico, they're beginning to degenerate."

"Go on—better and better!"

"The Atlanteans who landed in Asia civilized the Chinese, but they had no reason to congratulate themselves for it; as they refused to marry indigenes, whose vulgar appearance shocked them, the latter, out of spite, wove intrigues against them. They represented them, in the eyes of the powerful, as ambitious people avid for honors and responsibilities, and, harassed by his court, the emperor excluded the "red foreigners" from all functions. They made the decision to withdraw to Japan, where thy confined themselves in the isles of Yeso, and like their brethren in America they entered into decadence a few centuries later. Their posterity is presently dying out in wretched villages of fishermen and woodcutters. The Atlanteans of Egypt, on the contrary, spread out with an exceptional success. It was them who extracted from barbarism the Chaldeans, the Khitis, the whites of Troas and Mycenae, the blacks of Ethopia and those of austral Africa."

"The blacks of the south?"

"Yes, dear disciple, the Hottentots and the Bushmen, whose empire became most flourishing in the epoch when supremacy passed from the Pharaohs of Memphis to those of Thebes."

"Excuse my bewilderment, but..."

"Bewilder at you ease. There were adorable poets and artists of genius among the Bushmen. There were even Richelieus, if not Millerands—yes, great ministers. If ever your British carry out excavations in the Transvaal, what fine surprises they will have! Although, in the Transvaal...the English...oh, it's gold, vulgar gold that they covet."

Neurocyme fell silent. Immobile, she seemed to be reflecting. Soon, she resumed with passion:

"Oh, my friend, the people who are presently proud of their Disraelis, their Reynolds and their divine Shakespeare, the people of Chamberlain, Burne-Jones, Oscar Wilde and Jack the Ripper, will perhaps be beneath the Hottentots in a few centuries!"

"If Saint-Dolent could hear you!"

There was another silence. Then Monsieur de Sothermès interrogated: "The Atlanteans enjoyed a transcendent spirituality, you told me. How is it that they didn't destroy fetishism when they became masters of Egypt?"

"They didn't even try. The adepts who led their chiefs had advised them, on the orders of Trismegistus, to respect the local religions. In order to direct those peoples it was necessary not to contradict their superstitions. Now, adepts have to direct peoples; that is the mission they have received in the Ether. That explains the occult operations to which they devote themselves for the wellbeing of humans, without the later having any suspicion of it. Every adept must to have to his devotion some influential individual, and employ all means possible to achieve his ends."

"The social role of the adept is, therefore, that of high politics?"

"Even higher. He must exert an influence on princes and prime ministers. The beliefs of the masses and the philosophies of mandarins are of scant importance; the essential thing is that the adepts succeed in making use, as they understand it, of mandarins and masses. That is why religious beliefs remained crude in Egypt."

"It will be necessary, then, for me to take astral ascendancy over a minister of sub-prefect, and get mixed up in politics?"

The dilettante lowered his nose. He had spelled out the last words in a quavering voice. He could already see himself, in a black frock-coat and fresh butter gloves, cooling his heels in the antechamber of Monsieur Waldeck-Rousseau, or ringing Pierre Baudin's doorbell in the Avenue Rapp...

"Does that displease you?" asked Neurocyme.

With a kind of morose sincerity, he replied: "Between us, I prefer literature, because politics...isn't exactly my element...like metaphysics, in fact. Nevertheless, what would I not accept, daughter of Viviane, in order to become your husband?"

"You're too kind," she said, smiling, "and you'll see, as you advance in the doctrine, that you'll become passionate for the transcendental."

"By dint of gazing into your eyes...perhaps I'll get there," he murmured, in a surge of vague hope.

"It's necessary, in any case, for the work to which you're destined," she suggested to him, in a warm and sonorous tone. "Oh, you're going to see the outline of grandiose events, dear disciple. The era of adepts is about to open."

"Isn't it open, then?" he asked, reanimated.

"Their reign cannot commence before humankind has emerged from childhood, and it's scarcely adolescent. When it has inaugurated the virile age, they will guide the world. It will be a hundred thousand times more magnificent, Enogat, than the times of Atlantis!"

Enogat listened to Neurocyme as a child listens to stories, sometimes a little frightened, often charmed and almost always avid to hear more. He accepted candidly everything that she said to him, as much by virtue of mental idleness as amorous passion; he had never cared so little about great problems and dialectics.

They went back. They found their camp assailed by a horde of indigenes. What did all those Bedouins want?

The first who detached himself to approach Enogat and Neurocyme was a tall, lanky fellow with a proud visage and a resolute gesture, carrying in his gaze the insolence of a Spanish mendidalgo.

He introduced himself: "I am the sheikh of the Pyramids,"

The elemental threw him twenty sous. He picked up the baksheesh, pocketed it, and drew away superbly.

Then the others, chocolate or black, approached. Some proposed services as various as they were paradoxical; others sketched disquieting concerts; all of them demanded: "Baksheesh! Baksheesh!"

They became so numerous, so tenacious and so agile that the Arab servants could not succeed in driving them away, even by making use of the whip. It was necessary to distribute small coins and dates. Alas, however, even when departed they were not entirely gone. They had left something of their Bedouin integrity: the camp was swarming with insects.

In vain, the tent was transported to the vicinity of the ruins of Memphis. Other indigenes arrived, weeping, wailing, sniggering and yapping: "Baksheesh!" It was necessary, to put them to flight, for Enogat and his servants to show them revolvers.

There was another peril, perhaps even graver: the curiosity that the elemental had provoked in rival in Gizeh remained keen, and immense. A few tourists maneuvered in order to encounter the sensational couple, as if by chance, in the serapeum. An Englishwoman, who appeared to be simultaneously the elder sister of her Gracious Sovereign and the first cousin of the Tawarets,[59] opened fire by begging Neurocyme to teach her to read hieroglyphics. It was necessary to engage in dialogue, to negotiate, to accept and render visits in the course of which the Beloved and hr disciple were overwhelmed with cups of tea, ginger-nuts and questions.

Ow! Were they carrying out a mission for the French government? Were they, on the contrary, studying for their individual pleasure? Were they innovating an original reportage for some powerful ultra-Atlantic *Herald*? Were they simply devoting themselves to the comfortable emotions of automobilism?

And how many embarrassing words, naturally, emerged in these conversations. When old Mistress Victoria Tawaret once said to Neurocyme: "Your husband," referring to Enogat, and the elemental exclaimed: "He's my brother," Monsieur de Sothermès felt an indescribable malaise...

Abruptly, they packed their bags and fled, in a northerly direction, as far as Saqqarah. That was to fall from the Thames into the Garonne. As they were exchanging their learned impressions of the tomb of Neferhotep, a monsieur of amiable

---

[59] The Tawarets were a class of fertility goddesses, depicted with the body of a hippopotamus and the head of a crocodile. Given that Queen Victoria was 81 when the story was written, likening the tourist to her elder sister is also a trifle unflattering.

appearance rushed toward them and, almost throwing his arms around Enogat's neck, exclaimed: "Ah! Dear compatriot! What luck, by God! I heard your reflections; it's incontinent what I thought! To encounter French people so far from the Opéra always gives pleasure."

And the monsieur insisted on their sharing his "modest lunch." Oh, he wouldn't take them far! In the meantime, where were they staying? How long had they been touring the land of the Pharaohs? Had they news of "the homeland." Amusing, this corner of Egypt, although a little hot. One couldn't find a single newspaper, not even the *Charivari*, nor *L'Illustration*...apart from that...

"But pardon me, let me introduce myself," continued Monsieur Ernest Valcambilhe, of the Smart Club. "I was born in Toulouse, like Pedro, like Jean-Paul, like Antonin and all the rest,[60] but otherwise, I've been living in Paris for thirteen years."

He fell silent for a moment; then he repeated: "Ernest Valcambilhe."

The dilettante was obliged to state his name.

"What!" said Valcambihle. "Enogat de Sothermès, that's you! It's you who gave those unique fêtes, to which the elite of Parisian society flocked sumptuously in hyperhistoric costumes! And Madame is the Egyptian princess whose beauty and wit our chroniclers have celebrated! For once, the eulogies of our chroniclers fell short of the verity. Oh, your fêtes! Didn't I agitate all my connections to obtain an invitation! To think that I've never been introduced to you in Paris, and that we meet here in a cave. Very chic! A cigar?"

---

[60] The "Pedro" born in Toulouse was the philosopher Pierre Grégoire (1540-1597), author of the encyclopedia of occult sciences *Syntaxes artis mirabilis* (1578); the others cited are the painters Jean-Paul Laurens (1838-1921) and Antonin Mercié (1845-1916)

"Thank you, but I no longer smoke since occupying myself with the occult sciences," said the aspirant adept, with a grave civility.

"You do magic? More and more chic! How I bless the hazard—as our forefathers said—for have contrived this incredible meting! A true *coup de theâtre*!

"In the genre of Blum and Pierre Decourcelle's *Robinson*," sighed the elemental, inaudibly.[61]

Valcambilhe escorted them until nightfall. There were obliged to keep him at dinner; when the excessively gracious companion took his leave of them he threw them the suave promise: "*À bientôt!*"

"Another day of that sort," declared Neurocyme, and I'll go mad."

"What a bore!" groaned Enogat. "There might be only one Frenchman in Egypt at present, and it's on us that he falls!"

"My dear, it's necessary to decamp tomorrow without waiting any longer," said Neurocyme, imitating their companion's southern accent."

"Already..."

"You're not determined to visit all the tombs, I suppose."

"Certainly not."

"In any case, they're all alike. My friend, let's go."

"Where to, his time? To El-Lahoun, to explore the virgin pyramid?"

"No, indeed! That would be to tempt indiscreet curiosity more than ever. As it appears to me to be impossible to pursue our studies in peace in this country where the English have replaced the crocodiles..."

"And where even Frenchmen come!"

"...We're going to leave Egypt."

"So quickly?" said the dilettante. "Are you serious?"

---

[61] *Robinson Crusoé*, a drama by Ernest Blum and Pierre Decourcelle was premièred at the Théâtre du Châtelet—famed for its stage gadgetry—in October 1899.

Very seriously, Neurocyme continued, in her golden voice: "Furthermore, this Egypt has a monotony that might have had some charm when the ancient cities rose up in all their splendor, but which emanates an atrocious bitterness now that they're in ruins. Everywhere the same appearances, and always the same effects."

"There are corners that aren't bad, though, on the banks of the Nile," Sothermès insinuated, meekly. "You know, dear, I suppose that toward Philo...by having a smart, spacious villa constructed there..."

"On the banks of the Nile? Oh, dear disciple, when one thinks that on that ever sacred river, the river that mirrored Cleopatra, the Cook Agency is ferrying gentleman in veiled helmets and ladies in impudent sunglasses, one can only have one desire if one still conserves some estheticism: to flee as quickly as possible. Egyptian landscapes? I advise you not to talk about them."

"Oh! What I said about them..."

"A sea of imbecile plains, from which villages of mud emerge at intervals and trees bristling with romantic plumes. Good for Marilhat or for Valcambilhe! Stones, rocks and sand—for I don't say anything about the desert plants. Have you seen them, the desert plants? And to think that the good Schweinfurth went to tell Europe that he had found an unusual variety in these dunes! And of course, Europe believed him. Who knows? Perhaps even you, poor friend, still believe him...you still have so many superstitions! At least, if you believe that there's sun, there is—and it's violent. Oh, these scenes that one can only contemplate through smoked lenses, aren't made for enjoyment, Enogat, admit it!"

"But by isolating ourselves in a well-situated palace, my dear..."

She stamped her foot and tightened her nostrils. "No, no, no! The places where a soul of transcendent intellectuality might reside are like 'historical sites,' my dear. The Muslims dishonor them, when it isn't the English. There are people who vitiate the air by their presence, you understand? We shouldn't remain on this noxious soil a moment longer."

"At your orders, my friend. And…where are you taking us?"

"Chaldea is only a few steps away; let's take them. It's quite simple."

As soon as the sun rose the following morning, Neurocyme gave the order to break camp.

Everything was packed when Valcambilhe arrive, radiant, carrying a bouquet that he offered to the elemental. Then he coughed and, after an imperceptible pause, he said: "Great news, dear friends. I've received information from Cairo that Jean Lorrain has set forth for Gizeh. He should already have arrived, it seems to me. If he's come back, it's because it's beautiful. Would you like to go and meet him? That would be nice, eh? We represent the French colony in these parts! Hold on, an idea—what if we were to offer a banquet to Jean Lo…"

"Impossible," replied Neurocyme. "An unexpected and very important reason summons us in the opposite direction."

"We're leaving in a few minutes," added the dilettante. "Look, Monsieur Valcambilhe." And he showed him the servants loading the last packages into the trunk of the automobile, the engine of which as running.

"Oh, what are you telling me? I was planning a party…I even thought of taking you to Bulaq. After all…are you intending to return to Paris this winter?"

"We don't know yet."

"In any case, remember me, won't you? When you resume your fêtes… I'll describe your automobile to Jean Lorrain."

With that, Toulousian handshakes were exchanged. The Beloved and her disciple hoisted themselves on to their dragon. The monster moved off. A few seconds later, it had vanished in the dust.

XI. The "Affair"

They fled toward Alexandria like cashiers running away with the receipts, without dallying on the way.

Neurocyme's first concern on arriving in the large and noisy city was to look for a ship departing for Syria. Several steamers were in the port; she granted her preference to the one that was to raise anchor first. It was a small commercial steamer that had just completed loading in order to depart the following day for Beirut. A magnificent gratification persuaded the captain to take aboard, at the last moment, passengers whose unusual luggage had frightened him at first. At daybreak, therefore, the dilettante was able to sing Queen Hortense's well-known tune appropriately.[62] That was, if not the only, the most important incident of the crossing.

Having need of a new guide, the Beloved and her disciple had only kept one servant. The man in question hastened to make the acquaintance of several Arab passengers, one of whom had no sooner learned about the projects of the "French" than he offered to guide them. He was returning to Bagdad, and he had accomplished the journey enough times, with caravans, to know the road well. As for the route from Bagdad to Hillah, it was no less familiar to him. He also undertook to guide the couple to Tello.

Neurocyme made the man talk, scrutinized his physiognomy, and, satisfied with that double examination, engaged him. Thanks to that fortunate encounter, the elemental and her disciple were able to stroll at their ease when they set foot on

---

[62] The reference is to "Partant pour la Syrie" [Departing for Syria], a song composed in 1807 by Hortense de Beauharnais—the niece of the Empress Joséphine, who married one of Napoléon's brothers—which was set to music by Alexandre de Laborde. It became the unofficial French national anthem during the Second Empire, while the *Marseillaise* was banned.

land. Unfortunately, Beirut had nothing to charm them, and they hastened to leave it.

The fuming dragon was launched in the direction of Tadmur; from Tadmur they headed for the Euphrates, across a bleak and dismal country. There were entire days when they did not encounter a living soul, and the dilettante was regretting Egypt keenly when they arrived in the vicinity of Al-Kalim, in sight of the river. They crossed it further on, at Tanah, on a flat-bottomed boat. Once on the other bank, they resumed their course, raising an implacable dust on the roads everywhere, and, at intervals, a great excitement in the bosom of the populations.

Soon they reached Bagdad, where their vehicle and their persons had no less success than in Gizeh. Nothing pleased them in the degenerate city of the Caliphs; neither the Pacha's palace nor the customs-house gripped their gaze for an instant. Enogat was simply shocked by the ordure in the streets; her nerves taut, the elemental declared that the vulgarity of the inhabitants was only equaled by that of the architecture of the English consulate. Having renewed their provisions, they set forth again hastily without wanting to visit the cadavers of Seleucia and Ctesiphon, because, Neurocyme affirmed flatly, those cities had never existed.

A few days later, their tent was erected at Tello, near the palace of the patesi Gudea. Exceedingly ruined ruins! Chaldea is the country in the world where the ruins are the most ruined. Undoubtedly there was, far beyond, the firmament, always turning always splendid, but for an elemental and a dilettante what is the firmament?

After a glance cast like alms on the heap of bricks and earth that constitute the ruins of the temple of Ningirsu, the elemental and her disciple wanted to go to Hillah. As they were on the point of departure, however, Enogat perceived that they were about to run out of gasoline.

"We're in trouble!" he exclaimed, anxiously "We'd have to go a long way to find a grocer selling that liquid!"

"Oh, my friend! To talk about grocers in the ruins of Tello!"

"However, dear..."

"As you're embarrassed by such a trifle," Neurocyme interrupted, "I'll make you some gasoline myself."

"You?"

"Of course. An adept is able to extract anything—absolutely anything, you understand—from matter, because all matter is one."

"You're teaching me so much."

"Had you, by chance, another concept of matter?"

"No, no, I confess...these questions and me..."

"My little operation will show you what true magic can do."

"And you have no need of a furnace, an alembic, a matras..."

"I only need heat."

"A high temperature?"

"Very high."

"Then I'm curious to see how you'll obtain it, for this region seems to me to be devoid of combustible material."

"I don't need wood or coal."

Then, having sent away the servants, Neurocyme approached a mound of earth and stone. Gravely, almost hieratically, she made a brief evocation. Then she stamped her foot three times. Flames sprang from the ground; they were gnomes! She gave them orders in a language that Enogat did not understand, and when they had disappeared—which is to say that the flames had gone back into the ground—she evoked Willis.[63] The latter immediately flew from the depths

---

[63] Willis are fantastic creatures of Slavic mythology, somewhat reminiscent of Greek nymphs. The label was borrowed for application to elemental spirits by German Romantic writers, and borrowed from them by the French Romantics Théophile Gautier, in the ballet *Giselle* (1841) and Alphonse Karr, in the short story "Les Willis" (1856).

of the horizon in the form of light clouds, and, one minute thirty seconds and a quarter later they stopped in a semicircle before the elemental. Monsieur de Sothermès was surprised to find a vague human appearance in them; their head seemed to be formed of snowballs, and their face, where a sensual mouth never stopped smiling, was reminiscent of Cypriot statues. They seemed to be clad in long robes of cloud.

The elemental communicated her desires to them by means of an expressive mime, and they started dancing in cadence, sometimes flying into the sky like eagles, sometimes skimming the ground like partridges.

"What choreography!" said the dilettante. "See how the ground is fuming at the place where the transmutation is in preparation."

"Then that smoke indicates that..."

"My friend, it's gasoline that is being fabricated down there. Fetch the can quickly—the operation is reaching its conclusion.

She spoke, and the Willis ceased their entrechats on seeing little blue flames emerging from the ground. As soon as the flames were extinct, the elemental lifted one of the stones of the mound, and Monsieur de Sothermès hastened to collect the limpid gasoline that started running from that orifice. They also filled a water-skin with it, and while Neurocyme replaced the stone, her disciple transported the two receptacles to the automobile. The burden was heavy; scarcely had he lifted the can than he had to put it down again. He was about to pick up the water-skin when he saw the can move on its own and go directly to the trunk of the vehicle.

"It's a phenomenon of levitation," the Beloved shouted to him, laughing at his amazed expression, "and it's to the movement, again, that you owe it. Look up in the air, my friend."

Enogat, raising his head, perceived the Willis in the process of weaving an ineffable can-can. It seemed to him that clownish legs were jiggling under the robes of cloud with the speed of a propeller, while the arms of marionettes, no less composed of cloud, were sketching colorless gestures above still-smiling faces. Before he had had time to spit out his surprise, he received a blow on the nose; it was the water-skin that was flying beside the gas-can, describing a graceful parabola. Then, having descended to the ground, the spirits commenced a dance analogous to the Kaffir pilou-pilou—which, being, as everyone knows, the ancestor of the Hellenic pyrrhic, necessitates frantic steps and maneuvers.[64]

Soon, the dilettante found himself among the performers. An irresistible force carried him away. Suddenly, his legs were functioning involuntarily, with an elasticity that would have made Valentin le Désossé[65] green with envy; his arms were gymnastic, his torso dislocated; his entire being overflowed, cavorting in frenetic rhythms, and finally leapt into the air to accomplish a perilous double somersault. When the unfortunate landed on his feet again, it was to collapse; his head was spinning, and his heart too. It took him several minutes to recover consciousness.

The Willis bowed ceremoniously before him, with long reverences; then they advanced pompously, and, one after another, embraced him in a gluttonous manner. At the second accolade, the dilettante's garments were completely soaked; at the last, they were streaming.

"But...but...what's this?" he groaned, as soon as he found the use of speech again. "They've acted unbecomingly all over me, the guttersnipes!"

---

[64] The author had no way of knowing that the term "pilou-pilou" would later be adopted as the name of a French rugby football ritual analogous to the New Zealand team's Haka. It was also the name given to Popeye's fantastic pet, Eugene the Jeep, in the strip's French translation in1937.

[65] "Valentin le Desossé" [i.e., the Boneless] was the nickname of the dancer Jacques Renaudin, immortalized by Toulouse-Lautrec as the partner of Louise Weber, alias La Goulouse, in his posters for the Moulin Rouge.

"Have no fear," said Neurocyme. "It's simply their nebulous vestment, which has changed into water—the purest water, have no fear—on contact with your material body."

"What specimens! Those Willis...!"

"They wanted to show you all their talents and honor you with dances."

"Thanks a lot...my dear! In the meantime I'm catching cold and exhausted."

"A few fluidic passes will cure you, dear delicate. In a few minutes, you'll be as robust as one of Assur's warriors."

Enogat was, in fact, fortified by the passes. Nevertheless, he remained rather sulky during the journey to Hillah. His adventure with the spirits of the air had upset him. Should Neurocyme have permitted that buffoonery? No, she should not! Was the Fay amusing herself in the fashion of art-students in 1830? Those were her distractions! He promised himself to have his revenge when he was an adept. Alas, would that be soon?

The sight of the tels of Babylon changed the course of their ideas. Sothermès became literary again. He recited a few lines of Raymond de la Tailhède:

On sands of azure and old, rare perfumes
Swirled in large cups, slowly...

And when the elemental had told him that the wall of the vanished city had once stood a few meters from where the automobile was quivering, and that the hovels that were blurred by a golden dust on the horizon stood on the site of the venerable Taman Babylon, Monsieur de Sothermès could not help crying out with the poet of *Lis noirs*:[66]

Sacred numbers, infinite rhythm, swaying
Of stars bathed in the flux of the somber ether,

---

[66] Albert Jounet, alias Jhouney, again; *Les lys noirs* was published in 1888.

Glory and decline of nations, course of years,
Float, passing by regally and sadly!

A few days later, as they were strolling on the banks of the Euphrates, they were surprised by a storm far from any natural shelter. They were obliged to go back to their lodging under an insolent downpour that soaked them to the bone, while the mud of the path splashed them all the way to the spine.

Neurocyme had only brought one masculine costume; she therefore resumed, regretfully, the feminine attire that she had been wearing on the morning of their departure from Paris. It was a delightful surprise for Enogat to find her once again in a dress. At the sight of her in trousers and a reefer jacket for so many weeks, he had ended up considering her as an androgyne. Now he felt, again, that she was really a woman.

And what a joy it was to contemplate a costume of the purest Parisianism in that desert, where the fair sex was only represented by Arab housewives! She wore that costume delightfully, moreover, with poses that recalled the great fêtes of yore. In truth, it was a transfiguration as radical as it was charming. Yes, the Beloved became a coquette again; she resumed her strange smile, her profound eyes, her fluttering eyelashes, her semi-sphinx-like attitudes. The meek disciple could not weary of contemplating her.

Until nightfall he enveloped her and caressed her with his amorous gaze; he breathed her in so much that he ended up being intoxicated by her.

Madly intoxicated! After dinner, they went for a walk under the nearby date-palms. The storm had swept the sky, and the stars were dancing there like the one that danced when Titania was born. Neurocyme leaned on her friend's arm; he drew his fingernails through her hair. Madly intoxicated! Oh, certainly, he would not otherwise have dared to renew his gallant attempts, held back by the severe attitude of his "initiator," impeded by the incessant "lessons" and, on the other hand, ill-served by events. All the successive displacements were scarcely favorable to amorous enterprises—but this time, the occasion seemed propitious: the night was superb; the earth exhaled balsamic freshness; the mystery, beneath the profound trees, was soothing and softening. Besides which, we repeat, he was intoxicated—madly intoxicated.

"On such nights," the elemental pronounced, in her Virgilian voice, "the adepts formed by Trismegistus take pleasure in teaching their disciples."

"Oh, sweet queen of my soul," the dilettante burst out, "what are stars to me, when I contemplate your eyes!"

"I hoped to make you understand that between us, nonsense was a cacophony," said the golden voice, less Virgilian.

"That's true, and you're a thousand times right, daughter of Viviane. I will tell you, therefore, without metaphor and without madrigal, that my love for you radiates such a warmth that I can no longer live near to you without obtaining a kiss from you...oh, very respectfully...from time to time."

"Friend Sothermès, why return to that theme? The initiate must conquer the grades one by one."

"Have I not yet given sufficient proof of my constancy to merit the favor of pressing your lips...?"

"The being who is climbing toward the light must restrain his senses."

"I'm restraining them, I assure you. Never has a frantic lover been seen, it's certain, to restrain them so harshly."

"History cites the case of the gallant knights, and even simple laborers," Neurocyme argued, "who waited for their beauty for years, and decades..."

Then, after collecting herself, she intoned, solemnly and mysteriously:

If you love, make it an occult desire
With a sole hope of innocent ectasy.
A hope, if you wish, that is a memory.

But do not lift up your quivering hands

Toward the frail face with the absolute gaze.
There is no other amour than of absent things,

The little that presages and all that is no more.[67]

Sothermès listened to it, shivering, and went very pale.

She took pity on him, and said to him, almost coaxingly: "Besides, what does a vain kiss matter to someone who is able to love truly?"

"Much more than you seem to think..."

"Come on! Elevate your spirit above the terrestrial plane; gaze no planetary space, and learn patience by meditating on the harmony of the spheres. The day will come when they will melt into the sun that engendered them, and for which they aspire; but that will only happen after the accomplishment of their evolution. Souls are like the spheres, my friend; each of them, at a moment of its existence, burns with amour for a soul that is its sun; it ought then to gravitate around that star, until it is in a condition to be united with it."

"The planets can easily wait, damn it, since they're retained by laws."

"Human souls can wait too, since they're endowed with will and reason."

"Eh! All that doesn't prove that a poor little kiss can bring about a catastrophe, Neurocyme..."

"Dear impatient, there was once, in Sirius, a Romeo and a Juliet...first, let me show you Sirius..."

The elemental raised her lovely head, turned it to the right and then the left—and, in the later movement, a wisp of hair brushed Enogat's cheek. Then the latter, no longer able to contain himself, abruptly took the Beloved in his arms. He clasped her to his heart. He clasped her harder. He tried to kiss her—but before his lips had brushed Neurocyme's nape, the

---

[67] These lines are subsequently credited within the text to Fernand Mazade (1861-1939), whose first three collections of poetry appeared in the 1880s.

latter had freed herself, and held her disciple's arms with a force and a violence of which he had not suspected her capable.

Menacingly, she declared: "Wretch, who only exalt your will in order to enmire yourself more deeply in the hylic sewer, quell the fury of your senses or you'll lose me."

"What are you saying?"

"You'll lose me—and forever. Do you think that beings of my kind can be treated like your prostitutes? Fays are not whores; it's necessary to merit them. We are a recompense."

"Oh, if you could see the fire that is devouring me..."

"I can see it, and I'm delighted by it; it is purifying you. Let yourself burn, then, in order to be reborn. Come on, dearest, more courage! This is only a petty crisis, a storm like the one that traversed the sky just now. Think that from the height of all those stellar worlds, many adepts are observing you and making incantations for your triumph. Do you no longer want to merit a place in their heart?"

"Yes, yes—and above all, in yours..."

"Now you've become a man of intelligence again." She smiled. "It's a good sign, my friend. You're saved."

"Saved? Perhaps..."

Certainly exhausted, however, a ram become a sheep, he allowed himself to be brought back to his bunk, meekly.

The next day, Neurocyme decided to calm him down by means of an excursion—a long excursion. They went by automobile to the bank of the Euphrates, and, leaving the dragon in the care of servants, they went to Kifl. There, not far from the supposed tomb of Ezekiel, they rested briefly; then, as the heat was beginning to fatigue Enogat, Neurocyme directed their march toward the date-palms of Zayd ibn Ali. A miserable hamlet cut across their route.

"It's not pleasant here," said Enogat, after having zigzagged conscientiously between the heaps of filth that make a leprous carpet in all Arab settlements. "It's not pleasant and it doesn't smell good. Why, then, choose this place rather than Nineveh? At Kuyunjik or Khorsabad we might have discovered new bas-reliefs; at any rate, we'd have seen the palace of Sargon..."

"First of all," the elemental interjected, "the land of Assur is profoundly antipathetic to me, because it serves as an abode for a population of obtuse mercenaries; secondly, in the localities you've just cited, we'd have bumped into nuisances, as in Egypt. Here, at least one can study in peace."

She had scarcely finished speaking when they suddenly discovered, under the last date-palms, a European house, of iron and bricks, built between a courtyard and garden. At the sight of them, a bulldog that was dozing in front of its niche got up and gave voice. Immediately, a stout fellow with a rubicund face heightened by flavescent side-whiskers appeared in the doorway; he was the concierge. Perceiving correctly-dressed Europeans, he almost raised his hat, and disappeared, telling the bulldog to shut up.

The bulldog had fallen silent, and the travelers were about to resume their walk when a young gentleman, the proprietor himself, emerged from the house and came toward them. After having bowed courteously, he said, with a pronounced British accent: "Either I'm mistaken, or you're French, are you not?"

"You're not mistaken," Enogat replied.

"I am, myself, a British subject," the gentleman said, "and I wish you welcome."

Monsieur de Sothermès bowed, saying: "We're pleased to meet you."

"Undoubtedly, you're looking for me, to pay me a visit?"

"We were, on the contrary, far from suspecting that this clump of trees concealed a European dwelling," Neurocyme replied.

"What! No one mentioned my home to you, in Hillah?"

"We're not staying in Hillah," Sothermès explained. "We're traveling through the region rapidly, and we lodge far from towns, in a tent."

"Admirably practical, a tent, while traveling. But since good fortune has brought you to my home today, do me the honor of resting here for a little while."

The gentleman introduced them into the room that served him as a drawing room and, without delay, the stout rubicund man brought whisky, sherry, brandy and pale ale. The conversation, after having covered Mesopotamia and its means of communication, soon turned to confidence. As soon as he knew that his guests were neither commercial travelers nor archeologists, but were traveling for their pleasure and their desire to see the world, the Englishman let them know that he had settled near Hillah with the aim of devoting himself to a grandiose and colossal speculation.

It was a matter of buying the land over which Babylon and Nineveh had extended and reselling it in lots, as much to States as to individuals, when colonists wanted to rebuild a city.

"Ah! Evidently..."

"There's already talk of it in England. You understand me, don't you? Each of these locations is crying out for a city."

"That's true."

"New Babylon or New Nineveh, with railways, electric trams, steam-boats and gasoline-fueled tricycles! And seven-story houses, with elevators, and crystal palaces, and majestic docks on the very ground where the proud edifices of the sons of Nimrod once stood! To trace a Victoria Square, a Gladstone Park, a Chamberlain Street, a Roberts Road—what a beautiful dream! And to erect on the vestiges of the Tower of Babel an Eiffel Tower, much more considerable! Oh, wouldn't that be truly beautiful?"

"Yes. There's something to be done..."

"A great many things."

The dilettante and the elemental promised to think about the "affair," and then withdrew, effusive in thanks—the sherry was not bad—and congratulations.

"He's got a lot of imagination, that John Bull," said Enogat to Neurocyme, when they were alone under the date-palms.

"He's a Celt," she replied. "A race of artists."

"He interested me greatly, and while I was listening to him, I conceived a project too..."

"You're frightening me."

"I told myself that it might perhaps be clever and noble to buy a plot of land at Hillah, and to build on it."

"It isn't in this country, with or without a modern city, that we'll settle, I warn you. It would take a century to repopulate Mesopotamia, and if Europeans ever settle here, they'll plant factory chimneys before replanting trees. Believe me, for a long time yet, this accursed region will have no other décor but wilderness, with old bricks instead of flowers, and any delicate individuals who take it into their heads to stay for longer than a month in these gray plains will be afflicted with an incurable spleen. Even if it would be easy for us to change into gardens of Armida this noxious land where even your Raffaelli couldn't find anything to sketch, I'd still say to you: don't found anything here! Sâr Péladan has made these banks ridiculous forever."

"I think you're severe."

"On the Sâr or the region?"

"On both."

"*Your glory, O Babylon, I have manifested!* As for Péladan, he's a Nîmois journalist who thinks he's a hierophant."

They set forth again in a southerly direction. In a few stages, the travelers arrived at Basra, there they crossed the Shatt al Arab. Once on Persian territory, they headed for Shiraz. The roads were suffering from the rigors of winter, and it took nearly two weeks to get from the border to Persepolis.

Amused, at first, by the novelty of the décor, Enogat did not take long to find the journey utterly insipid. From Endian on, the road became uneven without appearing any more picturesque, and the cold increased in intensity. They had to buy goatskins and good astrakhans in order to support the rigors of the temperature, very capricious in March. The dilettante, whom the bad weather tested severely, thought that his initiatrix had wanted to teach him a lesson and he was on the point of asking her to turn back several times.

As there as nothing more to see in Persepolis, the elemental offered to take her disciple into the valley of the Polvar, to the site of the ancient Parsagardae.

"What's the point?" Enogat replied, "Since here's nothing to be seen but vague sepulchers. Wouldn't you prefer Suse, the Apadana of Artaxerxes?"

"Everything of interest there was in Suse is now in the Louvre."

"Then take me wherever you please, in a milder climate."

"You're becoming reasonable again. Let's return to the automobile."

"Immediately?"

"Immediately."

"We're not staying for two or three days?"

"This décor gives me gooseflesh, my friend. What is there to do here? Trail around like demolition contractors in a construction-yard, though rubble whose only virtue is to have passed through the hands of the entrepreneurs of Darius, Xerxes and Artaxerxes Ochus! Run around the suburbs to give ourselves the spectacle of the indigenes, or chat with some boring functionary—no thanks. In any case, Madame Gottglauben,[68] strolling around here in her trousers, has rendered the county antipathetic to me; at the thought that I might be mistaken for a plagiarist of that pedantic schoolboy, I can no longer stand still; the ground is burning my soles. Let's go!"

---

[68] This name translates as "Mrs. [or Frau] Godbelieving," but it does not seem to have had any conventional currency in19th century France.

A few minutes later, the automobile was ready to take the road to Shiraz. Bewildered by that abrupt departure, the servants exchanged glances with one another that the oldest ended up translating in the form of an apopthegm:

"Cracked, our bosses!"

Then silence.

And forward the dragon!

XII. A Few Mysteries are Unveiled

For league after league, Enogat de Sothermès remained taciturn, reciting verses to himself that he strove in vain to expel from his thoughts. Oh, that night under the date-palms of Tell-el-Kuraineh! Oh, Neurocyme, solemn and mysterious, intoning under the stars:

If you love, make it an occult desire
With a sole hope of innocent ectasy.

And then, even if they were married... She had said:

But do not lift up your quivering hands
Toward the frail face with the absolute gaze.
There is no other amour than of absent things!

Devil take those who make verses, and those who recite them!

And for even more leagues, he was bleak, depressed and sulky.

Finally, in Shiraz his face straightened, and brightened slightly. As Neurocyme turned the automobile on to the road to Bushehr, he asked her, graciously:

"Are we changing the itinerary? Where are you taking us?"

"Guess, my friend."

"Toward the Persian Gulf?"

"That's right. The Persian Gulf, where we'll embark for Bombay. I'm taking you to the ancient land of the Brahmins!"

Enogat received that reply with a sincere, even lyrical joy. Hindustan was a land to see. It made you a man. At least they would find a society there. Heaven and earth! He had had enough of desert.

Damn! he thought. *Just as long as she doesn't take it into her head to drag us into the jungle! I won't go!*

At Bushehr they dismissed the Arabs, of whom they had no further need, and embarked on a steamer bound for Bombay.

Until the Strait of Hormuz, they had a relatively calm sea, but scarcely had they moved into the Gulf of Oman than they ran into a rather nasty storm. The aspirant adept as gripped by a significant malaise, by which Neurocyme did not seem to be unduly moved.

"One can preserve oneself from sea-sickness by an effort of will—read Dr. Farès," she suggested. "But once the sickness is manifest, there's nothing to do but resign oneself to it."

"That's me!" Enogat moaned.

"He lay down in his bunk, and, when Neurocyme offered to have him undressed, he gathered all his remaining energy to stammer a refusal. He did not even want his shoes or gloves to be removed; the slightest contact caused him intolerable suffering. For three days—the wind continued to blow furiously—he remained dressed, shod and gloved, sometimes whimpering like a baby and sometimes muttering the most acerbic plaints, imagining that he was exhaling his last sigh.

The Beloved, whose nerves were overexcited by the state of the sea, found him complaining, annoying and ridiculous, and made only brief appearances at his bedside. To give herself some distraction, she opposed by means of an imperious dialectic two Englishwomen whom the frightful swell had spared—disdained, Neurocyme said—and flirted, very slightly, with one of the ship's officers. Finally, one day late, the ship came into harbor in Bombay. It was just in time. Weary of turning over in his bunk and utterly exhausted, Enogat wanted to die.

Forty-eight hours of rest for the dilettante.

While he came back to life in a good hotel bed, Neurocyme traced the plan of their journey, procured maps of the particular regions of which she was dreaming, and occupied herself with the search for servants. Her choice settled on two parsis of honest appearance.

"Have you recovered, dear?" she asked, on the morning of the third day, placing her leonardoeque hand on her disciple's brow."

He replied affirmatively. Nevertheless, it would have been, if not dangerous, at least cruel to impose a long railway journey on him, or tiring marches. The Beloved thus arranged for their first excursion a series of pleasure trips. They went in a boat—a good, old and gentle boat with oars—to Karanja, and idled there in the shade like schoolboys playing truant.

Nine hours from Gharapuri there were subterranean sanctuaries in the territory of Tanna in the hills of Kanheri. They were taken there. The apes that decorated them annoyed them. They had a whim then to travel the few kilometers that separated them from other sacred caverns, those of Monpezir.

As they were following a trail traced through wild ravines, a tiger suddenly emerged from the long grass twenty meters from Enogat. Before the dilettante had recovered from his surprise, the animal was on him, and had knocked him down.

Oh, to die! To die so young! To die before having…his lips…Neurocyme! Incapable of the slightest resistance, Monsieur de Sothermès was about to faint when—a last surprise!—the feline threw itself backwards, intimidated.

"Have no fear, dear friend," modulated the caressant voice of the elemental at the same time. "It's nothing, a simple alert. Wild beasts, as I've told you, obey my voice. That one will offer you its apologies."

And, having helped her disciple to his feet, the Beloved turned to the tiger and, hr eyebrow arched, gave it orders in an unusual language both soft and sonorous. That is why the feline, its tail between its legs, returned in a contrite manner toward Enogat, knelt as best it could at his feet, and licked them copiously. Leaning on the arm of his "dear," the dilettante, his cheeks livid and his eyes wide, watched the enormous, sanguinary tongue that was so patiently polishing him.

A thank you would doubtless have been too much, but a few words of pardon seemed indicated. In spite of his desire to proffer them, Monsieur de Sothermès remained silent; he was choking, his throat devoid of saliva. When the tiger also ran out of saliva, it flattened itself before the elemental, who, after a stern admonition, sent it back to its long grass, repentant.

"I owe you my life, dear!" stammered the aspirant adept, pressing the hands of his initiatrix with all the courage and vigor that he could muster.

"Let's not dwell on such trivia," she replied, with a slight grimace of disdain. "Soon, you too, Sothermès, will be able to command wild beasts."

They resumed the march, but Enogat was advancing with difficulty, as if the bitter drool of the tiger had weighed down his feet. He did not really recover all of his strength and all his innate elasticity until they arrived, at Monpezir, in the temple that had been devastated several times, where, near a Hindu fresco, a composition painted by Portuguese Jesuits was still displayed. The dilettante, however, no longer had any appetite for that life of insensate journeys and continual dangers. As soon as he had conquered his "dear" via the adeptate, he would refuse energetically any expedition of that kind. And, absorbed by those tragic thoughts, he only accorded a distracted and sad attention to the images of the sacred cavern—which were, in any case, much deteriorated.

They took the same route to return to Tanna, and when they passed the area of the licked feet, Enogat could not help going pale.

"What do you expect?" he said to the Beloved, who was smiling. "I'm a dilettante, not an explorer, and the existence we're leading is changing my habits so much..."

Then, becoming serious, she replied to him: "You have already suffered violent emotions because of me, my friend. They were necessary, be sure of that. This is tempering your character. They are the unavoidable ordeals of your initiation, and you needed them."

"If they're the unavoidable ordeals..."

"I'll give you, in any case, some compensations. Don't forget that I'm going to take you to the doyen of adepts."

"Certainly, quite an honor! Will it be soon?"

"Very soon."

With its cheerful gardens and its colorful houses, Poona produced an exquisite impression on Sothermès. Malabar Hill, in Bombay, had seemed to him to be a "Plaine Monceau" with exotic villas. Poona was a true Hindu city. After the imbecile plains crossed by railway, it appeared to him as an ideal oasis. The surroundings! He was seized by a fit of lyricism.

"Oh, my dear!" he exclaimed, "to build you a palace, a delightful palace in the Mogul style in the midst of this nest of verdure, a few minutes from the railway! Tell me whether you accept!"

"How do you know that we won't find something better elsewhere?"

"Is that possible?"

"I affirm that it is."

"To what shores to you want to guide me then?"

"To enchanted shores that you don't even suspect. Don't ask me anymore."

The dilettante drew away from Poona with regret. His spleen increased when the automobile had devoured a few kilometers on the road to Ahmednagar. The banality of the scenery aggravated his sadness. On the other hand, Ahmednagar, where they arrived at the end of the second day amused Monsieur de Sothermès with its constructions in a hybrid style, half-Hindu and half-Pathan. He was even more seduced by the mosques with minarets and the terraced palaces of Aurangabad, which they reached after another three-day journey through interminable fields of cotton. "A veritable décor for retired bonnet-makers," he grumbled.

"Look, dear friend, the center of Atmapur was there; the dogs are seeking their nourishment among the debris thrown over the walls of proud palaces. And this Hindu Hillah does not have a single stone of the Babylon that it has replaced.

Thus are punished cities that scorn the teachings of the doctrine."

Five days later, as the automobile reached the mount of Pipal Ghat, the elemental said: "Look at the flagstones paving this road; they're all stones stolen from the surrounding temples, and the author of that theft was a former rajah of the province. He committed it in order to pay court to English functionaries, and had no lack of imitators. You can see that the Hindus are no less vandals than the Europeans. Believe me, dear, it's not in this degenerate country that it's appropriate to build our palace."

At the summit of the slope they traversed a plateau where majestic trees covered with a dome of foliage a ruined necropolis of Muslim marabouts, and they stopped near a certain village that Enogat complimented with the epithet "pleasant."

"This place is called Rauzah," said Neurocyme, "Which means 'Paradise.' It needs to be a place of delights, though. Epidemics are rife here. We've almost reached our destination; Ellora is displayed on the western slope of that hill; we'll be there tomorrow morning. Today, I'll take you, after lunch, to the tomb of the great Mogul Aurangzeb and the mausoleum of a famous descendant of the prophet, the marabout Burhan-ud-din. The reception center of the tombs is one of the most exquisite for talking of metaphysics and rendering one insensible to the mirages of the world of Maia."

Then an emotion of a complex order invaded the aspirant adept, and when the fuming dragon had penetrated into the hamlet of Ellora, Enogat de Sothermès had hollow cheeks and a brow furrowed by anxiety. Another few turns of the wheel and he was about to see Him, the brother of Trismegistus! With that master of masters, it was no longer a matter of talking literature.

After having passed the temple of Kali, the Beloved stopped the vehicle, and for the first time on Hindu soil they set up camp.

Were they going to stay long? At least a week.

Seven days? Could one spend seven days with the doyen of adepts?

Neurocyme fell silent. That afternoon, however, she gave her disciple his final instructions

Then, abruptly, she said: "Come. I'll take you to His Transcendence."

"You haven't yet told me his name," said Enogat, trembling. "Is it forbidden to know it?"

""Not at all. Our brethren call him Patishtha, and the Hindu theosophists, who have piously retained the memory of his civilizing work, designate him by the title of Ancient-of-Days. But they believed him to be a demiurge returned to the astral, and scarcely suspect that he's living at this moment on the hill of Rauzah."

"And until when will he remain down here?"

"Until the times are accomplished my friend."

"Will that be soon?"

"At the appointed hour, my friend."

Enogat understood that it was necessary not to insist, and orientated his questions toward other points—no less obscure, however.

"The illustrious master is expecting us, you told me yesterday, daughter of Viviane. How does he know about out visit? You haven't written to him, that I know."

"It's by telepathy that I informed His Transcendence; it's by telepathy that he designated the place of the encounter to me."

"We're not going to his house?"

"His house is everywhere. In general, when he makes a tour of inspection in a province, he stays with our brothers. For the moment, as he's carrying out an investigation in a locality devoid of adepts, he has no fixed abode. When night falls he hides his hylic body in a thicket or a grotto and sends his astral body to repose in the ether."

"All the same, if that were reported in a newspaper..."

"Avoid reflections of that sort, I beg you, before His Transcendence...but I perceive that we've arrived. Let's go into this Buddhist monastery; it's this ancient enclosure that he's chosen for the rendezvous."

They found the vihara absolutely deserted, no tourist staying in Ellora that day. As they finished making a tour of the principal room, a gentleman crossed the threshold and headed straight toward them, brisk and prompt.

"His Transcendence," said the elemental, bowing very low before the brisk and prompt gentleman.

Immediately, remembering his dear's instructions, the dilettante threw himself to the ground and lay down in the fashion of Orientals saluting their monarch. Then Patishtha exchanged a few words in an esoteric language; then, addressing Enogat, he told him in French to get up.

"Prince of Adepts," pronounced the latter, in a trembling and atonal voice, "I pray Your Transcendence to accept the homage of a Will that aspires to the supreme initiation, and the oblation of a Force that is given entirely to the secret doctrine."

And the Prince replied, promptly and briskly:

"Dear microcosm desirous of the supreme methesis, what I have learned about your Self from your eminent initiator"—he indicated Neurocyme—"gives you my initial sympathy. Let her radiation sustain you during the magical askesis."

The Prince resumed speaking in the secret language, and while his speech lasted, Enogat studied him. What had he imagined, then? An eternal Father with a long snowy beard, romantic hair, a haughtily limping gait, a kind of Maubant costumed as a rajah? Profound error! He found himself confronted by a healthy and well-preserved quadragenarian, his face as glabrous as Forain's, his head covered with blue-black hair like that of Gandara, as correctly dressed and gloved as Caran d'Ache. What a surprise! A brown frock-coat, well-tailored, designed his powerful torso; his mouse-gray trousers fell with impeccable creases over aristocratic varnished shoes; a fine panama took the place of a diadem. Although he spoke with great authority, his tone always remained affable.

"Now you are one of ours," he said, "and you are dependent on my supreme power. The obedience that you have sworn to your initiatrix, you owe to me, even more complete. It is necessary, therefore, that you know who I am. Do not forget that a frightful and rapid death will punish the slightest indiscretion on your part."

"The candidate bowed so deeply that he nearly fell over.

"I was before there was a non-Being and a Being, before any atmosphere and any sky, before any light and any order, before life and death," said Patishtha. "The One respired calmly, self-sustaining, and there was nothing that was different from him or above him. Everything was then in the uniformity of the waters. I have seen the One who reposed empty and enveloped in the nothingness develop by the power of his Will and the desire elevated within him, engendering mind."

For a moment, the doyen fell silent, looked at his gloves, then Neurocyme, then Enogat—who was open-mouthed with amazement—his thumbs in the armholes of his waistcoat.

"It was," Patishtha went on, "A spectacle of which human words and idioms can give no idea, even vague."

The Ancient-of-Days continued: "Since the destruction of Tadmur and Atmapur, it is me who has been charged with supervising the maintenance of discipline among adepts and the good execution of orders that they receive from supreme hierarchies. Are you firmly resolved to serve under my orders, Seigneur Enogat de Sothermès?"

"I am firmly resolved," replied the aspirant adept.

"Swear obedience to me, then, and, before your initiator, put yourself in my hands."

The dilettante dropped his knee to the ground and pronounced his oath of fidelity, in accordance with the ritual.

Then Patishtha, the Ancient-of-Days, said: "Now that you are bound forever to the light, Seigneur Enogat de Sothermès, redouble ardor in study and perseverance in practice of the works of the adeptate; above all, repress your hylic appetites; scorn all desires irreconcilable with our principles; it is necessary that you become an Eon—which is to say, a principle of incarnate will. Develop and embellish your Self. The Self is the primitive synthesis, the transcendent unity of consciousness. You have crossed the five doors if Intelligence; you are now, therefore, on the thirty-two ways of Wisdom. Redouble your energy; do not allow yourself to be defeated by any obstacle, and you will reach the hidden center. On that day, we shall circle our head with the crown of adepts. The session is terminated, Seigneur."

Noticing that Patishtha was no longer speaking, the dilettante set one knee on the ground again, and, his head oscillating, he stammered: "How I thank Your Transcendence...how I am..."

But Neurocyme dragged him rapidly outside. "Isn't His Transcendence suave!" she said to him, with conviction.

When they were back in the camp, Neurocyme, smiling exquisitely, approached her disciple, very closely, and said to him, in a voice of gold and pearls, viola and hautboy, the voice of Sarah Bernhardt in the epoch of *Le Passant*:[69] "You merit a recompense, tender friend; what can I offer you that will delight you?"

Was she going to allow him to steal a kiss? The dilettante paled blissfully, and is heart began to race. After seven seconds of hesitation, not without trembling, he exclaimed: "My greatest desire would be...His Transcendence embraced me, as you saw. May I not in my turn...?"

"I do not have the quality to give you the accolade."

"That's not what I mean. Could you not, dearest, allow yourself to be embraced? Does not my grade as a licentiate confer the license?"

"Your grade obliges you to refrain, more than before, from passions contrary to the preparation for the adeptate."

"However, when you're my wife..."

---

[69] Sarah Bernhardt had her first major success in François Coppée's *Le Passant* in 1869, in which she played the male troubadour Zanetto.

"On that day, my friend, you'll be an adept, and…you'll no longer be so grossly terrestrial. All that can be accorded to you, at the present moment, is to kiss my foot, and outside my buskin, dear, outside!"

Enogat did not have to be begged; he prostrated himself, and, docile and punctual, deposited a kiss…on the leather that sheathed the elemental's right foot. And as soon as he had accomplished that sweet—certainly sweet, but insufficiently sweet—act, Neurocyme said, without emotion: "You've heard His Transcendence's advice; become an Eon."

An Eon! While waiting to become one, the dilettante contented himself with exhaling an elegiac sigh. And he dined poorly and slept very little.

"We no longer have anything to do in these places," Neurocyme declared, the following day. "One of our brethren lives in the vicinity of Adjuntah, not far away. Let's go salute him—for I can now introduce you to adepts; it's one of the prerogatives of your new grade."

"Oh?" said the dilettante, with neither joy nor pain. And he made the gesture with his head that signifies: "My God, I wish…"

XIII. Further Mysteries are Unveiled

In the vicinity of Adjuntah, not far away, the sun was still shining when the automobile deposited them not far from the bungalow of Fatchpur, at the gate of a villa coquettishly nested between a garden invaded by camellias, rhododendrons and violet daturas, and a verdant park where aloes and Chinese nims mingled their foliage with that of papayas with plethoric fruits and "mohra gold" acacias with clusters of golden flowers.

An indigenous domestic introduced the visitors into a drawing room pretentiously decorated in accordance with the formula of William Morris. Almost immediately, the adept, Mr. Goodsnob, appeared. He was a man of about fifty, fat, pink and jovial, a staunch Scotsman. A wart dotted his rather large nose. His eyelashes were a blond so pale that they seemed white, but his eyebrows, like his long hair and side-whiskers, were the fine red offered by carrots in May: a true James Guthrie portrait.

Naturally, Mr. Goodsnob greeted his guests in magical language. Then, Neurocyme having informed him, after a silence, that Enogat did not know English, he hastened to speak French. After obligatory congratulations on his new grade, Mr. Goodsnob asked for news of Paris, where he had once frequented a few illustrious individuals: Monsieur Thiers, Madame Rattazzi, the worthy Stéphen Liégeard and the delightful Arsène Houssaye.[70]

"Deign to stay here for a few days," the Scotsman aid to Neurocyme. "I ask you as a favor, so much does your visit

---

[70] "Madame Rattazzi" (1831-1902) was the salon hostess baptized Marie Bonaparte-Wyse, briefly married to the Piedmontese statesman Urbano Rattazzi, and previously known as Marie de Solms. Stéphen Liégeard (1830-1925) and Arsène Houssaye (1815-1896) were writers.

rejoice me. After the period of labor that our young brother has just traversed, he seems to me to need a little relaxation. Take your vacation in this dwelling; it is at your disposal."

The Beloved accepted. And from the next day on there were esthetic excursions, sometimes on foot and sometimes in palanquin, to the temples of the Valley, and under the banyans, the pipals and the bârs of the neighboring forests.

"A delightful paradise! What an Eden!" said Enogat to Goodsnob, in the course of stroll they took alone. "How good it is to dream under this shade!"

He sat down at the foot of a baobab. The Scotsman, sitting down in his turn, replied while chewing one of his sidewhiskers: "This paradise presents fine scraps; unfortunately, it's becoming a sort of Fontainebleau of the Deccan. More and more cottages are being constructed here, and Fatchpour is overflowing with tourists. Nothing good can result from that for our old trees or our ruins. You've seen how the frescoes in the grottoes have been mutilated; we owe that to the English who all believe that they're obliged to carve themselves a 'souvenir.' What will happen when they form colonies here? Oh, dear brother, how heavy the Saxon yoke is for other Celts! I console myself with the thought that the hour is approaching when the adepts will have in their hands the diplomacies of all the great powers. That hour will sound the knell of mercantile Albion, that Carthage of modern times."

"Provided that between now and then, England hasn't conquered the world!" said Sothermès, in whose ears the words of the gentleman of Chaldea were ringing.

"England? She'll have enough to do conserving her ancient conquests, and the fruits of her various abductions. Oh, if the Celts were able to unite in the love of their race! How rapidly they would render those descendants of pirates to the Channel. But they lack a King Arthur and knights of the Round Table. Let's wait for the adepts to substitute for them..."

"Why will the triumph of our brethren led to the ruin of Albion?" asked the new graduate.

Scratching his nasal wart, Goodsnob said: "Because Albion is a lair of darkness and its sons will never listen to the voices of the disciples of Trismegistus. The latter will, therefore, have to commence by destroying Saxon power if they intend to develop and consolidate theirs. It's necessary for the radiation of the secret doctrine."

"Hatred is not extinguished by hatred," proffered a grave voice that seemed to emerge from the baobab.

Surprised the two friends stood up. At the same moment, an aged Hindu, decked out like a rich merchant, seemed to emerge from the trunk and came toward them.

"I was resting on the other side of the baobab," he said, in French, and your last words drew me out of my meditation. I understood that Gautama was ordering me to speak to you. You invoked the secret doctrine; are you unaware that it is the Law *par excellence*?"

"Certainly not," replied Godsnob. "We know all the laws, that of Karma as well as the others."

"Meditate on it, then, and convince yourselves that the sage must live in his village as the bee purveys nectar, without harming the flower, nor its hue, nor its perfume," said the unknown old man.

"When a gangrenous limb threatens the salvation of a body, who would hesitate to cut off the limb?" replied the Scotsman. "If you are aware of the work of light, you ought to be with us against the English invader."

"Every man thinks his wisdom immaculate, and every mother thinks her child beautiful."

"Open your eyes, old man, and perhaps then you will recognize the value of our arguments."

"One proof is worth more than ten arguments. The law of the Buddha informs us: the *Lalitavistara* is not of the domain of reasoning. It is outside ideas, has completely surpassed the five objects of the senses, does not deliberate, does not hesitate, is ineffable, has neither sound nor voice, can neither be articulated nor taught, is irrefutable, has completely surpassed all support, having prevented desire, without passion. It is the impediment; it is Nirvana."

"Crouch down, then, in tyranny, if that amuses you!" exclaimed the Scotsman, furiously. "But don't find it bad that we think otherwise, we who, amorous of health and liberty, have no desire to annihilate ourselves in Nirvana."

"The worst malady is vain desire."

"Adieu, old man! Remember that the Buddha had a horror of futile chatter."

The old man went on, indefatigably: "The true coachman, is the one who retains his anger when his horses bolt."

"Adieu, adieu, old man!"

"The true reaper..."

But Goodsnob and Sothermès were already drawing away with long strides, far from the inexhaustible source of aphorisms.

"What a bore!" exclaimed the dilettante, with a tone of certainty.

"That's the pretended esotericists of Buddhism, dear brother," replied the Scotsman. "And if you heard the theosophists! Fortunately, those people aren't proselytes! This country would become uninhabitable."

That adventure rendered Enogat de Sothermès' departure less sad, and he made no objection when the Beloved informed him that they were going to head for Calcutta.

"But don't worry," she added, "We'll use the railway, and we'll stop on the way. I don't want to impose hard fatigues on you, my friend."

They went to rejoin the Great Indian Peninsular line at Chandur, and obtained tickets to Benares. That long journey did not displease Enogat, the sleeping cars of the G.I.P. being comfortable. As for Neurocyme, she amused herself even more than she had during the journey from Paris to Marseille. She spent long periods standing at the window, like a young miss, and she rejoiced in the buffets in the alarm caused by her costume.

In Benares, they stayed with another adept, a certain Gnascher, a stiff and bilious Irishman, who appeared to be between thirty-three and forty-five. The elemental then donned feminine dress and the disciple put on his gentleman's livery, and they wandered through the holy city, whose "cachet" they recognized. As they walked, the dilettante recited at intervals phrases from *Akedysseril*.[71]

"The death of the star Sutya, the phoenix of the world, drew myriads of stones from the domes of Benares."

And then:

"Already, in Benares, in the depths of the path of Pryamveda, torches were running beneath the terebinths."

That same evening, they manifested their desire to know the society of the city.

Gnascher invited several notables: a local rajah, a Jewish banker of German origin, a few Hindu landowners, English functionaries and one Frenchman, "Professor" Auguste Coudon. The rajah spent the greater part of his time in Benares or the neighboring cities, bragging about is European education and posing as an art-lover. He invited Sothermès and the Beloved to come and see his collection of European trinkets and faiences.

"I only collect curiosities from Europe," he repeated several times.

The next day, as they were strolling through one of the squares of Benares, curiosity pushed them toward the window of a bookshop where numerous publications were displayed. A theosophical periodic attracted their eyes. They were scanning the contents when a voice fanfared behind them:

"Don't cut into those machines, at least!"

They turned round and recognized the Marseillaise "professor."

"Charmed to encounter you, Madame and Monsieur," Auguste Coudon continued, imperturbably, "and to encounter

---

[71] The 1886 novelette by Villiers de l'Isle-Adam.

you in time to prevent you from a disbursement in favor of that ineptitude..."

"Don't worry, Monsieur," said Enogat. "We're proof against those theories."

Coudon wanted to do the honors of the city and its environs to his "new friends" and imposed himself with so much amiability that they could not get rid of him.

"Come to my cottage," he begged them. "We'll chat there at ease and in the cool. Personally, I only like that. It seems to me that I'm in Marseille when I'm in my cottage. As cities go, Benares isn't too bad, but as inhabitants it only has bores, and one lacks company. And the existence isn't up to much! Fortunately, I have my cottage...country house!"

Once at home, completely conquered by Neurocyme's charm and Enogat's dandyism, and tormented by an ardent need to express himself in French to French people, Auguste Coudon told them his life-story and inundated them with torrential confidences.

A writer in the langue d'Oc in his adolescence, and then, having emerged from the École Centrale without a sou to his name, he had pounded the pavements of Paris and the macadam of its suburbs for a while before finding a job. After a long search he had succeeded in entering a chemical factory as "chief manipulator." Unfortunately, a year later, the place had caught fire after an explosion, and he found himself with empty pockets again. Then he had written scientific "copy" for a trade journal for builders and technologists that lived on advertisement-articles. Seeing one day in the announcements that a factory in Chandernagore required a machine designer he had offered himself, was accepted and left for Hindustan. After eighteen months the factory-owner had gone bankrupt and the stock was sold, but during those eighteen months Coudon had learned to speak English and was able to "go back" to Calcutta. He translated writings in French, at first for a scientific journal and then a theosophical periodical.

"Until then," he continued, "I had lived in ignorance of theosophists. I found their patter very droll, and to distract myself I read their classic authors. Interested, as if by a feuille-ton, I dipped my nose into the ancient Hindu books I was able to find in the library of Calcutta, and God knows, it's rich in them! Endowed with a prodigious memory, I became so well-read in the texts that I delighted those messieurs.

"'It isn't possible,' they said to me, when I chatted with them. 'You've been initiated in Europe.'

"I swore that I hadn't, still candid. 'Elsewhere, then," one of the bigwigs in the enterprise insinuated delicately, one day.

"'It was indeed elsewhere,' I replied, no less delicately. An idea of genius had occurred to me: that of extracting an honest profit from my knowledge of rare texts.

"I therefore recounted, with aplomb and mystery, that I'd been initiated into the most occult secrets by the best Mahat-mas in the Himalayas. According to tradition, those Mahatmas are the adepts par excellence, and they live in complete soli-tude on inaccessible summits, conserving the doctrine in all its purity. 'The Mahatmas regard me as their own son,' I af-firmed, 'and on my urging, they won't refuse to send the aid of their enlightenment to the valiant renovators of theosophy.'

"If you had seen them then, the colleagues! There was a delirious joy. 'Why didn't you tell us that sooner?' cried the doyen, a tear scintillating in his eyes.

"'Can you think so?' I objected 'Such secrets can only be revealed judiciously. Duty ordered me to study you first.' That response succeeded in conciliating those messieurs and their society solemnly decided to send me, at their expense, to the Himalayas."

Here, winking his left eye, Coudon caressed the tuft of blond hair that corkscrewed under his chin. He coughed, and then went on.

"So, I left in the capacity of the ambassador of the wor-thy theosophists to the Mahatmas and I went as far as Lahore. There I made the acquaintance of an intellectual Russian lady, very distinguished and very clever, who taught me the tarot and chiromancy, and gave me excellent advice regarding fabricating letters for the Mahatmas—for, after conversations that can't interest you in any way, I'd told her everything. We drafted the first missives together, and their effect was marvelous. They were translated into other languages.

"Then, as a consequence of events it's better to pass over in silence, my collaborator left Lahore, and I found myself in some difficulty with regard to composing my letters. I ended up, however, getting myself out of the affair by copying various old texts and seasoning them with commentaries. That worked.

"Then, as I was getting old in Lahore since I was living there alone, I came to Allahabad, and then to Benares, where, finally taking the title of professor, I had the idea of opening an establishment of divinatory studies—reading the future in the lines of the palm, cards and the stars, consultations of a psychological order, and the rest.

"At present I combine with petty commerce the evocation of spirits and disincarnated souls for the great consolation of the inconsolable, and I've had my lodgings adapted for that kind of exercise: cupboards with double backs, hidden trapdoors, cavities in the walls, phantasmal mannequins…my stage-setting doesn't lack anything. You'll see—it's delightful."

Neurocyme could not help laughing.

"Tomorrow," Coudon announced, "two of our worthy theosophists are arriving, and I'm going to offer them a sensational séance. Come along, dear comrades, if you're not enemies of pleasant amusement."

"Very gladly," said the elemental. "All the more so as I'm curious to pose certain questions…"

"To the colleagues?"

"To your theosophists."

The Marseillais professor winked his left eye again, and rubbed his hands.

"I've remained in communication with those excellent theosophists," he said, laughing, "and they're convinced that I've settled in this city to be closer to the Himalayas. Every two months or so I take a little break in the country, not far from here, and I do my Mahatmian Sévigné there. My letters are a great success in the two hemispheres, and they're translated regularly in the United States. I'll show you a few of them; they're worth framing, I tell you, along with the colleagues…my theosophists too."

The next day, at the appointed hour, Auguste Coudon introduced to his dear "comrades" the celebrated theosophists Susupish and Sundari-Croni. The first, a former notary, was sadly reminiscent of Bjørnstjerne Bjørnson; the other, an amiable a rich retired businessman, evoked the abundant surface of Oscar Wilde. They sat down ceremoniously, at first observing a silence that was rather solemn. However, Coudon having assured them that his compatriots were metaphysicians very favorable to theosophical ideas, the preliminaries of the conversation did not linger in commonplace banalities.

"You've returned from the Himalayas, precious master; how did you find our dear Mahatmas?" asked Sundari-Croni, with a pompous interest.

"Radiant in their serene wisdom, "replied the Marseillais, "and as beautiful as Devas. They repeated to me that they're very interested in your studies, and, very sensible to your homage, they renew the assurance of their great benevolence."

"What gratitude we owe you, dear friend," said Susupish.

"It's necessary to proclaim everywhere that our beloved brother Coudon has given a new life to our society," exclaimed Sundari-Croni.

With a modest gesture, Coudon said: "Let's leave it there, please, and listen to what the Mahatmas have told me."

Then, having picked up a piece of paper from the table, the Marseillais read in a grave and meditative voice:

"The Nucleoles are eternal, the Nuclei periodic and finite. The Nucleoles are part of the absolute. They are the embrasures of the somber and impenetrable fortress forever hidden from the eyes of humans and ever Dhyamis. The Nuclei are the light of eternity that escapes therefrom."

"There is an entire philosophy in those lines," opined Sundari-Croni, with an abundant gesture.

"Listen now to the explanations with which our venerated Mahatmas have been kind enough to follow their axioms."

Picking up his piece of paper again, Coudon obscured those abstruse texts with extraordinarily opaque glosses, on hearing which Neurocyme had some difficulty keeping a straight face.

However, his two naïve "colleagues" being avid to penetrate that fuliginous nonsense, the "professor" carefully, gravely and religiously placed his precious grimoire in a box. Observing with satisfaction that no one was looking at him, he quickly pressed an electric button dissimulated beneath stacks of paper. At the sound of bells that was heard he put a finger over his mouth and said, in a mysterious voice: "Shh! It's a spirit announcing its presence to me."

"In that case, we'll withdraw," breathed Sundari-Croni.

"Not at all, dear brothers," Coudon replied. "You can stay; it's a spirit with which I have frequent communications."

"Truly, we won't disturb you?" whispered Susupish, in his turn.

"Not at all, I tell you. It's a solar *pitri*, the venerable Vandakara, who is glad of the company of seekers of light."

"What an honor!" proclaimed the voices to the two theosophists, in unison.

Without appearing to touch anything, Coudon immediately plunged the room into a profound and complete obscurity; then, leaning on one of the walls, he swiftly activated a false partition, which, as it drew aside, allowed the sight of a kind of phantom of a human face, in a dazzling light: the *pitri*.

It was a soft wax bust bought from a hairdresser. Coudon had fixed it on a support and dressed it in a long white robe made from a bed-sheet. As for the head of the bust, which had originally represented a young woman with bicolored hair, the wily Marseillais had transformed it, by means of a Medieval wig, into an ideal young male lead.

The lighting was obtained by means of three reflector lamps placed too high within the pseudo-cupboard for any spectator to be able to see them. Their light traversed orange and canary yellow pieces of paper before being reflected from a tinplate sheet that covered the back of the niche, on which the theosophical pentacle was profiled. Pink and pale blue gauze, simply disposed to the right and the left and draped from top to bottom framed the luminous hole.

Finally, at the very bottom of the cupboard, perfumes were burning in several cassolettes, no less well hidden than the lamps, and the vaporous spirals rising from those cassolettes rendered the spectacle stranger and more mysterious. It was ingenious.

While the two theosophists, silent in their seats before that apparition—the first they had seen—held their breath, Coudon, remaining in the shadow, opened one of the drawers of his dressing-table slightly, uncovering the phonograph it concealed, and the delighted observers heard words take flight:

"By the Seven Procreative Powers, Maia, Oum, Haranguebehah, Porsh, Pradiapat, Prekat and Pran, may Karma flood you with delights beloved brothers..."

The phonograph reintegrated into its covert, the professor advanced toward the opening, pronounced a few words gravely in Hindustani, stepped back, bowing, went back to his origin place in the shadow and pressed the switch that closed the false partition. The room was once again in complete darkness—but the show was not over yet.

"Don't move!" Coudon exclaimed. "The *pitri* desires to leave you a small material souvenir of his coming.

And without quitting his station, the bold Marseillais rummaged in the curtain that he had close at hand there, as if by chance, and pulled a hidden cord. Immediately, the ceiling-rose came apart like a valve, and natural flowers fell on to the spectators. *Voilà!*

Coudon switched on the lights again. Then there were cries and gestures of joy, and everyone ecstasized over the beauty of the flowers and the delicate intention of the *pitri*. The *pitri* was ideal!

"Did you see?" said Sundaru-Croni. "It had all the features of an androgyne."

"And Susupish murmured: "What a supreme and unforgettable spectacle!"

While the two Calcuttans were narrating their impressions to the elemental, who was greatly amused, the bold Coudon came to sit down next to Enogat and whispered into his ear, tin the French of the Cannebière: "A good trick, eh, my lad! Did it succeed, or what!"

Neurocyme judged the moment favorable for interviewing the theosophists. That was why she insinuated: "If we reported to modern scientists the events we've just witnessed, I imagine, if I'm not mistaken, that they wouldn't fail to cry hallucination."

"The poor folk!" exclaimed Sundari-Croni. "They don't suspect that Maia is the scattering of a beam of light that reflects the double character of Parabrahm."

"Would you care to explain your concept of Parabrahm to me?" asked the elemental, with a feigned ingenuousness.

"Parabrahm is simultaneously everything and nothing," replied Sundari-Croni, majestically, "nothing in logic, everything in optics. It contains billions of potentialities, Layas points—which is to say, virtual centers of energy, which in developing, can become worlds; it's the immateriality filling all mater, the repose filling all life, the unconsciousness filling all consciousness."

"Yes, it's the filling *par excellence*," put in Auguste Coudon, insidiously.

The dilettante, immobile and somnolent, lowered his head. The zero total was still pursuing him...

For his part, Sundari continued: "Parabrahm is everything that human languages can say and everything that theosophical minds can conceive, plus everything inconceivable and everything that can never be said—in brief, everything that is, plus everything that might be: a synthesis of logos.

And all that is nothing, be certain of it, compared with what is."

"There," said Susupish, "we plunge into mystery. What Parabrahm is, 'it alone knows, and perhaps it does not know.' And, mystery of mysteries, that which is not is nothing, or rather, is still it, since it is simultaneously being and non-being."

"That's clear," said Neurocyme—but she thought it preferable not to persist. She simply thanked the messieurs, who declared themselves very honored by the attention she had accorded to their words.

After she had withdrawn with Sothermes, Susupish hastened to confide to Coudon that the "young lady" had appeared to him to be very intelligent.

"I believe," riposted the Marseillais, with a formidable aplomb, "that she's Katie King, neither more nor less."

"Bah!" cried the two theosophists, in unison, ectasized and open-mouthed.

"Yes, yes—but I couldn't tell you before the spirit; she insists on maintaining her incognito."

"What fine connections you have with the other world, my dear master!" declared Susupish, in a tone of increasing wonderment.

While Coudon continued to startle the two theosophists, Neurocyme, strolling in the sun, translated the Calcuttans' extraordinary verbiage for her disciple. He listened, yawning, until she had finished her translation.

"Those people are lame-brained," he muttered, "and there's truly no merit in putting one over on them. That Coudon appears to me to be an unscrupulous individual. To think that a person almost without literature—he knows Mistral, and that's all—that that blond Marseillais, that chemist-trickster, can deceive an entire society of honest seekers! For in the end, the sole fault of those philosophers is that of deluding themselves. How necessary it is to take precautions, when one occupies oneself with esotericism! Aiee! At least, dear, you're certain of the authenticity of His Transcendence, aren't you?"

But the Beloved straightened her lovely head, her nostrils quivering and her eyes sparkling

"You're question outrages me, incorrigible friend," she said. "Do you suppose that I could allow myself to be taken in by some trickster? Do you take me for a human?"

"I certainly hope not, soul of my soul!"

"Then?" she said.

He bowed his head. "A thousand pardons, dear daughter of Viviane! I don't know...I was afraid. Yes, the trickery that has just been unveiled to us caused me a painful anxiety."

"Your sensitivity will do you a bad turn on day, my friend. Let's go visit the rajah's collections; the sight of precious trinkets will finish dissipating your fears."

She had spoken—and they headed for the rajah's dwelling.

A disappointment, that visit! The trinkets, the famous trinkets, were frightful articles from Parisian bazaars: futile matchboxes and ash-trays, derisory tobacco-pots, pretentious flower-vases and other things only appropriate to concierges' lodges. As for the collection of faience and porcelain, it consisted of plates imitating the rustic or aping the style, and trays, bowls and cups from cheap restaurants or bankrupt boutiques. Compared with that flatly impertinent crockery, Monsieur Thiers' office could pass for a marvel of taste.

After having enjoyed their surprise, which he mistook for admiration, the rajah wanted to show them his treasure, the secret part of his "museum." With many precautions he opened a frightful casket, a sinister box fabricated by some old lady in the provinces, and triumphantly extracted from it photographs of the principal actresses of Paris. He had commenced naming them: Hading, Héglon, Réjane, Delna, Yvette

Guil…when the elemental and her disciple suddenly left it at that, without warning.[72]

In the street, the Beloved grimaced. "To rediscover in holy Benares the exhibitions of the Rue de Rivoli, as your compatriots put it, is terrible. Yvette Guil…oh, what horror!"

"And that's the use that those people make of their pension. In truth, I prefer the bourgeois who buys mass-produced Meissenware," articulated the dilettante.

They hastened to impart their disappointment to the stiff and bilious Gnascher.

The latter smiled bitterly, after which he took a toothpick from his fob pocket, inserted it in the corner of his mouth, and said: "There's no longer anything in Hindustan that can please the spiritualized. The English have pillaged the country and brutalized it. It's necessary to flee, far away. I don't know a single city in the entire empire where one can live honestly. In any case, the men accumulated in cities emanate suffocating atmospheres and accumulate monstrous ugliness. Fakery is everywhere, on the shelves and in the souls. Perhaps, when the reign of the adepts is firmly established, it will be possible to denounce it, but until then, the sage must isolate himself on some high plateau or in some unknown desert. My own resolution is formal: as soon as I can sell my house, I'm going to live on Gaurisankar."

To flee, far away! And Neurocyme and Sothermès took to the railway again that same evening. They did not stop until they reached Calcutta.

"It isn't to show you this fastidiously industrial city that I've brought you here, dear Enogat," said the elemental. "It's because it's necessary for us to take to the sea again."

---

[72] The name cut short is that of the cabaret singer Yvette Guilbert, a favorite subject of Toulouse-Lautrec. She introduced a fashion for risqué verse narratives that were recited rather than sung, which were still not considered respectable at the turn of the century, although Sigmund Freud and George Bernard Shaw both admired her greatly.

"Aiee!" objected the dilettante, with an eloquent facial contraction. "Will it be a long crossing?"

"Fairly long. We're going to Yokohama. However, if you fear that the sea might affect you again, we could, strictly speaking, go to China by automobile and take the boat from Canton to Hong Kong. From that port to Japan is a mere excursion."

"That project has all my preference," said Enogat de Sothermès, swiftly.

"Its execution will doubtless require a little more time."

"Oh, there's no urgency, is there?"

"Nothing any longer retains us. So, I'll put on my masculine attire and…off we go, my friend."

The automobile was quickly tuned up, and provisions for the journey stowed in the trunk.

As they arrived within sight of the Ganges, a diluvian downpour assailed them. They were, of course, equipped with waterproofs. Nevertheless, toward the middle of the afternoon, Enogat began to shiver, shaken by dolorous frissons. It was necessary to go immediately to the nearest bungalow and put the feverish dear to bed.

An initial philter having remained ineffective, the elemental summoned a few spirits from the earth and sent them to collect a few plants, with which she concocted an unknown beverage. Scarcely had the invalid drunk it than he fell into a deep sleep. Twenty-four hours later he was calm and on his feet.

"I feel quite different," he said, feeling his chest and then his cranium. "What marvelous elixir, dear, did you have me take?"

"The soma of the adepts," the Beloved replied.

"An incomparable remedy! I not only feel more vigorous, I feel…more lucid!"

"That's because the plants have mystic virtues; the hierodules of the rites of Sabazios made frequent use of them."[73]

"That soma also procured me a delightful vision."

"That doesn't astonish me. And what did you see, dearest?"

"A population of spirits, genii, beings simultaneously virginal and savant, supernatural and human, clad in gems, precious amulets, rare plumage or spangled gauze; and all those forms were moving, to the sounds of a music of which no words can express the sweetness, in magical décor that can't be described, round an adamantine throne where the most majestic of the princes of the Beyond was seated. Suddenly, I saw myself. Two adepts in amaranth velvet robes dressed me in a long white tunic and led me before Patishtha, who appeared draped in a fiery cloak. His Transcendence threw a crimson cape over my shoulders and led me to a clump of crystalline flowers before which fays were gathered. The prince made a gesture; the fays arranged themselves in two rows, and under an awning of old pink velvet—oh, ineffable surprise!—I saw you standing, as resplendent as a star. Then His Transcendence put your hand in mine and led us in great pomp to the throne of the young god of that abode. He poured magic words over us; I felt myself becoming a burning fire, but as I was about to press you to my heart, everything vanished. That enchanted décor seemed to me to be an image of the paradise of Indra."

But Neurocyme smiled. "Imaginative even in dreams!"

"In fact, what is Indra exactly, in Hindu mythology?" Sothermès asked. Doubtless some divinity of beauty?"

She smiled again. "I regret having to straighten out your poetry, but Indra is only a cow," the Beloved replied.[74]

---

[73] Sabazios was a Thracian deity sometimes assimilated to Dionysus, whereas hierodules were frequently reckoned to be temple prostitutes, so the use Neurocyme is suggesting is presumably in connection with bacchanals.

"A cow?"

"An alcoholic cow."

"Please!"

"Consult the *Rig-Veda*, Book Ten."

They set forth again. As far as Amarapura in Burma the journey was effectuated without difficulty, in spite of the incessant rain. Beyond the Irrawaddy, the roads became difficult. In the territory of Tonkin, the servants refused to go any further.

"All right, go! Leave!" Neurocyme said to them. Then, turning cheerfully to her disciple: "We'll be able to do our own cooking; it will be delightful, my dear."

It was delightful, the first time; indifferent the second, and a veritable bore after that. As for the installation of the camp, Enogat quickly came to consider it the worst of chores. After three days of jolts over frightful terrain under an obstinate deluge, they fell one vile morning into a pirate ambush.

The automobile was surrounded in a minute, and the bandits were already hurling themselves upon Enogat when the elemental, with a double magical gesture, discharged her fluid. Immediately, the aggressors began to leap about frantically, as if they had touched a hot iron plate; then they fell on the ground, howling in terror, and continued to leap up again, as if harassed and driven from cover.

Neurocyme hastened to accelerate the automobile to top speed; once clear of the band she made another gesture, after which the bandits ceased their jig. On the other hand, they were seized by fits of uncontrollable sneezing, resounding coughs and tormenting diarrhea. Thus, it was in the midst of a concert of bronchitics lost on a road powdered with snuff that the disciple and the Beloved beat their retreat. Was it from cold or fear that Enogat de Sothermès, green and mute, was shivering?

---

[74] This is by no means an orthodox account of the Hindu god Indra.

"Come on, dear," said Neurocyme, cheerfully, "you're not going to keep that petrified expression? You're safe and sound, and there's no fear that the pirates will pursue us, having too much need of rest—not to mention that they take us for terrible sorcerers."

"What power you have!"

In the evening of the day that had commenced so dramatically, they arrived within sight of a French outpost, and that was a different matter. The sentinel, mistaking the dragon for a Chinese machine because of its draconian form, took aim at it and called his companions to arms. Twenty soldiers immediately ran forward, and their amazement was not small when they heard Enogat howl that he too was French.

The amazement in question was transmuted into bewilderment when the travelers related that they had come from Burma and had been attacked by pirates. The soldiers uttered various exclamations, in an unaffected manner, and the worthy sergeant-major who was in command of the detachment declared that it was "utterly superb" and that "I'll tell you one thing, my old colonist"—which was that he was "blue in the face."

The following day, astonishment could be read on those good red-pimpled faces once again when the elemental and her disciple climbed back into Léonidas' vehicle.

"The most amazing thing," the sergeant-major said to them, by way of adieu, "is that you've done that, being from back home. That, notwithstanding, bowls me over...."

Beyond that advance-post, the country evidently became safer. It did not become more amenable to automobile traffic. There were potholes further on and it was necessary to make unimaginable detours.

Finally, they reached genuine roads; but then they fell from one evil into another. The administration surged forth: vexation, recommendations, objurgations, *ifs* and *buts*, a few *becauses* and a great many *whys*. Why were they traveling in that singular vehicle during the rainy season? Why had they come to Tonkin via Hindustan? It wasn't usual. Why had they encountered pirates? Why hadn't their passage been signaled? One of the glorious pen-pushers even asked whether the so-called Sothermès had satisfied the law regarding recruitment. Why wasn't he at least carrying his military record-book.

"They'll end up throwing us in jail," Neurocyme anticipated.

Enervated, the couple decided to go into China. From Xieng Kok to Hanoi they went at top sped, and as far as Lang Son it was an almost vertiginous course. Although the beauty consented to reduce speed once on Chinese territory, she refused to prolong the halts any longer than the time strictly necessary for repose. Nevertheless, after crossing the Si Kiang, she finally consented to remain in the same place for a few days.

Harassed by the temperature and his domestic labor for so my weeks, the dilettante could no longer stand up, and he was so discontented with this new life that, for the first time, he refused, almost sharply, to take his lesson in esotericism.

"All right," said he elemental, unmoved, "curl up in your dream. I'll go to the nearest village to by something suitable for our agape."

She came back carrying a duck, and while she plucked it, Enogat asked her whether there were adepts in China. Surrounded by down, however, her bosom as if palpitating with red and blue feathers, Neurocyme replied with the magnificent disdain of a cook: "What! Do those things still interest you, dear?"

She had out the duck over the fire, and a few drops of grease were seen to burst to flame from time to time.

"What, exactly, is a yogi?" asked Monsieur de Sothermès, his face orange-tinted by the flames.

"He's a monsieur who imagines that his intimate sense and his individual Buddhi are united with the universal soul."

And they ate the duck.

As soon as they arrived in Canton, they went to see a Chinese mage who lived in a suburb of the city. On seeing him, Enogat started with an intense surprise. The old man's face bore an extraordinary resemblance to that of Verlaine on his evenings of sly absinthe.

"*Soubam astou sarva djagatam,*" said the Yogi, greeting them in Sanskrit, meaning: How fortunate all beings are.

"The renown of your wisdom has reached us, old man," Neurocyme pronounced in the same language, "and we have come humbly to implore your advice. It's claimed that you can cure melancholy. My brother here is afflicted by that malady; will you consent to give us a consultation?"

The yogi fixed his bright malign eyes on Sothermès and, having judged him, said to him in excellent French—for he had studied in Brussels—"You seem careworn, my son. Do you regret Europe and its barbarians?"

"You know who I am, then?" replied the dilettante, nonplussed.

"You are a heart that amour is causing to suffer."

"Can you read souls then, old man?"

"I can read everything that is legible, and that is how I know that you have come from the land of the Brahmins, after having left France in the hope of the supreme initiation, and not for love of wisdom but that of the two eyes."

"You can also read the past?"

"All that was, all that will is and will be, my son, is stereotyped in the astral light, the tablet of the invisible universe. Well, my son—believe in my clairvoyance—in wanting to enjoy felicities before having merited them, you are putting, as the old Hindu proverb has it, the cart before the ox. Kill passion, if you want to live in love; and for that, our great Tcheou-Kong assures us, there is nothing better than unpeeling the mysteries of numbers."

"I know the Pythagorean table," Enogat articulated.

But the yogi said: "That is not sufficient, my son. If you want to acquire Wisdom, it is necessary to know the Keo Ku. By that means, you will know the earth and will become sage and clever; and by means of the knowledge of the earth, you will acquire that of the heavens, which will render you *ching*—which is to say, wise and devoid of passions. The sides Keo and Ku have their numbers, you see, and it is those numbers that prove all things. Scrutinize these mysteries patiently, dear son, and you will find happiness. In any case, if you want to sacrifice to voluptuousness, make it a nourishing aliment. According to the words of an occidental sage, be like the Venus fly-trap, which, after having allowed itself to be tickled by the insect, closes its corolla and digests its guest."

"He gives the impression of caring little about the world, that yogi," said Enogat to the elemental, as they were returning from the suburb. "I promise you to be sage henceforth, in order no longer to be at risk of suffering such pathos."

From Canton, they embarked for Yokohama, and this time entered into a delightful sea. On arrival, the Beloved's first concern was to go and book two places on the next steamer bound for San Francisco

When the dilettante rounded his soft and timorous eyes, she said: "It's not to visit Japan, a country devoid of any interest from the intellectual point of view, only good for the antiquaries of the Hôtel Drouot, that I've brought you to this hideously modern port. It is, my friend, to take you to America, where, if you condescend to receive the enlightenment you lack, the supreme grade will be conferred upon you."

The aspirant nodded, and then bowed, his head, and made no reply.

XIV. In which the hero touches his goal
without touching it as much as he wished

That second crossing was less fortunate.

The heavy atmosphere that they had to endure gave Monsieur de Sothermès new fits of fever and overexcited Neurocyme's nervous system terribly. For a fortnight she was like a cat tormented by a storm, to such an extent that she ended up, if not scratching her amorous disciple, at least giving him gooseflesh, patient as he was.

She's no longer a woman and no longer a spirit, he said to himself, in long soliloquies, during hours when indescribable malaise nailed him to his nauseatingly swaying bunk. *She's turned into a hysterical feline. What egotism, and what demands! No, no, if this life goes on, I prefer to renounce the satisfaction of my passion. I've not only reached the end of my strength, I've reached the end of my forbearance. What a life for a dilettante! And I was grumbling in Paris! Oh, if anyone had told me that I'd resign myself to such travels, and to such conditions! All that for a woman...who isn't only a woman! Why the devil did I have to involve myself with occultism? At least with a pupil of the Conservatoire, a dancer, or even a divorcee, I'd be able to get what I want...whereas, with that elemental, who, in any case, might not be one...who knows? I wouldn't be wrong to write to Dr. Callidulus; I left him in an unfortunate state of mind, that worthy man, and I regret it. That excellent friend would give me good advice. But there! How can I write to him? If she sees me doing it, she'll never permit it. I need to find a way to go out alone, all alone, and then into a café. But where can he send me a reply? Horror! I no longer belong to myself...*

In San Francisco, they began to quarrel as soon as they arrived at the hotel. Neurocyme having talked about leaving by automobile immediately after dinner, the dear disciple dared to protest that that was bordering on madness.

"You're becoming irreverent, I think," she replied, acerbic and angry. "Do you intend to impose on me a sojourn in this accursed city where the dollar, the modern golden calf, is enthroned—the yankee calf with the goat's beard?"

"Would it be imposing anything beyond your strength on you, then, to ask you, in the name of humanity to let me get the rest I need after the malaise of the crossing?"

"But I'm stifling between these walls! Do you think, by chance that my carnal matter is exempt from suffering? I'll compose a philter for you..."

"No thanks! I don't want any more of them. Can't you see that I'm exhausted?

"Don't worry; we'll hire two servants, and we'll travel in small stages. We won't be traveling far from this city, in any case."

"You always tell me that, and then..."

"Our goal is Los Angeles, an enchanting corner, the Californian paradise."

"How long will it take?"

"Eight or ten days at the most, at moderate speed."

"You want to kill me, then?"

"You're becoming insupportable. If necessary, we'll install a cradle in the car."

"Thanks! What about the trepidation?"

"You..." She clicked her middle finger against her thumb, like Negans. In spite of everything, though, Enogat held firm. "No, no," he said. "Rather the hospital. Go on ahead, I'll rejoin you...next week."

At that moment someone knocked on the door of the room, and he stupefied dilettante saw Saint-Dolent appear: an extraordinary Saint-Dolent, with a high collar and a mauve cravat, spick and span. After a firework display of exclamations, incomplete questions and semi-responses, Saint-Dolent succeeded in explaining that he had just read their names on the list of travelers staying at the hotel where he had been lodged himself for forty-eight hours, sent by the *Paris Herald* to report on the San Francisco Exposition.

"And you?"

"We've come from China," Enogat replied, "after an exploration such as no one has ever hazarded."

"From China? It's exquisite to find you again like this, after such a long absence—for it's at least seven months since you left us. Why have you left us without news?" Saint-Dolent complained, like a mandolin. "Our friends are very anxious about you."

"How could we write?" the elemental put in. "We only ever quit deserts to take railways or steamers."

And the mandolin, as cheerful as only a mandolin turned in London can be, went on: "You can tell me all about it. I promise you to get some fine articles out of it, and not only for the *Paris Herald*. Now I can publish anywhere I wish."

They spent a part of the day together, and, on the insistence of Saint-Dolent, Neurocyme consented to remain one day more—but an incident occurred to bring forward the departure. After having dined with the elemental and her disciple, Saint-Dolent had hastened to mandolin to some Parisian colleagues that he had in San Francisco and a few yankee journalists that Neurocyme was an astounding occultist, in honor of whom the nabob Sothermès had given fêtes that all Paris was still talking about. Enticed, scenting copy, the colleagues wanted details, and each of them resolved secretly to interview the already well-known beautiful magicienne the following day.

At nine o'clock in the morning the correspondent of the New York *Herald* sent up his card. Twenty minutes later all the reporters of American and English newspapers present met in the hotel. The well-known magicienne sent word that she would not receive anyone. Immediately, the editor of the Chicago *Herald* sent her the following note:

Then please give us an article on the occult sciences, on any topic you choose, and name your own price.

She replied with these words traced across Enogat de Sothermès' card:

I make gold, not articles.

226

In the meantime, the two servants hired the day before—a Swiss and an Italian, both multilingual—came to obtain Madame's orders. Neurocyme told them to load the baggage into the automobile immediately and to have a hasty breakfast; they would be leaving in an hour.

"In an hour!" exclaimed Sothermès, sadly, when the domestics had gone.

"It's the only means of escaping the interviewers!"

"But we're supposed to meet Saint-Dolent at noon!"

"We'll make our excuses, that's all: unexpected business."

When she rang to order breakfast, there was a further avalanche of visiting cards, those of the French journalists.

"Yes, they get up later," she said. "The invasion is complete. You can see that it's necessary to leave."

The dilettante had a keen desire to send the elemental out for a walk and go down to chat with the journalists, but the fear of a row stopped him, and he contented himself with sighing, without making any reply. The waiter who brought up the breakfast announced that all the gentlemen of the press had gone, except for one, who had sent another card. Enogat read: *Georges Bocquois*, and, scribbled in pencil: *on behalf of Saint-Dolent*. Neurocyme scrawled on the card: *Impossible; a thousand regrets*.

"You're also refusing to see Bocquois?"

"I'm refusing," she said, emphatically, with a ferocious gaze.

"You remind me of Tomyris," murmured Sothermès.

And he nibbled his food like an anorexic and sulky child.

At midday, with the note of apology to Saint-Dolent written and not a journalist in sight, they installed themselves in Léonidas' dragon and crossed the threshold of the hotel. Seventeen automobiles and fifteen motorized tricycles emerged from the neighboring streets and lined up in their wake.

"Who are all those people?" the San Franciscans asked one another.

They were the journalists.

The beautiful magicienne was unwilling to be interviewed. What a joke! Unwilling! They would see about that—in fifteen motorized tricycles and seventeen automobiles!

Neurocyme did not notice at pursuit until they were some distance from the city, in the open land that succeeded the suburbs of San Francisco.

"They're following us, the Redskins!" she growled.

And she increased her speed. Immediately, the journalists urged their machines forward. Then, warming to the game, the beauty caused her dragon to a veritable gallop. The race became exciting. It seemed that an infernal tarantula had bitten all those iron monsters, speeding toward the misty horizon. Everywhere, before them, the peasants and villagers became alarmed, with a fear mingled with wonderment.

"It's a wager," they said.

Hamlets and towns were crossed in a matter of minutes, horses frightened, a diligence overturned, poultry killed. A wooden bridge clasped as the thirteenth vehicle passed over it and the fourteenth plunged into the stream, which was fortunately not very deep.

While the journalists in the last three automobiles and the tricycles went to the aid of their colleagues entangled in the debris of the bridge, the others began to find the pursuit a trifle long. They had not had time to have breakfast; their stomachs were announcing lunch time, and the fugitives still did not stop.

Suddenly, one automobile came to a halt, having run out of petrol; then it was the turn of the second, and then a third. A hundred meters further on, two more imitated them. Finally, at a bend in the road, a sixth vehicle ran into a pile of stones and overturned. Then, overexcited by the complaints of her disciple as well as the perseverance of the last survivors, Neurocyme resolved to put an end to it. She called the spirits of the air to her aid, and the car, carried away at the speed of a locomotive, had soon disappeared into the dust and the blinding sunlight.

"My God!" and "Damn!" cried the valiant reporters, not without some amazement mingled with a great deal of chagrin. And they wondered how an automobile, certainly very heavy because of its decoration, could have outdistanced theirs. By what marvel of mechanics? It was necessary to know! But where could they catch up with the fugitives?

At the first village they reached, they were told that the auto with the dragon's head—probably an advertising vehicle, the villagers said—had taken the road to Monterey. Night was about to fall, and the journalists were dying of hunger. They dined rapidly, bought provisions and climbed back into their vehicles, determined-duty before all—to spend the night on the road. As the nabob and the magicienne would have to stop in order to sleep, they would catch them when they woke up. In any case, the adventure was taking on an unexpected, quite sensational character. They could get at least six columns out of it.

They stopped at every inn on the road, not so much to drink as to obtain information, with the result that by morning they had discovered the place where Neurocyme and Sothermès had eaten supper the evening before. After their meal the travelers had wanted to continue their route, in spite of the profound darkness and the stubborn advice of the hotelier. They were in a great hurry, it appeared, to arrive at Lake Tulare, the objective of their excursion, and they had departed in the direction of the mountains.

"To Lake Tulare! Forward ho!" proclaimed the intrepid reporters.

They had been tricked. Neurocyme had devised that stratagem in order to launch them on a false trail. The beauty had hastened to regain the road to Monterey by means of a detour, and she, her disciple and the servants had spent the night quietly in an inn a few kilometers from that city. They were savoring a comfortable chocolate there while the journalists set off toward the mountains.

The Beloved made another detour to avoid Monterey; then, finding a pleasant enough location in open country, she chose it as a camp site. Her first concern, as soon as the "masters' tent" was erected, was to put on her trousers, their precipitate flight having obliged her to depart in a dress. As for Enogat, still grumbling, he hastened to go to bed.

In order that he could repose entirely at his ease, the elemental condescended to camp in the same place for a few days. Their nerves therefore had the leisure to calm down somewhat. The dilettante conserved, nevertheless, a muted rancor. He hardly spoke; he no longer smiled at all.

Determined to render him, no matter what the cost, his good humor and courtesy, Neurocyme decided, one morning, to mingle with his food one of the innumerable drugs whose preparation she knew. Then, in short stages, idling along the Californian coast, they went to Los Angeles.

An adept lived in that city. They stayed with him because he possessed an alchemical laboratory, and the time had come to initiate Enogat in certain operations.

They had only been there for three days when a gentleman presented himself, asking to speak to them. It was Georges Bocquois, renewing his attempt to obtain an interview.

After a second check in San Francisco he had hastened to rejoin Saint-Dolent, begging him to use his credit with the nabob to obtain a five-minute interview with the beautiful magicienne.

"Come with me," Saint-Dolent had replied, "And if I don't succeed, Neurocyme being rather capricious, we'll have recourse to a forced interview."

They had arrived at the hotel as the recalcitrants had just left, and there was nothing else to do but follow them by automobile.

"I know where they went," said Saint-Dolent, "And I'll tell you. Enogat and the beautiful occultist are going to Los Angeles overland. Take the sea road, and it's more than probable that you'll get there before them. Run to the port; I'll scribble the letter that will serve you as an open sesame."

Bocquois had had all the time necessary to get there first, but that persistence annoyed Neurocyme, and in spite of Saint-Dolent's letter she maintained her rigorous refusal.

For an entire week the elemental obliged her disciple to lie low in their host's villa, offering the pretext that the garden was vast and sufficient for hygienic walks. Only when Enogat was able to combine he elements of the philosophical stone did Neurocyme take him to visit the city. Since his initiatrix had made him take an anti-bilious potion, he had, in any case, resumed his former chivalric manners. Sometimes, languors invaded him. The city of rich villas pleased him enormously, and he could not help asking Neurocyme whether she would have pleasure in coming back to settle in the vicinity.

"It has, moreover," he was careful to add, "the best climate in the world."

"Climate matters little to adepts, my friend," she replied. "As for the city, it's pleasant, I grant you, but a little too much like Monte Carlo. Be patient still; the time is approaching when we can realize it."

"Oh, so much the better!" he exclaimed. "For, in spite of the horror that vile questions of the material order inspire in me, I'm obliged to confess to you that my budget won't permit us to prolong our voyage much longer."

"Is that all?" she smiled. "You're forgetting, my friend, that I know how to make gold."

"I had, indeed, forgotten. Certainly, if gold costs you no more to produce than gasoline..."

Closing his mouth, she promised him, seductively: "We'll do it together, as soon as you're my husband. Banish all dread on the subject of our expenses, therefore, and allow yourself to be taken further still."

"As always, your vassal inclines," he murmured, tenderly. "Where are you taking me now?"

"To the San Bernardino Mountains, where, in the company of souls frequented by the eagles, we shall complete your preparation for the examination of the second grade."

As they were about to take their leave of their host, two commissionaires brought a rather voluminous parcel addressed to the two voyagers.

"Sent by Saint-Dolent," said Enogat. "Here's his name on the label."

"This parcel didn't come by railway," observed the Beloved. "Can Saint-Dolent be here?"

At a sign from her the two domestics immediately removed the nails from the lid of the crate, and to everyone's surprise, a gentleman emerged from it.

"Madame," he said, bowing to Neurocyme with grave courtesy, "please excuse this theatrical manner of introducing myself to you. Imperious, not to say ineluctible necessities oblige me to it, be certain, and I was greatly encouraged in it, besides, by our friend Saint-Dolent, who believes in your generosity to all originality."

"My car is waiting for me, Monsieur, and my minutes are counted," said the beauty. "What do you want with me?"

"You are, our friend affirms, a great doctor in occult sciences. You would get me out of a cruel embarrassment by permitting me to submit a psychological case to you. It won't take long. However, if you're in a hurry, I would be sorry to cause you the slightest delay; I'm ready to accompany you if it wouldn't be inconvenient."

"Expose your case, without further delay," said Neurocyme.

"This is it, Madame. A friend of mine, something of a mage, has read in my hand that in my, imagination prevails over sane reason, and furthermore, an afflicting circumstance, he recognized, after having measured the phalanges of my thumb, that my will was not very...willful. I've consulted the occultists of Paris; they replied that it was necessary for me to cultivate my will-power, but since I don't have the will-power to do that, what can I do?"

"The occultists of Paris," said Neurocyme, pulling a face, "have some analogy with Molière's physicians."

"It also seems to me," replied the gentleman, "that those gentlemen are like the people who say that they are Spanish, as sung in a celebrated operetta. I mean that, my confidence being severely shaken, I resolved to cross the ocean and consult in America. There, learning from my excellent friend Saint-Dolent that you were, Madame, at least as strong as the Queen of Sheba, if not more, I..."

"Show me your hands," she interrupted.

"Too kind, in truth."

And the gentleman exhibited his carpals and metacarpals.

"Eh! But here's a will that isn't so bad. Look," the elemental said to Enogat, as attentive as a medical student at a clinical lecture, "this will obeys a logic that doesn't lack a certain roundness. See how fleshy the second phalanx of the thumb; that's the most fortunate thing that can happen to a naturally anxious imagination. Oh! The head line runs toward the moon; but it doesn't plunge into it."

"There's hope, then," said the gentleman.

"Certainly. The mounds are harmonious, the phalanges of intellectuality sufficient. In addition, you're rich in mercury."

"Ah! Indeed, you're filling me with ease."

"It will be sufficient to attract solar influences to you and to devote yourself, in a methodical manner, to reading and endeavors. Impossible to indicate to you now he regime to follow; time is pressing. I'll have them sent to you."

"A prescription. You'll really write me a prescription? How kind you are. I'll leave you my card."

The gentleman held out his card to Neurocyme.

"No need, Monsieur. You're Georges Bocquois—did you think I didn't know that? You're George Bocquois, and you wanted to trick me..."

"Oh, Madame, can you believe...you've closed your door to me as an interviewer, not as a consultant. One more word, and I'll go. Before being a journalist, I'm a man; what if

I were to ask you to inscribe me in the number of our disciples?"

The wily reporter was counting on that masterstroke to allow him to accompany Neurocyme for a few months, but he counted without his host.

"You oblige me to respond," the beauty said, becoming sarcastic, "that a rather long treatment would be necessary. Skepticism isn't cured in a day."

"Oh, I beg you," replied Bocquois, without departing from his gravity, "add that treatment to the prescription, Madame and dear doctor. And whatever the volcano might be where you establish a school, you'll see me come running."

And he made his exit with the correctness of an English diplomat.

Alone at last!

The elemental and her disciple camped for two weeks on one of the slopes of San Bernardino, where the last Atlantean adepts held their assemblies. On the fifteenth day, Patishtha arrived unexpectedly, still irreproachably dressed, shod and gloved, as if he had descended from a cab. And after having given a further examination to the pupil de Sothermès, he conferred the second grade upon him, the *agrégation*.

"It's the penultimate one," he said afterwards. "A few more steps to climb in the hierarchical mystery of light, and you'll be an adept, you'll separate the subtle from the dense, earth from fire."

Not too soon, thought the *agrégé*. And he allowed himself all the more easily to climb back into the automobile because the atmosphere on San Bernardino was chilly.

They transported themselves to the foot of Popocatepetl, and throughout the journey the *agrégé* was cheerful, charming, witty, attentive, even gallant, the dust and the sight of lovely señoras having restored his amorous fervor.

"Never, not since Thebes, I think, have you been so genteel," the daughter of Viviane granted him.

"It's because I've never loved you so much," he replied, with an imperturbable aplomb. "And as we're finally arriving

234

at the terminus of the voyage that will assure me of your hand..."

Three weeks later, the elemental declared to her pupil that he was ready to submit to the final examination, and they departed for Palenque.

"It's in the ruins of that august city, where the college of our Atlantean brethren stood, that you'll make you vigil of arms—for a mage is a knight—and you'll receive the adeptate."

"A mage is a knight," Monsieur de Sothermès repeated, proudly.

And the journey did not seem overly long...

Señor Pampico possessed a hacienda on the banks of the Usumacinta, near the ruins of the Palenquean temple; it as there that the disciple and the Beloved stayed. They found the señor himself there and another adept, the Toltec Chimalopa, a kind of savage prophet with the head of a necromancer, reminiscent of a redskin Klingsohr. The four individuals saluted one another with a great deal of ceremony.

When night fell, Neurocyme took her disciple into the ruins of the temple near the hacienda, and after having given him his ultimate instructions, she left him alone, without a weapon, under the stars.

The time for the vigil of arms had come.

After five minutes, the sound of his footfalls annoyed him. He sat down on a stone, with his back against the wall, and his reflections became bitter. He evoked Paris, is house, his library, his friends, his dinners, and his intimate fêtes. All that, in sum, had been good and he had quit all that. Why? Oh, certainly, Neurocyme had made him enticing promises. But looking at it coldly, what had he learned? The hidden meaning of things about which he did not care, a more-or-less hollow metaphysics—for after all, he did not know the value of the system imposed in the name of the doctrine, not being learned in philosophy. In brief, word, more words, and nothing but words. In practice, he had been taught the use of certain signs, the preparation of an alchemical, perhaps anodyne, cuisine, and finally, the culture of the will. His will! Hmm! It had been fairly good, once; had it changed? He had abandoned himself to such an extent to his initiatrix that he no longer felt the slightest moral energy. What, then?

The black shadows extended in the cold azure of the moonlight.

"Here I am, back in the state in which I was on leaving school," he groaned, "At the mercy of a skirt. And what a skirt! A woman who almost always dresses in trousers—a funny skirt!—and doesn't want to allow herself to be embraced—a funny woman! She's less a woman than a colleague. Madame Gottglauben, less the cigar. And that's the being I adore, and who holds my life!

Vanquished by fatigue, he dozed off for a few minutes.

When he opened his eyes again, it appeared to him that the shadows of the ruins were animated. Beings of indecisive form—phantoms, rather—were gliding silently along the ancient walls. He wanted to stand up, but his legs refused him any service. Almost immediately, the phantoms advanced toward him, three by three, processionally. He distinguished their features. They were figures without any precise age, constituted of gaseous material, like the soul of Petamounoph.

"Brother," proffered the phantom who was marching at the head of the procession, "We are the astral bodies of the first adepts formed among the Toltecs; I am Huthiacuri, the archimage." And, introducing the here souls that came directly behind him: "Here are Puriaca, Cosithuirichic and Chihuahua, my faithful collaborators of yore, and the entire troop of our colleagues accompanies us.

"Tomorrow, Brother, you will know what is expected of you. Count on our gratitude, as we are counting on your valor."

The astral bodies vanished, and before Enogat had recovered from his bewilderment, the Beloved ran toward him.

"Dear disciple," she cried, "you have emerged triumphant from the final proof."

They went back. He drank, and then went quietly to sleep.

At two o'clock in the afternoon, Neurocyme woke him up, and having take him b the hand, led him to the most sacred part of the temple. There, raising by means of her fluid a certain stone slab with hieroglyphic sculptures, she uncovered the first steps of a mysterious stairway.

"Let's go down," she said. "This stairway leads to the crypt of the sanctuary where you will be interrogated."

A little pale, the candidate descended without saying a word. At the bottom of the staircase, in a small room illuminated by a magnesium lamp, stood two adepts charged with assisting him: Señor Pampico and the Toltec Chimalopa, clad in zinzoline robes. They took a white robe from a cedar-wood box, in which they dressed Sothermès. The elemental donned a grenadine robe. Then, still in silence, the candidate was introduced into the main room of the crypt, entirely decked, for the circumstance, with gold and silver drapes. Under the lunar magnesium light, it was magically resplendent.

At the back, on a platform covered with black velvet, and beneath an ebon canopy ornamented with ostrich feathers, Patishtha was enthroned, clad in a very ample robe and a regal mantle of crimson velvet, his cranium circled by a diadem of rubies and sapphires. Around him were seated the four Toltec archimages. To the right and the left were grouped, vaporously, the astral bodies of the other adepts making up their retinue, and the light that they radiated eventually completed the transformation of the crypt into an indescribable incandescence.

The dilettante was so dazzled that he thought he had lost his sight. When his retina recommenced distinguishing forms and colors, he saw His Transcendence before him. Almost immediately, the interrogation began, and, the elemental having finished exposing to the Grand Master the candidate's entitlements to the supreme examination, he was a sacred adept.

Then his two assistants dressed him in a violet robe, and the entire assembly embraced him tightly. The Beloved herself deposited a kiss on his forehead. A simple kiss: but he had, on receiving it, the sensation of a burn.

While an invisible orchestra played poignant music, Neurocyme presented the new adept to his assembled brethren. Each of them saluted him in the style of the Beyond; he responded with esotericolyrical eumolopeias; it was as touching as it was precious. Scarcely had the last ecstatic chords returned to the harmony to space than, at a sign from the archimages, the ground was covered with exquisite flowers, and as if with frost. Patishtha stood up, and resumed speaking.

"Brother Enogat," he said, "your initiatrix has made known to us your desire to espouse her. Do you persist in that desire?"

"Certainly, yes, August Master," the new adept replied, blushing to the whites of his eyes.

"And you, dear sister Neurocyme, do you consent to unite your splendor with his magnificence?" interrogated the Ancient-of-Days, in his sententiously stentorian voice.

"I consent to it," said the elemental, with a Gioconda smile and the gaze of a Montépin heroine.[75]

"Well then, give one another your hands, and before the supreme council of the adepts of this hemisphere swear to reconstitute in yourselves the perfect androgyne," pronounced Patishtha, in a slow and solemn one.

"I so swear," said Neurocyme, hr eyelids unquiet.

And Sothermès repeated, full of impetuosity: "I so swear."

"Your declaration is inscribed in the astral. The supreme council taking action in me, Patishtha, transcendent and august

---

[75] Xavier de Montépin (1823-1902) was a prolific *feuilletoniste*. Although his multitudinous serials featured a great many heroines, given the context, the serial's original readers might have thought first of *Mademoiselle Lucifer* (1853) or possibly *La Sorcière rouge* [The Red Witch] (1876).

sire, commander of archimages, in the name of the Hierarchies that regulate us, I unite you. The secret doctrine orders you to live for one another in a complete abstinence; but in the case that the effort is above your strength, it authorizes you to divorce. Go; the ceremony is finished."

Enogat could not believe his ears; but he had to yield to the evidence. Patishtha himself came to offer his velvet-gloved hand to Neurocyme, in order to lead her into one of the rooms of the temple, where the nuptial banquet was set out. The two assistants opened he march. Enogat took his place behind his spouse, alongside Huthiacuri, and the procession of adepts followed in its habitual order.

As they arrived in the banquet hall, decorated with silver drapes and crystalline flowers, resonant brass instruments sounded—a troubling presage—the nuptial summons from Wagner's *Götterdämmerung*, and the meal commenced. It was then about eight o'clock in the evening—in the Rue Vaneau, dinner was at seven o'clock precisely—and after so many various emotions, Enogat de Sothermès felt some appetite. Only Patishtha and the two assistants took part in the feast with the spouses. The other adepts contented themselves with watching, astral bodies having no need to chew or swallow aliments. Confided to the elementals, the table service left nothing to be desired. Every dish offered a flavorsome quintessence, every beverage a delectation.

There was no reception after the dinner. Nevertheless, the soirée that followed was one of the most animated and most joyful. No human is as talkative as an adept in recreation, and at one moment, Chimalopa, Pampico, the archimages and His Transcendence were all talking at the same time. The invisible orchestra was heard again. Finally, solicited from all directions, Enogat recited a few fragments of poems.

> *Music, sometimes, takes me like a sea,*

he began, with Baudelaire; after which—the orchestra still playing—he cried with Robert de La Villehervé:

O music eloquent to speak the unspeakable,
Rhythms! charming accords that, in clement skies
Open to our gaze the inaccessible door
Of the palace where, like the arrows of a target,
Golden stars tremble in the depths of firmaments!

The dilettante concluded with this quatrain, so melodic, suppliant and seductive, by poor Lélian:

Listen to the very sweet song
Which only weeps to please you;
It is discreet; it is light;
A frisson of water on the moss.

Then, he contemplated Neurocyme tenderly; and he felt a sudden anguish, for he understood, by her seemingly abstracted attitude, the seemingly distant smile of her eyes, and the glacial curl of her mouth, that of all the members of the audience, she alone had not deigned to listen...

*XV. In which two accessory individuals return to Paris,
where a third prepares the denouement*

On returning to Paris, Saint-Dolent had nothing more
pressing to do than to go and ring Callidulus' doorbell.

"I've brought you news of Enogat and Neurocyme," he
announced, right away.

The doctor made a movement of joy. Inviting his visitor
to sit down, he said: "Speak quickly, dear friend. I'm listening."

"Yes," the other continued. "I encountered them in San
Francisco. What a city, San Francisco! What a prodigy! I was
initiated there..."

The doctor's eyes widened, fill of surprise. "You? What
has become of Enogat?" Callidulus was sincerely anxious.

Then Saint-Dolent told him that he had found Enogat out
there, very depressed and disenchanted.

"Disenchanted, you think?" interrogated the good doctor.

"Very disenchanted," the mandolin repeated, "and even
degraded." After a few more digressions, he concluded: "Our
friend isn't happy, my dear doctor, that's sensible and visible.
And the cause of the evil that's eating him away is that
Neurocyme. You know whether I know women. Well, I've
always thought it was necessary to mistrust that one."

As Saint-Dolent was leaving, Callidulus retained him by
the arm, and in a voice that was almost a whisper, he queried:
"The money?"

"What money?" asked Saint-Dolent, bewildered.

"Sothermès' money, of course! Is our friend living simply, or spending recklessly."

"My opinion is that he's ruining himself," the anglophile
pronounced.

The excellent doctor paled slightly. All day long he was
preoccupied and perplexed. But that evening he went to dine
in "high society," which changed the course of his thoughts. In

any case, should he attach any importance to Saint-Dolent's diagnosis? The man only had cheerful eyes when considering things Anglo-Saxon.

Let's wait, Callidulus said to himself.

But Georges Bocquois, interrogated on his return, confirmed Saint-Dolent's impressions.

"Certainly," he affirmed, "the beautiful *magicienne* piqued my curiosity sharply. I found her interesting, very sarcastic and exquisitely misanthropic. Nevertheless, I wouldn't confide my son to her, if he were twenty years old. The nabob Enogat disturbed me; he seemed to me to be dying of spleen."

"And do you know," Callidulus asked, "if the money...?"

"No matter how bad things are," Bocquois replied, "the nabob will still last as long as his fortune."

"Without an adieu…it's very sad."

And, shaking the hand of the prince of reporters, Callidulus headed for the house in the Rue Vaneau. His resolution was made. On the way, he met Marc Lepetit.

"*Salve*, dear Doctor. Bocquois *mihi fuit obvius*."[76]

"I've just left him."

"Our amiable host Enogat is finished."

"Not entirely," said the doctor. And he went on, rapidly.

In the Rue Vaneau he rang the bell, and Monsieur Jean opened the door.

"Jean," he said, "I've come on behalf of your master to see how the medium is doing."

"The old woman?" the valet replied. "She's still asleep, Doctor. Funny, isn't it?"

Beside Eloa Chevalier's bed, Callidulus shook his head with a tragic expression. He felt the sleeper's pulse and put his ear to her chest.

"I've arrived just in time. She's very ill, my worthy Jean."

"I have, however, followed Monsieur's…and Madame's…instructions to the letter. I've given her..."

---

[76] i.e. Bocquois is obviously avoiding me.

"I don't doubt it, my worthy Jean; it's the treatment that's no longer suitable. We're going to change it. I have everything I need with me. I'll only ask you for a very clean bottle."

Monsieur Jean went out, and came back with a bottle in his hand. Callidulus took it, and then found another pretext to send the valet away momentarily. Then he went into the bathroom and filled the bottle with pure water. Afterwards, he went back to the bed where the signora was asleep.

"Poor woman!" he murmured, very softly. "I regret it greatly, but in the end...and as Neurocyme's materialization depends uniquely on the potion..."

The doctor did not finish the sentence, even silently.

And when Jean came back into the room he handed him the bottle solemnly, enjoining him: "That, my worthy Jean, is what it's necessary to give the patient henceforth. Two spoonfuls every five days to begin with. Then we'll reduce the dose. Warn me if any alarming symptom becomes manifest. Oh, she's certainly very low."

In the street he felt a vague remorse. He nearly went back to change the prescription, but after having felt sorry for the signora, he suddenly felt sorry for himself.

What a petty man I am, he said to himself. *Frankly, I would have thought I had as much character as the colleagues...*

And, to encourage himself entirely, he continued: *It's the sole means of saving Enogat, the sole means of freeing him from that larva, that ghoul...at least, I hope so.*

Then he felt better, and, whistling, with his hands behind his back, he hastened toward Bellevue.

As he went to bed, he thought about the adventure again. He had, at least, only one dread, which was that Neurocyme might not die with the death of Eloa. And, while taking off his shoes and putting on his night-shirt, he muttered: "Can one ever know? That elemental has defied all our anticipations..."

And, putting on his night-cap: "Oh, the strongest among us are not yet eagles. Mystery envelops us, and we're very dense matter."

Then, having embraced his wife, he went to sleep.

Epilogue
Hymen! O Hyménée!

The nuptial fête went on long into the night. The freshening wind was even announcing the approach of rosy dawn when Patishtha, the Ancient-of-Days, gave the signal for the separation. To the sounds of a majestic warrior retreat, the adepts withdrew, both martial and solemn. The spouses, stripped of their magic robes, went back in a humdrum fashion to the Pampico hacienda.

They were alone. Day was breaking.

"Dearest!" quavered Enogat.

He placed his right hand over his heart, and held it there momentarily, rolling his dazed eyes. Then, opening his arm lyrically, he launched himself to embrace the Beloved, his wife.

"Eh! What's the matter with you?" she demanded.

"I love you," he said, a trifle disconcerted. "I adore you."

"I know. I'm very grateful to you for it, my friend."

Again, he opened his arms. She repelled the gesture. "No, dear friend, not here, not yet. Let's reserve that purely human satisfaction for…our wedding night."

"As you please," said the dilettante, with the anguished physiognomy of someone who has just received a cold shower. "Would I cease to be discreet in asking you whether you count on fixing for a near future the date of that nu…I mean, whether the moment of that so much desired night…"

"I desire nothing more than your happiness, dear friend; and if I ask you to support yesterday's life a little longer, it's because I want to celebrate our marriage in a palace worthy of me—worthy of us!"

"Oh, nothing more legitimate," he murmured, more resigned than convinced.

"You wouldn't want us to commence or honeymoon here?"

"We could commence it in our tent, installed in one of the enchanting sites that abound in this marvelous land," he suggested, feebly.

"No, no, that wouldn't be royal! I need a home now."

"Let's create that home, dear, and render it superb. I told you in Paris that my love extends to giving your sovereign beauty the life that it merits, the worship that it requires. Have you already chosen some region?"

"My choice is fixed on an Oceanian island."

"An Oceanian island! Why not install ourselves in southern Africa?"

"It's full of Europeans, and one also encounters reporters there. Besides which, the climate would accentuate your innate indolence. None of those inconveniences on *my* island. The ocean breeze and the absence of all civilization renders the abode delectable. In any case, one can get there from Honolulu in a matter of hours."

"Come on! You're joking, dear."

"It's not my habit. I know an entirely idyllic island devoid of volcanoes: that of Hermes, the most northerly in Hawaii. Once, in my voyages through space, I said to myself in contemplating that splendid tropical décor: that's a country where I would like to live if I were incarnate. Oh, the sun!— the sun and the flowers! You wouldn't dare, I suppose, to refuse to please me."

All of that was said in the most natural tone. Enogat made an effort to remain calm and gallant. He went on: "I intend to be agreeable to you. Permit one minuscule objection, however. Is that pearl of an island, Hermes, equipped for the life of two intellectuals of our sort?"

"It's you, dear, who isn't being serious. Everything is to be created on that island, and that's what delights me. We'll build a manor there: an ideal manor, of an unknown architecture, as befits a soil still virgin of monuments."

"Good, good—and what about the materials, sand the workmen?"

"We'll bring them from San Francisco. A fine affair!"

"Better and better—but all that will cost the earth."

"I'll fabricate gold as soon as we get back to Mexico, and we'll leave before this evening."

"But while waiting for the construction of that hermetic manor, will we continue to lodge in our tent?"

"No, dear impatient; I don't want to put off the night of our hymen until next year. We're going to write to the best factory of dismantable houses in San Francisco and obtain the finest model of that sort. I'll take charge of concealing its banality and making it a stylized nest, elegant and pleasant. Are you content with that?"

"I'll have to be."

In Mexico, after having placed orders with three couturiers, Neurocyme bought a few items of furniture and sumptuous fabrics for the decoration of their home. Everything—including the automobile—was confided to the two servants, who departed for San Francisco in order to take possession of the chalet and embark for Honolulu.

The ball having been set rolling, they decided to spend another two weeks in Mexico, in order to give their servants time to arrive on the island of Hermes and to set up the chalet. Enogat took advantage of that forced leisure to put his affairs in order, and to send instructions to Paris to transport his library and works of art.

"Shall I announce my marriage to Callidulus?" he asked.

"Announce it, dear," Neurocyme replied. "Announce it to all your friends."

For the first two days, Enogat wrote his letters without too much difficulty. On the third, he felt languorous and tenderly lively. Abandoning his correspondence, he lay down on a divan and allowed his thoughts to drift.

Why put off for a month, or perhaps two or three, the wedding night so much desired? The more he thought about it, the more excessive he found the reasons given by his "wife" for that delay. Since it would be necessary to lodge in a temporary home when they arrived on Hermes, could they not, in the seigneurial domain of Señor Pampico...

On the fourth day, he could no longer hold still, and, determined to exert his authority, he submitted that project to Neurocyme, in a very energetic fashion—but she opposed to it, in a peremptory tone, equally energetic, a flat refusal.

Enogat spent the afternoon wondering whether he ought not to divorce. That same evening, he threw himself at his spouse's knees. Neurocyme forgave him, but remained cold. During the second week she was taciturn, and her nervousness became fretful; she appeared to be suffering. The dilettante attributed the bad mood to annoyance, and only paid slight attention to it.

Finally, the day of the departure arrived. In order to avoid the rigors of a maritime crossing, Neurocyme had decided that they would leave in a balloon. They installed themselves in the nacelle joyfully.

"All away!"

The balloon quickly attained a good altitude, and the elemental steered it easily, by means of her fluid, toward the Hawaiian islands. They only took with them food for six days, a mat on which to sleep and their nuptial costumes.

At the height where they were navigating the temperature was delightful; a gentle breeze swayed them between the blue infinity of the sky and the blue infinity of the sea. Sometimes, they encountered eagles.

Their gazes lost in the clouds, Neurocyme repeated in an almost imperceptible voice the verses of Fernand Mazade that she had recited on a delightful and sad evening, by the dancing light of the stars, under the lovely date-palms of Tell-el-Kuraineh.

There is no other amour than of absent things.

Darkness fell. They did not converse any more that day. After having sighed two or three times, as much by conviction as in order not to lose the habit, Enogat lay down like a gun-dog on the mat and went to sleep, deeply and dreamlessly.

Almost as soon as he awoke he diagnosed a vague crick in the neck and a confused headache. With the intention of being encouraging, the espoused shook her luminous head and smiled, but he insisted on his distress; he confessed that he regretted the seasickness very keenly, and that he was experiencing, in addition to the crick in the neck and the headache, the deplorable sensation of having aged twenty years. The most direct and bitter reproaches were germinating in his mouth when his gaze suddenly discovered a little chaplet of islands.

"Look," said the elemental. "Ours is the little one, down there, at the utmost extremity."

"Whether it's that one or another...as long as we descend! Oh, what a voyage, my dear friend!"

They dropped anchor near a radiant site where, among the wild flowers, a pavilion in wood and iron stood: the new Kasbah. And immediately, their servants ran to meet them, with a dozen indigenes clad in the foliage of various unknown trees. Monsieur de Sothermès would gladly have embraced all of that ill-clad personnel. As if by enchantment his confused headache had dissipated, and his vague crick in the neck was becoming increasingly vague.

Well, the installation was still very summary, but at least they could already sleep in real beds; and that idea, and another, rendered the dilettante his innate courtesy and fundamental gallantry. That is why, as soon as dusk fell, he knelt at the feet of his wife and hummed a few lines of the canticle by Albert Jhouney, enveloped in tender harmonies by Ernest Chausson.

Wife with the radiant brow
Dusk is now descending
And pouring into your eyes
Rays the color of blood.
The magical twilight
Surrounds you with rosy fire...
Come sing me a hymn
As lovely as a dark rose.

Neurocyme listened to him, without anything more. A few alexandrines by Haraucourt were no more agreeable to her. In the following days, she appeared clearly chagrined.

Undoubtedly, in accordance with her promise, she would soon transform the wood-and-iron chalet into a "stylized nest," elegant and pleasant. A week sufficed for that. But during that week, she was singularly etiolated. It seemed that a strange consumption was undermining her.

The evening of the wedding having arrived, when Enogat, emerging from an aromatic bath, went with a light heart to the perfumed cella where his "dear" was waiting for him, he was struck by her spectral pallor.

Perfectly natural emotion..., he thought.

Tender and impetuous kisses were about to put it to flight, that emotion, and replace it with another, sweeter and more profound, sublime! For the hand of destiny had finally marked the hour of tender and impetuous kisses!

Ornamented with stones with multicolored gleams and clad in transparent silks, Neurocyme, in the attitude of an idol, illuminated with the glory of her white contours the nuptial bed on which fine lace displayed their grace, so precious, on such voluptuous satins.

Enogat knelt down next to the bed, and in a voice that resembled the cooing of a turtle-dove in the branches, he said: "I bring you the oblation of an amour more adoring, more intense than ever. My soul, dearest Fay, is a devouring flame!"

"Remain thus always, dear friend," murmured the elemental, fixing her hallucinating eyes upon him. "The adept ought to live in perpetual flames. That way, he is refined and fortified incessantly."

But, passing beyond that chaste prayer, the dilettante attempted to respond with a kiss. Without getting up, he enlaced the admirable torso of his wife with his concupiscent and coaxing arms; all he could perceive was her eyes, smoky emeralds within the fine gold of her lashes. And although he did not see her lips, at least he could hear them, stammering:

If you love, make it an occult desire
With a sole hope of innocent ectasy.

Shivering from head to toe, he raised himself up and leaned toward Neurocyme. The verse struck his heart like a dagger:

A hope, if you wish, that is a memory.

Then, as white as a shroud, he tried to draw her toward him, to press her against his tumultuous breast. He sensed that she was gasping.

But do not lift up your quivering hands
Toward the frail face with the absolute gaze.
There is no other amour than of absent things,

Bewildered, without letting go of her, he appealed: "Neurocyme!"

The gasp, which seemed to be drawing away, replied:

The little that presages and...

Nevertheless, Enogat embraced his wife. But was he really embracing her?

The gasp went on:

... all that is no more.

And Enogat perceived that he was only hugging empty space. There, instantly, in his very arms, Neurocyme had disaggregated. Her material form, that splendid body, scarcely glimpsed, those beautiful hands, that rare and seductive visage, that adorable mouth, magnetic and mysterious, those capricious, oppressive and resplendent eyes, that hair of a gold like no other in the world, all of that had vanished: a chimera, it had dissipated; a mirage, it had evaporated, dew touched at that moment by the rising sun.

Now, again, tottering and haggard, three times, and then ten times, Enogat screamed: "Neurocyme!"

A burst of strident laughter was the only response.

And the cella fell back into a sepulchral silence.

At the same moment, in the Rue Vaneau, Dr. Callidulus was at the bedside of the signora, who had just yielded her last sigh.

SF & FANTASY

Adolphe Alhaiza. *Cybele*
Alphonse Allais. *The Adventures of Captain Cap*
Henri Allorge. *The Great Cataclysm*
Guy d'Armen. *Doc Ardan: The City of Gold and Lepers; The Troglodytes of Mount Everest/The Giants of Black Lake*
G.-J. Arnaud. *The Ice Company*
André Arnyvelde. *The Ark; The Mutilated Bacchus*
Charles Asselineau. *The Double Life*
Henri Austruy. *The Eupantophone; The Olotelepan; The Petitpaon Era*
Honoré de Balzac. *The Last Fay*
Barillet-Lagargousse. *The Final War*
Cyprien Bérard. *The Vampire Lord Ruthwen*
S. Henry Berthoud. *Martyrs of Science*
Aloysius Bertrand. *Gaspard de la Nuit*
Richard Bessière. *The Gardens of the Apocalypse; The Masters of Silence*
Chevalier de Béthune. *The World of Mercury*
Albert Bleunard. *Ever Smaller*
Félix Bodin. *The Novel of the Future*
Pierre Boitard. *Journey to the Sun*
Louis Boussenard. *Monsieur Synthesis*
Alphonse Brown. *City of Glass; The Conquest of the Air*
Émile Calvet. *In a Thousand Years*
André Caroff. *The Terror of Madame Atomos; Miss Atomos; The Return of Madame Atomos; The Mistake of Madame Atomos; The Monsters of Madame Atomos; The Revenge of Madame Atomos; The Resurrection of Madame Atomos; The Mark of Madame Atomos; The Spheres of Madame Atomos; The Wrath of Madame Atomos* (w/M. & Sylvie Stéphan)
Félicien Champsaur. *Homo-Deus; The Human Arrow; Nora, The Ape-Woman; Ouha, King of the Apes; Pharaoh's Wife*
Didier de Chousy. *Ignis*
Jules Clarétie. *Obsession*

Jacques Collin de Plancy. *Voyage to the Center of the Earth*

Michel Corday. *The Eternal Flame; The Lynx* (w/André Couvreur)

André Couvreur. *Caresco, Superman; The Exploits of Professor Tornada* (3 vols.); *The Necessary Evil*

Camille Debans. *The Misfortunes of John Bull*

Captain Danrit. *Undersea Odyssey*

C. I. Defontenay. *Star (Psi Cassiopeia)*

Charles Derennes. *The People of the Pole*

Georges Dodds (anthologist). *The Missing Link*

Charles Dodeman. *The Silent Bomb*

Harry Dickson. *The Heir of Dracula; Harry Dickson vs. The Spider*

Jules Dornay. *Lord Ruthven Begins*

Alfred Driou. *The Adventures of a Parisian Aeronaut*

Odette Dulac. *The War of the Sexes*

Alexandre Dumas. *The Return of Lord Ruthven*

Renée Dunan. *Baal; The Ultimate Pleasure*

J.-C. Dunyach. *The Night Orchid; The Thieves of Silence*

Henri Duvernois. *The Man Who Found Himself*

Achille Eyraud. *Voyage to Venus*

Henri Falk. *The Age of Lead*

Paul Féval. *Anne of the Isles; Knightshade; Revenants; Vampire City; The Vampire Countess; The Wandering Jew's Daughter*

Paul Féval, *fils. Felifax, the Tiger-Man*

Charles de Fieux. *Lamékis*

Fernand Fleuret. *Jim Click*

Louis Forest. *Someone is Stealing Children in Paris*

Arnould Galopin. *Doctor Omega; Doctor Omega and the Shadowmen* (anthology)

Judith Gautier. *Isoline and the Serpent-Flower*

H. Gayar. *The Marvelous Adventures of Serge Myrandhal on Mars*

Louis Geoffroy. *Apocryphal Napoleon*

G.L. Gick. *Harry Dickson and the Werewolf of Rutherford Grange*

Raoul Gineste. *The Second Life of Doctor Albin*

Delphine de Girardin. *Balzac's Cane*

Léon Gozlan. *The Vampire of the Val-de-Grâce*

Jules Gros. *The Fossil Man*

Jimmy Guieu. *The Polarian-Denebian War* (2 vols.)

Edmond Haraucourt. *Daah, the First Human; Illusions of Immortality*

Nathalie Henneberg. *The Green Gods*

Eugène Hennebert. *The Enchanted City*

Jules Hoche. *The Maker of Men and His Formula*

V. Hugo, P. Foucher & P. Meurice. *The Hunchback of Notre-Dame*

Romain d'Huissier. *Hexagon: Dark Matter*

Jules Janin. *The Magnetized Corpse*

Michel Jeury. *Chronolysis*

Gustave Kahn. *The Tale of Gold and Silence*

Gérard Klein. *The Mote in Time's Eye*

Fernand Kolney. *Love in 5000 Years*

Paul Lacroix. *Danse Macabre*

Louis-Guillaume de La Follie. *The Unpretentious Philosopher*

Jean de La Hire. *The Fiery Wheel; Enter the Nyctalope; The Nyctalope on Mars; The Nyctalope vs. Lucifer; The Nyctalope Steps In; Night of the Nyctalope; Return of the Nyctalope*

Etienne-Léon de Lamothe-Langon. *The Virgin Vampire*

André Laurie. *Spiridon*

Gabriel de Lautrec. *The Vengeance of the Oval Portrait*

Alain le Drimeur. *The Future City*

Georges Le Faure & Henri de Graffigny. *The Extraordinary Adventures of a Russian Scientist Across the Solar System* (2 vols.)

Gustave Le Rouge. *The Dominion of the World* (w/Gustave Guitton) (4 vols.); *The Mysterious Doctor Cornelius* (3 vols.); *The Vampires of Mars*

Jules Lermina. *The Battle of Strasbourg; Mysteryville; Panic in Paris; The Secret of Zippelius; To-Ho and the Gold Destroyers*

André Lichtenberger. *The Centaurs; The Children of the Crab*

Maurice Limat. *Mephista*

Listonai. *The Philosophical Voyager*

Jean-Marc & Randy Lofficier. *Edgar Allan Poe on Mars; The Katrina Protocol; Pacifica 1, 2; Robonocchio; Return of the Nyctalope;* (anthologists) *Tales of the Shadowmen 1-12; The Vampire Almanac* (2 vols.); *The French Fantasy Treasury* (3 vols.)

Ch. Lomon & P.-B. Gheuzi. *The Last Days of Atlantis*

Camille Mauclair. *The Virgin Orient*

Xavier Mauméjean. *The League of Heroes*

Joseph Méry. *The Tower of Destiny*

Hippolyte Mettais. *Paris Before the Deluge; The Year 5865*

Louise Michel. *The Human Microbes; The New World*

Tony Moilin. *Paris in the Year 2000*

José Moselli. *Illa's End*

John-Antoine Nau. *Enemy Force*

Marie Nizet. *Captain Vampire*

Charles Nodier. *Trilby and The Crumb Fairy*

C. Nodier, A. Beraud & Toussaint-Merle. *Frankenstein*

Henri de Parville. *An Inhabitant of the Planet Mars*

Gaston de Pawlowski. *Journey to the Land of the 4th Dimension*

Georges Pellerin. *The World in 2000 Years*

Ernest Pérochon. *The Frenetic People*

Pierre Pelot. *The Child Who Walked on the Sky*

Jean Petithuguenin. *An International Mission to the Moon*

J. Polidori, C. Nodier, E. Scribe. *Lord Ruthven the Vampire*

P.-A. Ponson du Terrail. *The Immortal Woman; The Vampire and the Devil's Son*

Georges Price. *The Missing Men of the* Sirius

René Pujol. *The Chimerical Quest*

Edgar Quinet. *Ahasuerus; The Enchanter Merlin*

Henri de Régnier. *A Surfeit of Mirrors*

Maurice Renard. *The Blue Peril; Doctor Lerne; The Doctored Man; A Man Among the Microbes; The Master of Light*

Restif de la Bretonne. *The Discovery of the Austral Continent by a Flying Man; Posthumous Correspondence* (3 vols.)

Jean Richepin. *The Crazy Corner; The Wing*

Albert Robida. *The Adventures of Saturnin Farandoul; Chalet in the Sky; The Clock of the Centuries; The Electric Life; The Engineer Von Satanas*

J.-H. Rosny Aîné. *Helgvor of the Blue River; The Givreuse Enigma; The Mysterious Force; The Navigators of Space; Vamireh; The World of the Variants; The Young Vampire*

Marcel Rouff. *Journey to the Inverted World*

Marie-Anne de Roumier-Robert. *The Voyage of Lord Seaton to the Seven Planets*

Léonie Rouzade. *The World Turned Upside Down*

Han Ryner. *The Human Ant; The Superhumans; The Son of Silence*

Louis-Claude de Saint-Martin. *The Crocodile*

Frank Schildiner. *The Quest of Frankenstein*

Pierre de Selenes: *An Unknown World*

Norbert Sevestre. *Sâr Dubnotal: Vs. Jack the Ripper; The Astral Trail*

Angelo de Sorr. *The Vampires of London*

Brian Stableford. *The Empire of the Necromancers (1. The Shadow of Frankenstein; 2. Frankenstein and the Vampire Countess; 3. Frankenstein in London); Eurydice's Lament; The New Faust at the Tragicomique; Sherlock Holmes and The Vampires of Eternity; The Stones of Camelot; The Wayward Muse.* (anthologist) *News from the Moon; The Germans on Venus; The Supreme Progress; The World Above the World; Nemoville; Investigations of the Future; The Conqueror of Death; The Revolt of the Machines; The Man With the Blue Face; The Aerial Valley; The New Moon; The Nickel Man; On the Brink of the World's End; The Mirror of Present Events; The Humanishere*

Jacques Spitz. *The Eye of Purgatory*

Kurt Steiner. *Ortog*

Eugène Thébault. *Radio-Terror*

C.-F. Tiphaigne de La Roche. *Amilec*

Simon Tyssot de Patot. *The Strange Voyages of Jacques Massé and Pierre de Mésange*

Louis Ulbach. *Prince Bonifacio*
Théo Varlet. *The Castaways of Eros; The Golden Rock.; The Martian Epic* (w/Octave Joncquel); *Timeslip Troopers* (w/André Blandin); *The Xenobiotic Invasion*
Pierre Véron. *The Merchants of Health*
Paul Vibert. *The Mysterious Fluid*
Villiers de l'Isle-Adam. *The Scaffold; The Vampire Soul*
Gaston de Wailly. *The Murderer of the World*
Philippe Ward. *Artahe; Manhattan Ghost* (w/Mickael Laguerre); *The Song of Montségur* (w/Sylvie Miller)